She didn't pause to let him recover, just bit his neck on the side and made sure she had a good grip on it. Out of all the things she liked about her cat, the strength of her bite was one of her favorites. Once she got enough flesh pierced with her teeth, there was no getting free.

He tried to turn and dig his back feet into her side, but her much longer body was a plus as she stepped so he couldn't reach her. With his front paws, he tried shoving against her face so she would have to let go. Straightening, she backed up and dragged him. He was still for a moment and just like that her cat was bored and joined in by shaking her head. She lifted it to check if there was any struggle left. The creature hung from her jaw. Releasing it, she pawed him a few times and there was no response. Fragile little things, these hyenas, she thought. Grabbing the leather strap of his pack, she bit through it.

She smelled gun oil. Spinning around, she crouched down and then saw Griffin standing beside a tree. He was pointing a gun *at her*. Her cat tried to resist, but Blaise overrode her and grouched and gave him a warning growl. He had about three seconds to lower *her* gun.

ANIMAL SENSES

1 *Heart*
2 *Scent*
3 *Passion*
4 *Courage*
5 *Solace*
6 *Faith*
7 *Spirit*
8 *Fury*
9 *Pride*
10 *Torment*
(coming soon)
11 Honor
12 Beauty
13 Trust
14 Virtue
15 Hope

MAGIC SEASONS ROMANCE

1 *Beltane Magic*
2 *Solstice Heat*
3 *Harvest Dreams*
4 *Autumn Dance*
5 *Winter Mist*

MYSTIC GIFTS TRILOGY

Mystic Perceptions
Dream Visions
Inner Reflections

Dreams

Three steamy stories that started with a dream

Curses

Two tales of curses.

After the Silence
Volume 1 Bree

SINGLE TITLES
Solitary Witchling
Salvation
Café Serenity

Writing As: J. Risk

THE ALTEREALM SERIES

1 *The Huntress*
2 *The Seer*
3 *The Empath*
4 *The Witch*
5 *The Chronos*
6 *The Warrior*
7 *The Telepath*
8 *The Healer*
9 The Kinetic

THE SOLRELM SERIES
Concealed

(coming soon)

Unveiled
Undone

GEMINI LEAGUE

(coming soon)

Dark Moon

While I was finishing up Torment (Animal Senses Series) and Unveiled (Solrelm Series) I found out that I lost my editor and friend to complications following an accident.

Our paths crossed in 2012 when I was looking for beta readers, and then she offered to help me 'pre-edit' before I sent my books off to the publisher's editors. I thought that was amazing, of course, now I understand that her hair was probably standing on end and her body twitching with the mistakes in my writing. From that point on everything I wrote went through her before going anywhere else.

When I decided to get my rights back and go out on my own, she was there with me every step of the way—not just in my writing, but in all things. There were days when we would email each other twenty times. While we haven't worked together in the last few years, because she was too busy climbing the mountainous obstacles life placed in her path, she was still a part of my writing world and our weekly life updates.

I can honestly say not a single word of mine would be published without her help. I was ready to give up on the Animal Senses books while I was writing book 2. I messaged her and told her that things were straying from my original plan. Her reply was to rub raw hamburger on my wrists while writing to keep those tiger shifters in line.

When I bounced the idea of Gemini League books off her, she made me promise that I would base one of the characters on her. I didn't get the chance to tell her because I wanted her to read it for herself and just know that Capri was her, because she was magic, as the character is.

This one, and all those that follow, are for you, Lady. I don't know where you've moved onto, but I know you will organize the hell out of the place.

Published by Exordium Books (FRP)

ISBN: 978-1-990763-21-2

TORMENT

Animal Senses Series Book 10

Jacqueline Paige

Chapter One

Blaise put the truck into park and blew out some of the tension. As drives went, that one had been intense. Visibility at best was five feet in front of the vehicle. Her truck was built for off-roading and it was a good thing, much of the drive had been through snow that would have bogged down her Alliance ride. Even the few times she could see, she wasn't sure if she was on a road or making her own. There hadn't been any gaps that could have been a turnoff, so she hoped this was the place. The snow was blowing so much she couldn't see *anything*. Was there a house here? There had to be. Why did they send her here?

Grabbing her phone, she messaged Kenzo, her boss. Maybe now he'd give her some details. The cryptic instructions she'd been given were to get here any way possible, tell no one, and then she'd be filled in. The strangest part of it was she was told to use her own vehicle and not one from the Alliance. Why? It had taken her a day and the weather had done all it could to prevent her from going anywhere. She hadn't stopped, afraid she wouldn't get going again. She couldn't remember a snowstorm like this before. She kept hoping she'd drive out of it eventually but hadn't. If anything, the closer she got to this mountain the worse it got.

Her phone rang, and she answered without pausing to see who it was. It wasn't like many called her.

"Blaise." It was the boss.

"I made it." She had already told him that in the message, but after that drive, she'd thought it bared repeating.

"You used your own vehicle, right?"

"That's probably the only reason I got through it."

"Good. There's no way you were tracked then."

She grinned, "good luck to anyone tracking *anything* in this weather."

"Yeah, it's a mess."

"Why am I here, Kenzo?" She put the window down a few inches and tried to see through the blowing snow. A gust of wind blew snow in her face. She closed the window.

"If you're at the end of the road," Blaise tried to see if she could go any further, but could only see snow. "Roughly twenty feet into the bush there's a small shed. I'll send you the key code to get in. There's a sled inside to get you up the mountain."

Blaise leaned forward and caught glimpses of 'the mountain'. The wipers were pushing snow, but not able to keep up with it. She was going up there?

"Raymond says you go straight up from that shed, there's a trail cut through the trees, so you'll know if you stray. When you can't go any further, you hang a left and it will take you to the cabin."

"Raymond Hardy?"

"Yeah. This is his personal getaway spot."

Blaise raised both eyebrows and looked out the windshield again. "What am I doing at this cabin?"

She heard Kenzo suck in a breath and blow it out. "Watching Aiden Tomas' half-brother, a half-breed, until we can figure out what we're doing with him."

"I'm sorry, did you say Aiden Tomas' brother is a half-breed?"

"Yes, I did. Tripp and Amari got him."

Blaise stiffened, the exhaustion from her long drive was

gone. She opened her mouth and then closed it. "How long have we had him?"

"Just before the storm hit."

"Does Tomas know?"

"He has to by now."

She started to ask if he wanted her to 'persuade' information out of him, but he cut her off.

"Hold on."

There were other voices in the background making her wonder where her boss had gotten snowed in. All the teams were stuck in various areas, and their plans to breach Tomas' locations and free their kind had come to an abrupt halt. No one was happy about it. Blaise had been escorting a few collared rescues when the storm hit. Fortunately for her, the center was near HQ and her own ride had been parked in an underground lot she used when she was there.

"Tell them to go see if they can find their vehicle and tag it." He cleared his throat, "sorry, Tripp saw a bit of action this morning."

"Everything good?"

"Yeah. They were somehow tailed in this storm and thought they'd catch them off guard at dawn."

Blaise smirked, "How'd that go for them?"

"Tripp took one out, Amari," he snorted, "got the drop on the other. Trying to get clean up there right now is going to be a nightmare."

Blaise had dealings with Amari a few times and she had nothing but respect for her. "Amari's out of control, I like her style."

Kenzo laughed, "well, her mate, Tripp, isn't sure he does."

Her eyes widened, "they're mates? That's awesome." She chuckled, "he's outta control too. Good match." Lately, everyone was finding their *fated* mate. She rolled her eyes at the thought. A part of her was happy for them, but then there was her reality, which didn't leave room for happy, gooey thoughts and fantasies of 'what if'.

"You can say that because you don't have to try to control

Tripp."

"I don't think anyone can control Tripp, Boss."

"Don't I know it. At least you don't openly defy *every* order. Message me when you find the cabin. Graham Watts from Raymond's team is there right now, but he is needed elsewhere. Take all your gear with you, I don't know how long you'll be up there."

She nodded, "any instructions on what I can or can not do with the prisoner?"

"Unknown at this time, we're waiting on word from Devin Addison. He is tagged though, by Tomas, so he can *not* leave the Faraday cage he's in. And have care with your phone, signals can be detected in the rest of the building."

"Tomas tagged his brother?"

"He's a half-breed, Blaise, given how the Tomas family feels about our kind, we're still astonished he's been allowed to live."

What kind of life would that be? To share blood with a man that thought of their kind as pets? "Yeah." Was the only response she gave him. She couldn't talk about Tomas or what those they rescued went through. It just sent her into a murderous frenzy. *Focus on the task.*

"Objective until further notice, keep him safe and alive. You good to head up now, or do you need a short rest?"

"I'm all aces, boss."

"Good. Probably an hour's ride in this weather, so get your bearings and head up now."

"Will do." She listened as he hung up. "Aiden Tomas' half-brother." She blew out a breath, "this is going to be a helluva ride." She glanced at herself in the mirror her green eyes were flecked with amber, telling her that her cat was close and ready for some fun. At least now she understood the secrecy. Turning the truck off, she stowed her keys in her run pack and grabbed a hair elastic. She made fast work of getting her hair braided and off her face all while avoiding looking at herself in the mirror again. The dark skin on the right side of her body from her jaw down didn't bother her anymore, but that didn't mean she wanted to *see* it either. She'd accepted her life, but then again, she had no choice. No one with a brain dared ever call her a mixed breed, but that didn't mean it wasn't true. The secrecy in her own family regarding that topic told her it was one hundred percent fact and someday, she was going to find out all the nasty details about it.

She felt the truck rock in a gust of wind and decided to find the snowmobile before hauling all her gear there. She stared at her phone waiting for the code to be sent. Once she had it, she'd put it in her pack.

Had Kenzo purposely chosen her to do this? Get the abomination to watch the half-breed? She didn't know, but it didn't matter. He didn't treat her differently and she respected him for that. Besides, she had orders, and she'd carry them through without question. She owed Kenzo a lot, he'd recruited her when she was at a crossroads in her life. One direction on that road would have led to the end of her existence, and further humiliation for her family. Today, she'd proceed like any other day, follow her instructions and not deviate from them. If she got to beat someone or kill something along the way, even better.

Chapter Two

Griffin stood there facing the window that was an inch away from the cage. To his captor, it would appear he was looking out at the blustery weather, and that's what he wanted him to believe. The light was just right in this space to allow him to use the clear pane as a mirror and watch the other man. He wasn't locked in the room by any physical walls, just wire. His father, Alberto Tomas had put a tracker in his body. How had he not known this? When had he done that? At first, he thought it was a ploy to keep him cooperative and stay in the cage and then a big man named Raymond had shown him with a bug detector. He scowled and looked at the floor for a moment, did his *brother* watch his movements and only display false trust in him? Trust was the wrong word, Aiden had never hidden his disdain for their shared blood.

Flicking his gaze back to the glass, he watched the man that was here to 'protect' him. They had him in a cage. It was roughly eight feet by eight feet and contained a small cot. He knew the size because once his head had cleared from being knocked out, he'd paced it *a lot*. The wire was to keep any signal from his transmitter from being detected. Graham, he only knew the man's name because the big man, had called him that, had been left to watch over him and feed him.

Three days ago, he'd been sent to retrieve an alpha woman and had woken up here. He was glad for one part of this at least, that Aiden hadn't gotten the woman. It would be one Griffin wouldn't have to watch as his brother's lackeys crushed her free will and erased all that she was, and turned her into an empty shell. He hated seeing when the light was no longer in their eyes, when they'd broken and given up hope.

He turned and watched Graham sit down and look at the small tv screen. His own fate was questionable at this point. He hadn't been asked any significant questions, threatened, or beaten since he'd woke up in the back of the vehicle with the alpha woman and the man, that as it turned out, was not working for his brother, but was part of the Shifter Alliance. He'd been scanned, fed, and for the most part, ignored. He was used to being ignored, had been for most of his life—but having nothing to do but sit in here was going to get to him if it went on much longer.

This wasn't the Alliance that his brother swore about and insulted often. He expected feral lunatics based on the information he'd overheard, but so far, he'd only seen intelligent, reasonable people. What worried him more than anything was that they couldn't keep him indefinitely in this cage. Then what happened? He'd overheard a quiet conversation, and as far as he knew they were waiting for a doctor that could safely remove the tracker that rested in the muscle at the back of his neck. If removed wrong, it could paralyze him. Reaching, he ran his fingers along the muscles, trying to feel it. There was a small lump, but he'd always had it—moving his hand he felt the other side. There was no lump. His father had had it put in when he was quite young because it had been there for as long as Griffin could remember. Other than that, he hadn't overheard anything pertaining to his current situation.

Why would it matter for him to have this inside his body? At what point had he ever been able to wander free? Never. The pickup for the Alpha woman had been the first errand he had been sent on alone. The reason for that was that things were happening to *finally* stop what his family was doing and there hadn't been anyone free to 'escort' him.

His one guard had told him some of what was happening, how the shifters were fighting back, and for the most part, winning. He'd had to clamp down on his emotions and not cheer out loud when he'd been told. It was about time that someone did something to stop his family and the others that worked with them.

He turned around to look directly at Graham again. *Family.* Could he even call them that? Family did not torment and humiliate other members. Not that he had a lot of proof of that, he didn't know anyone outside the immediate circle that worked with his brother. Even thinking the word brother made his stomach churn. Aiden was no brother, just as his father hadn't been a dad either. A sire would not parade his child around like a showpiece of 'look what I did,' not in the evil sense he had. Griffin couldn't relate to those he shared blood with at all.

The sound of Graham's phone chirping dragged him out of his thoughts. He went over and lay on the cot and closed his eyes, not wanting it to be obvious he was going to listen to the conversation.

"Yeah."

While this vacation from Aiden was nice, and no one was barking orders at him, Griffin hoped that soon someone would communicate with him, maybe give him a clue what fate had in store for him. Graham gave off the vibe that he wasn't interested in conversation, so he'd used the last few days to sleep, because for the first time since he was a child he could without worrying about something happening to him.

"Visibility is next to nothing up here." He chortled, "when do I panic and worry she's out there lost in this?"

Someone was heading here. Was it the medic to remove his tracking chip, or tracker, whatever it was called?

"I've never worked with her, but I've heard she's straight-up scary." He laughed, "yeah, we'll be fine." He heard the chair scrape the floor. "You want me to head back down?" The sound of the tv was lowered, "yeah, might take me a day to get there, so tell him to wait. These machines are solid, so it shouldn't be too difficult." A few moments of silence, "sounds good, boss. Yeah, still chilling and catching up on sleep. Will do."

He heard the man's boots on the floor. "Hey. Do you want a shower before I go?"

Griffin opened his eyes and looked out through the cage at him. "Yes." He swung his feet to the floor and stood up. Grabbing the silver blanket from the end of the cot, he wrapped it around his shoulders. He didn't know what it was made of, just that it was heavy, and blocked any signals. For whatever reason, the only spaces protected in this place were his cage and the bathroom. Who put their bathroom inside a Faraday cage? He didn't know who owned this place, but they'd obviously built it with captivity and privacy in mind. He glanced out the windows as he walked. There was nothing to see but white in any direction when he looked out.

Graham stood at the door for a moment before locking him in. "I'm going to be heading out soon." He put his hands on his hips and looked at him, "look I can't imagine being a half-breed, but just take a bit of advice, be straight with them when they start asking questions." He shrugged, "I've heard the prince is a fair man."

Griffin was going to meet the prince of the Alliance? He would process that later. He made sure the blanket covered the back of his neck, "like I'm in a body that is the wrong size." He told him. Graham's confused look almost made him smile, "what it's like being a half-breed." He clarified.

Graham nodded, "that's got to bite, man. Sorry."

Sorry? He was apologizing like he had played some part in his father's sadistic world. He shrugged it off, "take what you're given and make it work." He mumbled it and turned his back to the door, so Graham wouldn't try to strike up any sort of conversation. Right now, he needed the solitude the shower offered him. Hot water sluiced over his skin and the sound drowned out all noise. He smirked when the door closed, he knew his mother wasn't one of those water people, or he'd still be able to hear in the water. At least that was his assumption.

He didn't know what they planned for him, or what was next in this life for him, but he did know that he was never going back to a life of torment with his *family*. Even if the cost was his life.

Chapter Three

Blaise stopped and turned to check that her gear was still secured. Tugging on the glove, she pulled it off and wiped her hand over her numb cheek. It was going to take hours to thaw out once she got to the cabin. Briefly, she was missing the warmer climate she grew up in where it never snowed—until she remembered why her family had left there in the first place. She'd take the snow any day.

Working the glove back on, she was thankful she'd grabbed them and the snowsuit from in the shed. Raymond Hardy thought of everything, otherwise, she would have headed out in this storm dressed as she was and would have frozen to death. She did regret not taking one of the helmets. It would have kept her face warmer. Pulling the collar up, she tugged it over her mouth and then revved the machine. Turning it slowly to the left, she throttled it up and crouched again. She'd already found out the hard way that sitting made fast movement harder and as a result avoiding trees almost impossible.

She wasn't sure how long it had been, but when she saw the lights, she blew out a hot breath that traveled down to her neck inside the material. She'd made it and could still feel most parts of her body. Her feet were questionable, none of the boots in the shed had fit her, so she'd had to wear her shitkickers. Normally she loved her boots, but the steel plate in the toes had been the first thing to freeze. She wondered if shifting to rejuvenate was a good or bad idea when she was this cold. Maybe she'd message and ask Kenzo; he probably had more experience with it—considering his animal was more than comfortable in the snow and cold.

The cabin looked nothing like what she'd pictured, in fact, it looked more like an above-ground bunker than a cabin in the woods. She stopped in front of the shed beside the *cabin*. Getting off, she opened the door and checked if there was space enough to pull in.

Going up onto the deck, she hefted her gear awkwardly with numb arms and went to the door. She didn't bother knocking, Graham would have been told she was on the way up—and right now she just wanted out of this weather. That feeling wouldn't last, she couldn't be indoors for long. Her home, of sorts, was a testament to that.

The shocked look on Graham's face told her how frosted over she must look. Lowering her gear to the floor with a *thunk*, she started to work off the gloves and dropped them to the floor. Her hands were red. Glancing, she saw Graham walk over to the woodstove and open it up. By the time he turned back around, she was working her arms out of the cold material.

"Pretty bad out there?"

She only nodded, or it felt like she was, but it was hard to tell.

"Shit, I was hoping it only looked bad up here."

"It's everywhere down there." She peeled the suit down her legs and then stopped when she reached her boots. This was going to suck, she thought. Shuffling over, she sat on the bench beside the door and began to work the frozen laces loose.

"Okay, I'm going to head out before it starts to get dark then."

"You have orders?" She glanced over at him, then back to

her boot, and winced as she pulled her numb foot out. It burned like nothing she'd felt and silently vowed to grab some winter gear and stow it in her ride from this point on.

"Yeah." He cleared his throat, "quick rundown here, that cage and the bathroom are the only spaces that block signals."

She glanced at the cage and the man sitting in it before looking back to her other boot.

"Any trips to the bathroom, he has a blanket to wrap around him, most particularly his neck, and shoulder area," when he paused, she looked up at him again and nodded so he'd continue. "Check-in is every two hours. To Illias."

Blaise paused before she pulled off the boot, "supplies fully stocked?" She was beyond hungry. It had taken a lot of energy trying not to freeze. How did one forms do it without animal heat to tap into?

Graham smirked, "there's enough here to survive an apocalypse. Boss is ready for anything."

She smirked and then regretted it because it made her cheeks burn, "good to hear." She looked over at the man that was Aiden Tomas' half-breed brother, "and him?"

Graham shrugged and then looked at him, "he's no trouble," he turned back to her, "then again, where is he going to go?" He motioned to the window.

She clenched her teeth together and eased the boot off slowly. When she pulled her legs free of the suit, she stood up and wished she hadn't. Hanging it up, she walked awkwardly to the stove with her boots, each step hurt. Setting them down, she dropped down on the chair to the side of it. Yanking her hat off her head, she saw it was frozen in the shape of her head and dropped it beside her boots. "Is there an objective yet," she jerked her chin toward the captive.

"Nothing yet." Graham went over to a bag and did it up, "I think the weather shit on any plans that were going to happen."

"Yeah, the teams are cooling their heels waiting for it to clear."

He went over to the door and grabbed a suit from the hook, "Boss's gear is through there if you want to check on the weather or anything."

"Thanks." She glanced around the space, it was furnished sparsely, with a couch and one chair, a small table and a couple of chairs in the corner, and then the caged-off area. What exactly did Raymond do here? She'd pictured, a fireplace, a bookshelf, somewhere to relax away from the rest of the world, this was not meant for any of that. Then again, her own home followed no norms.

Nothing else was said until Graham was standing at the door ready to go out, "don't tell anyone where you are, and don't make any calls or texts without authorization."

Blaise stood up and nodded, "got it. I'm just hanging out here until I have orders."

He grinned, "it's a peaceful gig so far. I was okay with a few days' downtime."

She nodded, despite not needing downtime. Something like that led to thinking and that always pissed her off or broke her heart. "Safe travels," she grinned, "or warm ones at least."

He laughed, "I'm used to the cold."

She had no idea what clan he was from, but being part of Raymond's team, he probably got to travel a lot. Or had, until all out-of-continent travel had been halted. When word reached her that other continents were working with the Tomas organization, she'd almost laughed out loud. Her family knew firsthand about corrupt ambassadors working against their people.

Rolling her shoulders, she stood up and moved a little closer to the stove. Thawing out was almost as painful as the freezing part. She shifted to the side of the stove, so she could check out their prize captive as she waited for feeling to return to all of her body.

He sat on a cot in an otherwise empty space. She didn't know what she'd expected, but he looked perfectly normal, which annoyed her. Being a half-breed, she'd expected, no, hoped for some visible flaw. His skin was normal, and his hair was dark and not mixed shades. She couldn't see the color of his eyes from here, but they were a human shape and not noticeably odd.

"If you move around, you'll warm up faster."

She stared at him across the space. He stood up and crossed his arms over his chest. Looking away, she flexed her hands over the stove. "I'm fine." It was a lie, she told often, for many reasons. There was nothing fine with her or her existence.

Chapter Four

A woman. They'd sent a woman to watch him. Griffin was so surprised; all he could do was watch her. Of course, staring at her without pause made him feel even more awkward about it, so he did it from various positions in his space, hoping it was less obvious. The window reflection, sitting and appearing to glance around, even laying on his side on the cot.

He wasn't used to being around females, and definitely not alone with one. Thirty-three years and he could count on one hand the number of times he'd had a conversation with a woman. Did ten to fifteen words count as a conversation? He wasn't sure.

She was tall for a female, at least she appeared to be from this perspective. She hadn't come near his cage, so he wasn't one hundred percent on his guess of her height. She wasn't talkative as he thought girls to be, but he had no real-life data to corroborate that observation, only hearsay from other males. His father, his brother, and all his human lackeys had made sure Griffin wasn't near any of the females alone, ever. The few times he'd managed it, whether, through their lapse in judgment or his own, it hadn't been under normal circumstances. Most females he'd been around were being held against their will and the women in those instances had been captives of the sick deprived individuals that in his opinion were lower than parasites on the scale of evolution. There hadn't been conversation, only fear—of him and human women that didn't shift; he'd only seen briefly in passing. It wasn't like he went to social functions.

She stood up and stretched and then reached to pull her hair up. He wasn't sure what color to call it. It wasn't red, at least not plain red. Would it be called auburn? There were lighter streaks through it, making him wonder what sort of shifter she was. He'd observed that many of their hair held some clue as to their creature side's color. Her skin was pale, not in a sickly way and there were freckles dusting the bridge of her nose and cheekbones. The overall structure of her face was feminine and appealing. She was quite lovely to look at. Along her jaw and neck, her skin was darker and not as fair as the rest. He'd noticed her one hand was as well. He wasn't sure what caused it and wondered if it would be appropriate to ask. Despite the contrast in the two skin tones, she was still lovely in his opinion.

She hefted her bag onto the table Graham had sat at and began pulling things out of it. He couldn't hide his surprise to see it was weapons. Two handguns and several knives. She fit them on her trim body without pause, telling him that she was more comfortable with them than without. He watched as she assembled with quick, smooth movements a type of rifle he'd never seen before. It was smaller, like it had been altered to be that way. When she checked the magazine, the sound broke into the silence with a startling effect. Once done, she lifted it and looked through the scope before nodding and placing it beside the door. His mind was all over the place. They'd sent a woman to watch him. A woman with guns and knives adorning her body.

He cleared his throat, "do you do this a lot?" He paused when her gaze pinned him where he stood. "Babysit." He clarified. The hard look in her eyes had thrown him for a few seconds it was such a contrast to her delicate and lovely face.

"I do whatever is required." She looked him up and down a few times and then went into the kitchen.

An alliance soldier, he thought. He was still shocked that they had female soldiers. He'd overheard conversations from some of Aiden's men about the female team members, even women Alpha's that were in charge of entire clans. He knew the women that were taken were not the helpless beings his brother spoke of often. He'd seen gouges and injuries on some of Aiden's men that told him how much they'd fight for themselves.

Had he ever fought for anything in his life? Blowing out a breath, he went over to look out the window. After a few rebellious moments when he was a child, he'd learned to keep his head down, his mouth shut, and stay off his father's radar as much as possible. Of course, doing that with Aiden had proved more difficult. His younger half-brother resented every cell of Griffin's body. He'd repeatedly proven that by giving him the worst possible tasks. One of those was collaring the men, no boys, that would be forced to work and hold their own kind in captivity. That was the one that Griffin hated the most. Each time he secured one around another being's throat, he felt like he had just sealed their fate and stollen their lives from them. He hated it even more than the ones he was ordered to kill. At least in death, he was granting them freedom from all the sick, twisted injustices they had suffered or would had they lived as Aiden's possession.

He smirked briefly, remembering the first few reports of the houses holding captives being raided. Aiden had gone ballistic, ranting like a complete lunatic. To Griffin, it was just his true colors showing. He didn't know how they'd been found or their whereabouts now, but was silently cheering them on and hoping they found a life worth living now that they were free.

"Do you want coffee or anything to drink?"

He jolted and turned to see her standing at the kitchen door.

"A coffee. Thank you. Black." He pushed away from the window while trying to think of something else to say. She didn't give him the opportunity to and was out of sight before he could speak another word.

He felt a tremor in his hand and lifted it to see it shaking. It had been happening a lot the past two days. He knew the reason but wasn't sure if he should say something about it. He turned and looked at the locked box his belongings had been placed in. Passport, driver's license, phone, gun, and his medication. He'd always taken it, and now he had the chance to see what happened if he didn't. He had no idea what the pills were as the bottle was unlabeled, the tablets unmarked, but he'd been told since he was twelve that they were wholly necessary so whatever animal DNA he had would stay dormant.

He'd always complied for fear that if whatever he truly was came out, he'd find himself locked up, a collar around his neck, like the hundreds whose lives were stolen from them. Tucking his hand back into his pocket, he stared at the floor. He should probably ask for one of the pills. The idea of whatever was inside him coming out scared the hell out of him. He wasn't a young boy whose body would give way to shifting. Doing so now could cripple him. Or worse, he may only half shift and then he'd be stuck like that for the rest of his life.

The woman came out of the kitchen carrying two cups. Griffin had a quick flash of what life should have been if he'd been normal—until she set one on the table and opened his *cage*. That canceled out any fantasy thoughts he had. Setting the cup on the floor inside the wire, she stepped back and closed it again.

Griffin reached down and picked up the cup. "I'm Griffin Ballard," he blinked at his own stupidity, "which I'm sure you already knew."

She stood behind the table and looked across the room at him for a few seconds. Sitting down, she pulled the locked box over and glanced at her phone, and punched the code in on the pad. "Blaise."

That was it, no eye contact at all, just her name.

He couldn't very well say pleased to meet you like they were at a social gathering of some kind. With a nod to himself, he sat on the cot and sipped the coffee. It burned his mouth but was made the exact way he liked it. "Thanks." He waited until she looked over at him, he lifted the cup, "for this."

She held his look for ten seconds at least and then jerked her chin once in an abrupt acknowledgment that he's spoken at all.

Oh, yes, he was brilliant with women.

Chapter Five

Every time she glanced in his direction, he was staring at her. It wasn't odd for people to gawk at her. It had been happening her entire life. She'd gotten used to it, but still hated it. This time she wasn't just annoyed, she was keenly aware of it and it was really starting to bother her. Setting his gun, which she noted was well maintained, aside, she picked up his wallet. His driver's license looked legit, just like her own ID. She studied the picture, his was good. No one's ID photos were ever good, but his was. She resented him for that. Her own looked like she'd just taken a punch to the gut when the flash blinded her. His last name surprised her. She'd expected it to be Tomas. Points to him for not using *that* name. She read the address and sneered at the card in her hand, "*suite*," she looked over at him, "you live in some posh *suite*?" She scoffed.

He sat there for a moment, just looking at her. "It's decent. Warm in the winter, cool in the summer."

"I bet." She dropped the card into the box and pulled out another one.

"Does it say that the *posh suite* is guarded? That I am locked in it unless I'm required by my *brother*?"

It wasn't hard to detect the disdain in his voice at the

mention of his half-sibling. "A real victim of circumstance, huh?"

He set the cup on the floor and stood up slowly. "I'm not a victim. The real victims are the ones that are taken." His tone was soft, with no sign of emotion.

Normally she was good at picking up on others' tells that they were hiding when their expressions were voided. He had none that she could see. "We'll get them all." She was done talking—or thought she was, but her mouth had other plans. "We're onto your rat." She wanted him to know that it was going to be over soon. Once all those innocents were brought home, those responsible would pay for all they'd done.

"My rat?"

"The spy that was leaking information to your *brother*." Why was she even talking to him?

He stood there for the longest time and then blinked twice, "you found *one* rat?"

"Yeah." Still, her mouth was blabbing.

"My father had more than one in place on the inside," he chortled ridiculously, "seeing as I don't plan on ever being there again," he motioned around him like she hadn't noticed he was in a cage, "I can also tell you that some of those *victims* you rescued are plants as well and will find a way to get information back to my br—Aiden."

Blaise sat there staring back at him for a very long silent moment. Why was he telling her this? They could have wanted him to be taken to feed them false information. She frowned. Knowing he'd be a sacrifice in the end and wouldn't be returning. "Do you know the names that go with your theory?"

He moved over to the cage and grabbed the wire and looked out between it at her. "No, I don't have names." He clenched his jaw for a second. "I know faces. I've been present for meetings and thought to be out of hearing distance while they spoke."

She got up and went around the table and perched on it. "We'd know if we'd pulled out one-forms." She'd seen those they'd gotten out. None had been in a good state.

He gave her an amused look, "I didn't say they were human, or just human."

"A shifter? You're saying a shifter is working with Tomas, without him holding a family member hostage or something?" Some of those abused men were working *for* the man that had abused them? Why?

"Some taken young enough are raised differently than the others. If they don't know of clans and your world, and believe what they're told, why wouldn't they work with him? We're all told stories of how feral and uncivilized the clans are."

She studied him for a moment. He held her look without faltering. It was insane, but also made perfect sense. She needed to let Kenzo know. They could be housing spies along with the captives. "Why are you telling me this?" There had to be a catch. She trusted no one, not completely.

He smirked, "I'm never going back. I may live in a cage for what's left of my life, but it's still better than the life I've had up until now."

"Your life's been hard? Have you seen those we're fighting to get back? Their lives are hard." She could only think of Emersyn as the words came out. What she'd survived made her the strongest person she'd ever known.

"You think I agree with it? What they're going through? I could do *nothing* about it any more than I can the weather." His tone was deeper, but his expression was still blank.

"I'm not saying you did it—but you were there. It's *your* family."

"Aiden is *not* my family. Having the same father does not make us family, but hey, I'm not complaining. I'm the best of both worlds. Right?"

His words said he was pleased to be, but the expression on his face said otherwise. What was it like to be half one thing, but not fully? She glanced at her darker hand, she was half and half. At least she could shift, that was a blessing—of sorts. If she hadn't been able to, her life would have been something altogether different.

"Ballard? Is that your mother's name?"

A cold look replaced the indifference on his face. "That's my assumption." He sneered, "dear old dad certainly didn't want me to use his."

She nodded slowly, "your mother, what clan was she from?" She tried not to think of how this man in front of her had come to be. If her mouth kept asking things like that it was going to be hard to do. She wasn't a dreamer, but maybe there was a chance it was with consent.

"I have no idea. I never knew her." His expression blanked again.

Had he been ripped from her arms at birth? Or maybe she didn't make it after the birth. This was a dead-end conversation. Regardless of what he said, she knew she was going to be pissed off. Should she voice how sorry she was he hadn't known his mother? She didn't think she could go there. She couldn't develop a soft spot for this man. "So, your father raised you?"

"If that's what you want to call it. It was more of an education than nurturing relationship."

"It's still better than those we've rescued from those houses."

His expression darkened. "You seem to think I had a choice—I didn't. Okay, I did. Either do as instructed or live in a cage with a collar around my neck." He started pacing in the small area. "Do your people think I *wanted* to be an errand boy? Answer my father and brother's beck and call?"

She didn't need him agitated, then she would be, which could lead to bad places. "Can you shift any part of you?"

"No. I've never tried either. I wouldn't try. I didn't want to be their show and tell as well."

"You don't know what clan your mother was?"

"No. I don't know anything about her. I could be wildebeest for all I know." He looked at her again, "Is there such a clan?"

"Not that I know of." She fought the grin, so he wouldn't see that picturing him as a wildebeest amused her.

"Look, even if I wanted to, I can't or couldn't." He pointed to the table, "I've been taking those since I was twelve so I wouldn't."

She picked up the bottle of pills, "these stop you from shifting?"

He nodded and then glanced at his hands and jammed them into the pockets of his creased pants.

She examined the bottle closely, then opened it and inhaled. The pills were tinged with a chemical smell. "Do you know what they are?"

"Oh sure," he scoffed, "I analyzed them in my lab the first chance I had." He gave her a hard look, "I have no idea what they are." He was back at the wire looking at her through it, holding her gaze, "look when I was sent alone, which has never happened before—to pick up the Alpha female, I was supposed to kill Darrel," he shrugged, "which I had no problem doing, he deserved it. He was a lowlife that made a living abducting people." He huffed out a breath, "they already knew that your people found the campsite where she had been held." He paused and took a deep breath and then exhaled slowly, "I was going to kill him and free the woman and then use the money to disappear." He snarled and tapped the back of his neck, "I had no idea I had a tracker in me." Pushing away from the cage, he went over to the window. "I wouldn't have made it very far."

Blaise looked at his back and then down at the bottle she still held. She needed to tell someone about this. She needed to tell *everyone*. Everything he'd said was game-changing and pissed her off at the same time. She looked at him, and then around the room. The bathroom was a dead zone, she wasn't going outside to make a call. Turning, she glanced at the door Graham had pointed to. "I have to check in with my boss, don't do anything stupid while I do."

Griffin snorted and motioned to the window. He didn't turn to look at her, "where am I going to go? If I didn't freeze to death, somewhere out there is a bullet waiting for me."

Blaise looked out the window. He was right. They would

come for him and wouldn't stop until his life was forcibly expired. If there were all these spies he was talking about, they probably already knew where he was, and the storm had gotten in their way.

She went over and opened the door and then stopped and looked around. Maps covered one entire wall. There was a lot of equipment in the room, but other than a computer, none of it was plugged in. She didn't know what half of it was for, but Raymond must have set it up in the cage before they brought the half-brother here. She shrugged, Raymond Hardy was at the top of all the Alliance teams, so it made sense that he'd be well-equipped.

Pulling out her phone, she turned and leaned back against the table. Glancing up, she paused and then smirked; if she wasn't mistaken, there was a cattle prod hanging on the wall. She couldn't even imagine what he'd need that for but was sure there were some stories to go with it. Opening up her contacts, she hit dial beside Kenzo and put the phone to her ear.

"Blaise?"

"Boss. I have things to share."

"Oh? How important? And tell me you didn't beat it out of him."

She smirked, "I didn't touch him. He's pissed off and that makes him chatty."

"Interesting. Hold on, I'm going to get Illias to add Devin to this call."

She heard a few clicks on the line and wondered how Illias could just add someone to a call she made. Then again, she knew nothing about technology. To her, it either worked or was a piece of shit situation."

"Devin, Blaise has been talking to our special guest."

"Is he still breathing?"

Kenzo chuckled, "she hasn't touched him."

"Just thought I'd check. Some of your team are a bit rough."

Kenzo laughed at that, "we do our job in whichever manner is the most efficient.

Blaise smirked, she'd never heard her team leader put things so politely before.

"Okay, Blaise, what have you got for us?"

She wasn't sure where to start but didn't want to keep the prince waiting too long. Which part was the most important? She looked at the bottle but decided the spies merited first mention. "Some of those we've retrieved are working *for* Tomas. From what he said, I'm going to say any that were born after their mother was taken or they were taken very young."

"Wait, you mean some of those that wore collars that we're freeing?" Prince Devin didn't sound so calm now.

"Yeah." She scowled at the floor, "I'd start with the ones that were the youngest, like how old they were when they were taken, ones that wouldn't know much about clan life and reference it with their state of health when we got to them."

"Overall health, the condition of their necks from the collar," Kenzo added.

"Yeah, I got it." Devin's tone was low and lethal.

"And," she blew out a breath, "he says his father had many placed on the *inside* of the Alliance."

"His father? So they've been working for the Alliance this long?"

"Does he have names?" Kenzo interrupted the prince.

"No, but he says he knows faces." She frowned, "he was supposed to kill that one that organized Amari's abduction." She looked at the door, wondering what he was doing out there, "he *says* he was planning to free her and then take off with the money."

There was a long pause.

"He didn't know about the tracker." It wasn't a question. The prince was a smart man.

"His apartment or whatever was a fancy prison for him, he says he was locked in and guarded when he wasn't needed."

"I can get someone to check that out. Clarify it." Devin sounded a little calmer now.

"Does the Alliance know about the drug they use to prevent shifting?" She looked at the bottle of pills again.

"We knew there was an injection used on the women."

She shook the bottle. "He's been taking these pills since he was twelve."

"He can shift?" Kenzo sounded surprised.

"He doesn't know. He's never tried or," she rolled the bottle in her hand, "he's never had the chance to try."

"What clan was his mother?"

"Unknown." She didn't want to think about his mother again or how she did or didn't get pregnant. "It's her last name that he uses."

"Illias, search Ballard in the clan directories."

"On it."

"Has he had any of the pills since we got him?"

Blaise shrugged, "I don't think so."

"Does he want them?" Kenzo asked.

"I can find out." She remembered what she'd gone through when she didn't know if she would shift of not. It was awful and she didn't wish that anguish on anyone. As far as she knew only clan that could fully shift were on all the Alliance teams. For good reasons, she imagined, acceptance of those they were policing was the only thing she could think of right now.

"We need those pills to figure out what they are, but do we want to chance his shifting if we don't know what he is?"

"Blaise can handle it." Kenzo sounded confident.

It pleased her that her team leader believed in her.

"I am so glad someone entered all this into the system. I can't imagine going old school and having to flip through actual paper records." Illias laughed, "there are two Ballard families listed. One has never had a family member taken or disappeared. The other had a young girl vanish," Illias blew out a breath into the phone, "about forty years ago."

"That fits," Devin said quietly, "given that if the age on his ID is accurate. The girl would have been an adult when—" he stopped for a second. "What clan was she from?"

"Kermode bear, or sprit bear is the preferred name, sir."

Blaise blinked, she'd never heard of that shifter clan before. The wild animal, yes, but a clan of them, no.

"Are there any of that clan left?"

"Uh," Illias made a ticking sound, "yes. On an island out West sir. Twenty members. Communication is sparse, but the last check-in with them was four months ago."

"Are there any Ballard's left?" Blaise wasn't usually one to care about things like that, but the man that had never known his mother might have family out there. If you didn't count Aiden Tomas and she was starting to believe Griffin didn't count him at all.

"There's two in the clan, uh, an uncle and aunt possibly. I'd have to do a deep dive to see how they're connected exactly."

"Do that and let us know," Devin ordered.

"Are you thinking we can dangle information in front of him and get more out of him?" Kenzo spoke quietly.

"I don't know yet, I just want all the facts." The prince replied.

Blaise frowned, "I don't think he'll have a problem sharing," she had no evidence to prove it, she was just going on a hunch.

"How did he tell you all of this, Blaise?"

She straightened, the prince might not be in front of her, but he was still a top-rank member of the Alliance. "He was agitated," she shrugged, "pissed off."

"That's good." Kenzo injected, "I'd call bullshit if he were calmly spilling his guts."

"I don't," she bit her lip for a second, trying to decide if she should continue, "I don't think his life has been much better than those we've been pulling out, sir. He was treated like a pet by his *father*," she sneered just thinking about Alberto Tomas.

"That wouldn't surprise me." There was a short pause. "Keep track of anything he shares. Leave it up to him if he wants those pills—but we need some to analyze. We're hoping the surgeon can get there in the next few days to take the tracker out, and then Nate has said he may be able to trace where it's being monitored."

"Oh, a challenge." Illias was amused.

"Okay." She thought of what he'd said, "sir, boss, he said they already knew about the campsite being found when Amai was taken and that there would be a bullet waiting for him as soon as the weather—"

"Shit. They knew Tripp found the campsite? How?" Now Kenzo sounded annoyed.

"We need to purge the Alliance of all these spies," Devin growled.

"I'm going to see if Uri can get one of his to keep an eye on your location, Blaise. I'll tell them to stay out of sight, but you'll have some kind of backup if you need it."

Blaise exhaled, "okay, boss. I can keep him alive, but that tracker complicates shit if they move in on our location."

"Only five people know your exact location, so unless they did manage to get a direction when he was being transported, you should be good."

That made her feel a slight bit better, but she also knew the extremes the Tomas family would go to.

"Can we leave you in charge of him until everything is sorted out and the medical team can get there? Are you okay with that?"

"I'm all aces, sir. Good to go."

"Great. I need to go fill in my father and then I'll be in touch."

Blaise nodded, "sounds good, sir."

"Good work, Blaise." Kenzo added and then the line went quiet.

Chapter Six

She hadn't spoken since she came back out of the room. Griffin didn't know what the walls were made of, but he hadn't been able to hear what was being said. That was unusual for him. Since he was a teen he'd been able to hear things that most could not. That handy skill had probably saved his life more times than he could keep track of. He would hear what was going on and be able to adjust his behavior to avoid conflict or in most cases punishment. Of course, it didn't work on Aiden as it had on his father. To Aiden, his existence made him guilty of *everything*.

He moved over to the window and leaned against the cage, ignoring the wire cutting into his shoulder. He had no real proof that Alberto Tomas was his father, other than being told he was. There was no resemblance at all to the senior or his full-blooded son. He'd never seen so much as a picture of Aiden's mother, but he had to assume he took after her. Many hours of his life had been spent wondering about his own mother. What had she been like? Not what she shifted into, but the type of person she had been. He was going under the assumption she no longer lived, because he'd never heard speak of her in any way.

The older women were moved to the camps where they

took the young girls. Had his mother been sent there at some point? He'd been to the boy camp as punishment for a year when his father was mad at him. There were no women there. He wondered if the girls were treated better than the boys were because, honestly, he wouldn't wish what he'd been through on his worst enemy. Aside from the physical torture they suffered, from starving to being beaten, the main purpose he'd concluded of the camps was to brainwash the young males, making them believe that females were the lowest form of existence. Good for breeding, nothing else. He smirked as he wondered what Blaise would think of that, he was sure people would be hurt for telling her something like that.

Glancing at Blaise, he saw that she was watching him again. What had she found out during her call with her boss that caused her to look at him like she was dissecting him? He pushed away from the wall and moved to the other side of his space. "Is everything all right?" Cocking his head, he studied her for a second. She was tense now when she hadn't been before. "You're looking a little tense."

"I'm fine." She got up from the table and crossed her arms over her chest. She was anything but fine, but he wasn't going to push his luck. "How are you feeling?" She motioned to the table with a jerk of her chin. He looked at the bottle sitting there. "Any side effects from stopping these?"

Griffin debated for a second whether he should tell the truth. "A little shaky." He pulled his hand out of his pocket and held it out to show her the slight tremor. "I don't think there's anything else." He'd thought for a while his sense of smell was improving, but decided that was because he was shut in with no ventilation outside from the storm. Ever since she'd arrived, he could smell something spicy and sweet, light but dark at the same time. Which made no sense, unless it was something on her clothes.

"Do you want the pills?" She shrugged, "it's been a few days, but it's up to you." She smirked so briefly he wasn't sure she actually had, "it's not like you're going to suddenly shift without notice."

In his entire life, he didn't remember someone asking him what he wanted, pertaining to anything. "What is it like? To shift that first time?"

Her eyes widened for a moment, "it's scary, of course, the not knowing part gets the better of you," she shrugged, "but the adrenalin rush of that first time is like nothing I've felt since."

Holding his hand out, he turned it over and looked at it, "chances of me even shifting is, pretty much zilch, I've been told."

"And yet," he looked at her as she picked up the bottle and shook it, "they made you take these, so I wouldn't say zilch, or they wouldn't have made you," she watched him closely, looking for a reaction. He knew from experience that any reaction that portrayed your true thoughts or feelings was dangerous. "I'm pretty sure they made you take them."

Tucking his hand back in his pocket, he studied her for a moment. How much did he tell her? "Up to a point, yes. I had no choice," he looked down at the cup on the floor, then bent down and picked it up. It was cold, but he still drank the last coffee before answering her. "Until I did."

"Until they gave you a choice?"

"I don't," he set the empty cup down, "think I had a choice. I had no idea what my mother became; so after a few curious thoughts as a young boy, I chose to not chance it."

"You didn't want to know?"

He didn't know how to explain it to her, "I was just trying to survive. I was ten when I gave up my fantasies of shifting into some powerful beast and escaping my life for a shiny new one." He hadn't meant to be so sarcastic; allowing emotions to burst free was unlike him. He watched her for a negative reaction, but it was like she hadn't even noticed it.

"Okay," she said slowly as if she was filtering her thoughts before speaking, "would you like to continue to take it, or not." She held up the bottle, "the choice *is* yours."

Choice. He was being given a choice. Did he want to see what happened without them? No, he didn't, but he was going to do it anyway—merely because he was given a choice. "Not right now." He looked at his hand again, "I don't know what happens without them, so…"

"Don't worry. I have tranq darts if weird shit happens." She turned on her heel and went over to her bag on the table and pulled out a handgun. It was bulkier than the one strapped to her leg. She waved it around and then set it on the table.

"Pass. The after-effects from those are not pleasant."

She smirked. "I'm told the headache afterward is pretty rough."

"That's one way to describe it."

Chapter Seven

Blaise hadn't known she'd decided to tell him until the words were coming out of her mouth. "They're pretty sure they know what clan your mother was from—if her name was really Ballard."

He froze. Didn't move at all, she wasn't sure if he was still breathing. "They do? You, ah," he motioned to the door of Raymond's other room. "You found that out just then?"

"Yeah. Do you want to know?" He may be part Tomas, but for the part of him that was a shifter, she wanted him to know. She knew what it was like to wonder what was inside you. To not know all the pieces of yourself was a very heavy thing to carry.

"I," he blew out a breath and stood there with his hands on his hips and looked at the floor. "I never thought there was a way to find out." He looked back at her, "I used to ask the ones looking after me when I was young, but—" he clenched his jaw, "that landed me in some bad situations." He blew out another breath and nodded slowly. With a look of trepidation, the motion of his head increased. "Okay. Yeah. Tell me." He grimaced, "wait, it's not like some awful thing like a large rat-like creature—that-that would be very anti-climatic after years of imagining other creatures."

Blaise couldn't help the smirk. She cleared her throat, "no. You're not a rat, well," she shrugged. "Kermode bear."

His expression changed three times before he spoke. "A what? I don't know what that is."

She frowned and glanced at her phone. The orders for unnecessary use were still in place, so she couldn't search and show him. "Spirit bear, I believe they're almost white or very pale. They're rare, only one clan on record, and pretty remote," she shrugged, "on an island in Western Canada."

He hadn't moved or made a sound.

"You might have relatives; they're looking into it."

"Actual relatives?" She wasn't sure if he was saying it to her or himself. "not that it matters, right? I'm from the enemy, and being mixed, it's not like they'll throw a welcome home party. I'm a mutt in the shifter community and an abomination in the human one."

What he said hit every chord inside her. If anyone understood the feeling that you didn't belong, it was her. "They didn't think I would be able to shift." He turned and looked at her. "My family."

"Why?"

Had she meant to go here? To bleed out her angst on a stranger? No, but it was too late now. "Somewhere in my family tree, way back, two from different clans got together." She didn't know the details, but she could fake it. Lifting up her right arm, she held it out making sure he could see the darker skin. He glanced at it and then back to her face. Scowling at him, she scoffed, "I'm a mixed breed." It was the first time she'd ever said it out loud.

"You shift?"

She nodded.

"To what?" he frowned, "what clans?"

"Tiger." She looked at her own hands and then dropped them to her sides. "My best guess is two different tiger species."

"Everyone's okay with it? You?"

She snorted, "I stopped caring what others thought when I

was ten."

"What does that mean for your children?"

Turning quickly, she went back behind the table, "I don't have any children."

"Fine. Your future children?"

"That won't happen." She glanced at the kitchen, not wanting to look at him. Should she ask if he's hungry? She huffed out a breath, regretting the entire conversation. "I got myself fixed so I don't have to worry about a child going through what I did." With stiff movement, she went into the kitchen and then changed her mind, and turned around. "I will take a hot poker and expunge that from your brain if you ever think about repeating a word of that."

His mouth quirked like he wanted to smile but didn't want to take the conversation lightly at the same time. "I understand."

Blaise spun back and went into the kitchen. She stood there and looked at the counter. What possessed her to say any of that? She'd never told anyone that she had made sure she would never have children. No one should have to go through the humiliation she had growing up. Other children were cruel. They didn't care if there were reasons you were different, just that you didn't fit into some checkbox that they did. Some adults weren't much better. She remembered the mothers telling their children not to get too close to her like her mixed DNA was contagious or something.

She looked at the door. What kind of life had he had? She knew just from him saying he was an abomination that the Tomas' hadn't exactly accepted him into their family with open arms. Shaking her head, she opened the cupboard to see what she felt like making. It wasn't her job to care about his life, or what his feelings were on anything. Her job was to keep him alive for the time she was here and then move on to the next assignment.

Chapter Eight

Was this day five? He didn't think he could handle many more in the cage, without air and being able to move around. "Am I going to be asked any questions?"

"That's not my job."

"What is your job?"

"Today? To keep you alive and safe."

"Safe?" He scoffed. "You think I'm safe here? There is nowhere safe from Aiden. Trust me on that."

"I'm not here to trust anyone or thing."

He shrugged, "smart. Look, give me a pen and paper and I'll write down everything I know."

"Do I look like an office worker?"

"No. You do not."

"You're serious?"

"Yes. As I said, I'm never going back—alive at least. I want to help—end what he does." He inhaled slowly, trying to slow his heart rate, "a map, if you have one I can mark cities and towns that I know Aiden has people or houses in."

With a skeptical look, she glanced around and then got up and went into the other room, he had no idea what 'gear' was in there, but if she came back with paper, he would write everything down that he could remember. He remembered a lot. Things that any rescued guard would never know.

She came back out with a notebook and a map. Stopping, she looked down at the sharpie in her hand and then at him. "If I give you a pen, you won't do anything stupid, right?"

"With a pen?" Griffin smirked, "what am I going to do with a pen?" He actually could think of a few things, but knew saying them was not the right move.

"Why do this? You know your future isn't looking great right now."

"I want to help." He backed away from the door, so she wouldn't be spooked opening it. "I know things. I could talk until my voice is gone and no one would believe a word I say. I get it, I'm from the enemy camp, but I *know* things that will help your people stop him—them." She still looked skeptical. He got it. "I learned the hard way that appearing oblivious is the best course of surviving this life I've been given. It took many painful occurrences to learn how not to react like I've heard something I shouldn't hear. I have a good memory. Let me help."

Tucking the paper and map under her arm, she pulled out her gun and opened the door. Keeping the gun aimed at him, she held out the other items.

He moved slowly, not wanting to set her off. "You know, I could take that out of your hand, right? Being a half-breed among full shifters growing up, I had to learn to defend myself." He clicked his teeth together, no sure what possessed him to say that.

She smirked, "don't underestimate me because I'm a girl."

He held out his hand for the items. "I would never."

She snorted and then backed out the door and closed it quickly.

Griffin was very intrigued. She was nothing like any female he'd been around. She was strong, but there were little slices of vulnerability there mixed in with all that strength. He didn't know if she was aware of it, but considering the number of weapons she had on her, he decided not to find out how well she used them by provoking her.

Turning around he rolled his eyes, there was no chair or table. Floor it was. Kneeling he spread out the map and looked at it. It was only of North America, so he'd have to just make notes about the other locations he was aware of.

He flipped the page and continued writing. It wasn't organized in any way, just point form with names, or an address, along with several codes and routines. The last twenty years of information was pouring from his mind, giving him a cramped hand.

Pausing, he straightened and stretched. Who knew kneeling on the floor, hunched over a notebook would be so painful. Rolling his head from side to side, he glanced over at Blaise. She was looking at him. Scowling, she got up and walked into the kitchen. Her moving past his cage caused him to pick up her sweet, spicy scent. A chill moved through him. Looking at the window, he wished for fresh air. The longer he knelt here, the more agitated he felt. Remembering everything was bringing up a lot of memories he didn't want to relive. Not just the injustices he'd personally suffered, but things he'd seen. He'd remember them for the rest of his life, there was no forgetting. Being closed in wasn't helping him at all.

Griffin looked down at the page in front of him. Next, he would share the companies they funneled money through, and then the transport systems they used. They'd changed over the years, but he still knew which ones were in operation and which had closed down because of technology. Even criminals knew when their methods had to be modernized or given up.

He was startled when the cage door opened. Blaise set a cup on the floor. He didn't need to ask what was in it, he could smell the coffee from here. "Can we open a window or door for a minute? I feel like the walls are closing in."

She closed the door. "It's because your meds are almost out of your system. Shifters don't do well inside or with confined spaces."

Leaning back on his heels, he looked around. "I didn't think of that."

She shrugged, "you'll get used to it. The anxiousness, when you're inside too long."

His chest tightened, "all of the others". He stared at the floor but didn't really see it. "The ones kept inside all the time…"

"Yup." She turned on her heel. "Now you're starting to understand. You'll probably have a lot of body aches too. For the first time in your life, you'll be the *real* you and not some medicated version."

Griffin glared at her back until she sat down and then he looked back to the notebook. *The real me?* He didn't know what the real him was, but helping end the tyranny of his sadistic brother was a good. Cleanse all the old part of his life. He took a sip and reread the last page, so he could pick up where he left off. The old part of his life kept scrolling through his head like a news ticker.

When he thought that, he'd been fantasizing about having some sort of life. There wasn't going to be a nice home and new life. He glanced at the wire. His future didn't look much different than his past.

Chapter Nine

Blaise flipped a few more pages and skimmed what he'd written down. He hadn't been kidding, he knew a lot. She wasn't privy to what the Alliance knew, but she was sure his information was going to change everything. Setting it on the table, she got up and went over to the window.

Was the storm finally moving on? It was hard to tell now that it was night. Wiping her hand over the glass, she leaned closer. With the blowing snow, it was impossible to see if it had or not.

A thud from the bathroom made her spin around. Going over, she listened outside the door.

"Are you good in there?" There was no reply. She couldn't hear any water running either. There was no way he got out the window. She'd tried the bars on it and hadn't been able to budge them at all.

Grasping the doorknob, she tried it. It turned, which was good. Breaking down the bathroom door in Raymond's getaway spot would have been embarrassing to explain. She opened the door a few inches, not wanting to get an eyeful of anything that they'd both regret. The door hit something and wouldn't open any further. Looking down, she saw blood on the white tiles and a leg stopping her from opening it further. Shoving the door, she saw the man she was in charge of lying on the floor. Blood was all over his hands, the side of his face, and his neck.

Dropping to her knees, she reached over and grabbed a towel. Had he fallen and cracked his head open? Running her hand over his head, she frowned; there was no bump or blood there. A steady stream of blood ran down his neck. She dabbed at it with the towel. Leaning over, she saw the source of it was a hole ripped into the skin near his spine. Pressing the towel over it, she looked around for the source of the puncture. He must have slipped and shanked himself on a sharp corner or— what looked like a spring lay on the floor. One end of it had been straightened and it was covered in blood. What the hell? She looked around and spotted what was left of the toilet paper holders roller lying on the floor.

Holy shit.

Holding the towel firm with one hand, she pulled her phone out of her pocket and set it on the floor. Hitting Kenzo's number, she tapped speaker and slid it so it would clear the door and allow a signal.

"Blaise?"

"Boss. I have a 911 situation here." She tucked her hair back from her face and then cringed and looked at her hand. It was covered in blood. Scowling, she raised it to her face and inhaled. It smelled like —

"Details," Kenzo said impatiently.

Shaking her head, she looked down at the unconscious man and put her fingers against his throat. His pulse was weak. "Where is the tracker in our *friend*?" She still didn't trust the phones to say too much.

"Back of his neck. Why? The surgical team will get there once the roads are passable..."

"He tried to cut it out with a spring from the toilet paper holder."

"What?" She heard a door slam.

"He's unconscious and," she moved the soaked towel enough to see, "bleeding all over the place."

"Shit. Hang on. I'm getting Illias to call medical."

She glanced at the phone for a second. *Hang on? And do what?* She looked around to see if there was a med kit in the room. Stretching, she opened the cupboard and almost sighed to see a first aid kit. Squatting over him, so she could keep the towel in place, she grabbed it and dropped it on the floor. It slid away from her as she tried to open the zipper. Snarling at it, she braced it between her knee and his back, so it would stay put.

"Blaise."

"Still here. I found the first aid kit." The stupid thing finally opened, and she dug in it, "there's no wound seal in here to slow the bleeding, boss."

"Doctor wants to know where exactly it is."

She straightened, "back of his neck."

"Yes. Where? How close to his spine, is it in muscle?"

"Uh, I don't know. Anatomy really isn't my thing." Causing injuries was more her thing, but she didn't say that. Kenzo was well aware of her *skills*.

"Assess and give us an approximate."

Blowing out a breath, she knelt and moved the towel to one side, she had to override the sarcasm and remember it was her boss on the other end, "two fingers width from the spine." The amount of blood was starting to freak her out. She moved the towel the other to see the other side and then pushed along the slippery blood-soaked flesh. "It doesn't feel like it's in any big muscles." She could hear talking. Flipping the towel, she rolled it to a dry spot.

"That's not good." He finally said.

She sneered at the phone. "No shit, boss. It's still leaking steady."

"It will be impossible to stitch it up without help."

She nodded, she wasn't sewing anyone's skin, with or without help.

"They want you to cauterize it."

She glared over at the phone, "with what?" The idea of burning his flesh made her stomach roll.

"Uh, Illias says heat a blade on the stove burner."

Clicking her teeth together, she looked out at the woodstove. If she stopped applying pressure, he could bleed out before she got back to seal it. "Shit, shit, shit. I'm going to have to drag him closer, or he's going to bleed out on the floor."

"Do it."

Standing up, she grabbed a few more towels and wrapped one around his neck, but not too tight. She rolled him gently on his back and set the other towel under his head, she placed the first aid kit on his chest. Despite him being part of the Tomas organization, she still apologized in her head when she lifted his feet and started to drag him out of the bathroom. Pausing, she dropped her phone on his chest and started backing up across the room. "How do I go about cauterizing?"

She reached the stove and positioned him close so she could reach both him and the blade she would heat. Glancing around, she spotted an oven mitt in the kitchen and jogged over and grabbed it. She didn't have time to shift and heal any injuries caused by stupidity.

Pulling her knife from her ankle, she set it on the wood stove's edge and knelt to check the bleeding. "Heating the blade now."

She unwrapped his neck and saw it was still oozing blood. Putting the towel back over, she held it in place as she moved her phone and the first aid kit from his chest so she could roll him onto his side.

"The blade is going to have to be close to red hot," Kenzo told her. "Doctor says roughly five seconds to seal it."

"And that will seal it inside and out?" If something went wrong with how she did this, she would be responsible for losing the biggest lead to date in stopping Aiden Tomas and all his sicko buddies.

"He says it should."

'Should' was not a comforting word right now.

"Is there some kind of antibiotic ointment or salve in the first aid kit?"

Reaching over, she flipped it upside down so all of the

contents spilled onto the floor. She picked up a tube and read the label, "yeah."

"After, put that on it and try not to cover it up unless necessary." Kenzo cleared his throat, "was he trying to take off?"

"Boss, I don't think he has any intentions of taking off or going back there." Blaise looked over at the cage he'd been in for days, "I think he just wanted out to move around. Those pills wearing off has been making him really restless."

"Oh? How can you be sure?"

She glanced at the blade and wondered how long red hot took. "He's been writing down details," she glanced down at him, "that will save us a lot of guesswork. If he planned to take off, why would he tell us?"

"Interesting."

"He marked locations on the map too…"

"How's his pulse? Did he pass out from loss of blood, or did he faint?"

She checked his pulse again. It wasn't the strongest, but it was still enough she felt a little of the panic ease. "I can't be sure, boss. Pulse is decent enough."

"Okay, good. How's the blade?"

Rising to her knees, she looked at it. How the hell was she supposed to check it?

"Rinse the area before you seal it."

She quirked an eyebrow at the phone. "Right." Cursing in her head, she rose , bolted for the kitchen, grabbed a bottle of water off the counter, and slid back beside him. Holding the towel in place, she wrestled the lid off with her teeth and then paused. "When you come to, I'm kicking you in the ass." She mumbled. Setting the water down, she put on the mitt, using her teeth to pull her hand all the way on it. Picking up the knife, she dipped her finger into the water and flicked it at the blade. It hissed on contact. She put the blade back on the stove and nodded, looking down at him. "Doing it now." She hoped the blade was hot enough because doing this more than once was not happening.

Moving the towel, she picked up the water with the hand in the oven mitt and poured it over the site. Setting it down, she grabbed the knife and then huffed out a few breaths to build up the courage to do it. She pressed the knife against his skin and winced for him. One. The sound of searing flesh, combined with the smell, made her want to puke. Two. She was definitely kicking his ass later. Three. Four. She blew out a breath again. Five. Pulling the knife away, she set it on the bricks around the stove. The wound looked worse than it had oozing blood, but it appeared to be sealed. "Okay, I think it's closed." Her shoulders slumped slightly.

"Get the ointment on it and get him back in the cage." She could hear other voices in the background. "Check for the tracker where he did it, just in case he got it out. I can't tell you how big it is, because X-rays were never done."

She lifted an eyebrow and opened the tube up. Her hands were red with his blood. The areas dry were dark now. She clamped her jaw together and then put the ointment on very carefully. He was an idiot, but something that angry looking deserved a little tenderness. At least until he was awake again and then she planned to press her knuckles into it, as payback for putting her through this.

"Keep whatever he's writing in a safe place. Call when he's conscious. I'm going to reach out to Uri and see what's going on with the one he was sending your way. I still think Tomas is going to keep looking until he finds him."

She nodded. "I'd appreciate a little surveillance on my location."

"As soon as he is conscious, get some liquids into him to help replenish the blood loss. You did good, Blaise."

"I'll call when he's awake." She didn't wait for any touching goodbyes, just reached over and hung up her phone. Pushing back from him, she sat on the floor a few feet away and studied him. "This can't be real," She whispered, "Because I haven't already been handed a shitty deal," she looked at the darkly pigmented skin on her arm, "now this."   She lifted her hand to her nose and inhaled. The blood had dried, and she couldn't be sure. Crawling over, she leaned close to his chest and took a slow breath. His scent hit her like a smack in the face, causing her to bolt upright and then get to her feet. Her mate was the half-brother of the man she wanted to see on the ground with a blade sticking out of his heart. Putting her hands on her hips, she looked at the floor. What the hell was she going to do about it?

Blaise stood with her arms crossed over her chest and her nose an inch from the wire, staring at him. He was still out. How long until he'd wake up? Should she be worried? Having already gone inside the cage three times and checked his pulse and the burn on his neck, she was beyond annoyed with herself.   She had a mate. For whatever lack of reasoning, she had always thought that because she was a mixed breed, there wouldn't be a fated one out there for her. Yet, there he was, unconscious on the floor a few feet from her.

Her mate was not only half-human, he was related to the family that had been hunting shifters for the last century, maybe longer, she wasn't into the history part of it. Obviously, in some past life, she had done some serious wrongs that she was paying for in this life.

If she was smart, she would get the hell out of here and never look back. She might have if it weren't for Kenzo and the Alliance. She'd never quit an assignment, or any task given to her and now was not the time to start. Especially with the weather the way it was, getting someone else here would be impossible.

Taking a deep breath, she blew it out slowly and reached for her cat. It was odd how quiet she'd been since she had inhaled Griffin's scent. Her animal was there, in a very watchful state. Why? Why wasn't she giving her opinions? Her animal was *always* free giving with her thoughts and feelings about things.

Stepping back, she turned and went over to the table. She wasn't going to check on him again tonight. She needed to grab a few minutes of sleep, or she was going to start losing it. Dropping down into the chair, she kicked her feet up on the table. Hissing out a breath, she got up and went over to the chair by the stove. If she sat in the other one, she'd spend the rest of the night staring at him like some kind of fool wishing for shit that could never be.

As soon as the storm let up, she would ask Kenzo to trade assignments. One of the guys watching him would be better. When he set a replacement, she would go take the information Griffin had written down to her team leader or the prince—anyone that would get her away from him.

Chapter Ten

He stood there looking at the portrait behind his desk. It was of his father and he felt like he watched over him. Most days, Aiden wished he was still alive, but lately, he was glad he wasn't. Things were out of control, and it pissed him off. Someone was sharing information and he wasn't sure who. The past several months had been one shit show after another. How were they finding the locations that had been operating for decades? They weren't linked to the family at all, so he knew the authorities weren't involved. There were many left, but now he was going to have to move them. Moving them was going to be a hassle, but it was going to have to happen. Of course, until the roads were open, that wasn't happening.

Stabbing the intercom button, he stared at the window.

"Boss?"

"I need a complete catalog of the sites that have been raided and all those remaining here in the US."

"I have them working on it, Boss."

"Good. Tell them I need it by the end of today." He hit the button again to end the conversation.

He needed to get the few that he trusted here for a little sit down to start planning this. Where the hell was Lindon? The house they'd been staying at was empty, with no trace of them at all. Of all those working for him, he never imagined that he would bail on him and disappear. He didn't know what rock he was hiding underneath, but they'd find it eventually. It was his own fault for letting him control where his clan was and never pushing to know the location. Not that it mattered in this instance. Lindon didn't seem to be attached to anyone, so holding clan safety over his head likely wouldn't have worked. The only thing Lindon cared about was planting his seed in every young female tiger they came across. Aiden didn't know how many offspring he had, but when he found them, they would find out if Lindon cared about any of them.

Unlocking his phone, he checked for messages. There was nothing new. His spy inside the Shifter Alliance was late reporting in. Scrolling through his contact list, he tapped on the one insider who had never let him down or let his father down. He would tell him what was going on. His father had been a genius, placing so many inside the Alliance before they stepped up the game and took this international. This *shifter's* stupidity had earned him a lifetime of serving the Tomas family. The one carnal sin that was never forgiven by these abominations was never kill your own kind—unless it's an Alpha challenge, or some kind of bull like that. This very reliable shifter had killed one of his own and actually believed Aiden's father would turn him in. To do that, he would have had to give a damn, and he didn't.

He glanced at the phone when the reply came, *New security system is taking me longer than I thought to get through. I'll let you know when I'm in.*

Aiden text back quickly, before the idiot did something obvious. *Don't wear out your welcome there. You'll be needed next week in Cancun.*

Got it, came back immediately.

Tossing the phone on the desk, he dropped into his chair , opened the center drawer, and pulled out the folder he'd looked through more times than he should have.

Flipping through a folder, he picked up one of the photos

and studied it. His men had said she wasn't where they tracked the car, yet here he was looking at her in this picture. She looked incredible, but then again, she always did. There was something different about her now that he couldn't quite identify.

It had taken five investigators to locate her, but now that he knew where she was, he had a way to keep track of her. Dropping the photo, he glared at the next one. She was with a fleabag shifter that he was told was the prince of their Alliance. He could only assume that she was able to shift after all. It was too bad, really; he'd hoped she couldn't. If she hadn't, then he could have kept her forever. Of course, his heirs would have been procured by a human mother. None of that half-breed shit was happening again. His father's lapse in sanity with Griffin was bad enough.

The intercom buzzed, "Boss. They found Griffin. The signal was brief, but they have a starting point now."

"Good, go retrieve him." He planned to teach him a lesson he'd never forget. No one ran from him. It was even worse than the fate he had in store for Lindon when he was located.

"Boss, it's mountain terrain. It's going to be impossible to get there in this storm."

Turning, he glared out the window, the snow still hadn't let up. "Send those new one who are eager to prove themselves. The," he scowled at the floor, trying to remember what atrocity they turned into, "the ones that Harley sent us from Europe."

"Okay, Boss, what are the orders?"

"Bring him back breathing, but I don't care if it's only just barely."

"Got it."

Slapping the folder shut, he brushed it back into the drawer and sat back. Folding his hands over the desk. They needed to stop grabbing women and children and weaker males. Turning the ring on his finger that his father and grandfather had once worn, he studied it. It was time to start going after their Alpha's and anyone else in a position of power. He was going to control the shifter world, one way or another. Taking females and children was not going to accomplish that.

Once he had control, he would have enough power behind him to take his family's 'business' and turn it into an empire. Adjusting the ring, he tapped his hand on the desk. It was time to start thinking about family. He would have married Rayne, not in a real ceremony, but could have kept her happy to play house with for many years to come. There was no time to dwell over a lost puppy, he needed a red-blooded human wife and children to teach them how the world really worked.

He stood up and stared at the painting. The idea of finding Griffin improved his mood greatly, it gave him something to look forward to, teaching his *brother* who was in charge.

Chapter Eleven

Opening the cage, Blaise went in and looked down at him. He'd been out almost four hours now and she was ready to jab him just to roust him. Squatting, she checked his pulse. It was steady and strong. Guess trying to drain all his blood was tiring.

She was about to leave when she noticed his hair. The dark black locks had white streaks throughout it now. Standing up, she put her hands on her hips and moved her gaze down over his body. Did he look bulkier now? His bear was closer than it had ever been. She looked at the wire surrounding them, her eyes widened. His bear better not make a full appearance, there was no way this cage would contain him.

Griffin moaned and shifted. His eyes opened slowly.

She blinked, her eyebrows raising, his eye color had also changed. Instead of blue, they were now closer to grey.

"Guess I botched it," his voice was hoarse.

Crossing her arms over her chest, she glared at him. "You were bleeding out on the floor when I got in there."

He opened his eyes wider and then touched his neck, "did you sew me up?"

She nodded. "No. Cauterized it."

His gaze flicked to her. "It doesn't hurt much for a burn."

Frowning, she reached down, grasped his head, and jerked

it to the side. She scoffed, "seems like your animal is helping with the healing." The burn was barely visible.

He shifted so she would release his head and sat up. "What do you mean?"

"It's mostly healed." She waved her hand above his head, "your hair has white in it now too and your eyes aren't blue anymore."

"What?" He stood up and teetered.

"Whoa. Park it until you get some food into you."

He dropped down onto the cot. The metal frame creaked.

"I feel," he flexed his hand and stared at it, "different."

Blaise backed toward the door. "I don't doubt it. Do us both a favor and try to get in touch with your bear. If you do have the ability to shift." She stepped out and closed the wire door. "This," she motioned to it, "won't contain a bear."

He gave her a gobsmacked look and then shook it off. "How do I do that? Get in touch with—" he looked down at his chest, "my bear?"

Blaise stood there for a minute, trying to remember how. She did it all the time but couldn't remember how it had happened that first time. "Uh, close your eyes, focus, if he's there, you—" she frowned, "you should feel a presence."

"And then I just talk to it," he frowned, "him?"

"Talk, think," she shrugged. "Drink that juice," she pointed to the cup on the floor, "I'll get some food."

"I'm starving."

When he looked at her, a shiver moved over her. Was it the different eye color, or was it something else? "You have to eat often. It helps control your animal."

"Okay," he nodded, a look of focus on his face, "this is," he smirked, "I never imagined this would be happening to me."

"I guess the pills work."

"Yeah." She stood there for a second, trying to decide if she was imagining things or not. "Do, uh," she flicked her hand in the direction, "do your clothes feel tighter?"

He frowned and then reached his arm out as he looked down at his slacks. "I thought it was all in my head."

Rubbing her hand over her forehead, she huffed out a breath. "No. Your animal is a whole other size than the man was."

"So, I'll stay this way?"

Nodding slowly, she stepped back, "probably. I don't know much about chemically controlling the change. I'll get that food." She spun on her heel and went into the kitchen.

Opening the freezer, she pulled out a pack of bacon and then a second one. Keeping him full would help. Slicing the plastic open, she peeled it back and dropped it into the pan. Turning the burner to medium, she opened the cupboard that was filled with boxes of protein bars. Grabbing a handful, she went back out. "These will help until that's cooked," she opened the cage and held them out.

Griffin stood up. He didn't look very steady on his feet, then again, he was driving a larger body now. It was going to take some time to learn how to move. She watched him inhale slowly.

"Bacon." It wasn't a question. A look of focus appeared on his face, "something else. Flowers and spices," he smirked, "how can I smell that trapped in this wintery hideaway?" He moved over to get the bars.

She cleared her throat and dropped them into his hand. "Could be shampoo or something." She went back into the kitchen fast. The flower, spicy smell was probably her. She lifted her arm and sniffed it. Her animal had a flowery smell? Surely that wasn't right. Glancing at the pan on the stove, she went back out. "I'm going to check the weather."

He paused with the half-eaten bar to his mouth and looked at the window. "They'll come for me when the storm lets up." They're probably halfway here by now.

"Let us worry about that. *You* talk to your animal and communicate that he needs to stay put." She went out the door so fast, that the cold took her breath away. She welcomed it. The snow was blowing, making it difficult to see more than a few feet. He was right. The storm was the only reason Tomas' people hadn't found them. *Shit.* Pulling her phone out, she quickly hit Kenzo's number. She didn't wait for greetings.

"Boss. He's awake, and his animal was very close."

"How do you know that?"

She turned, so her back was to the wind. "Uh, he's bulkier, his hair has streaks now, his eyes are a different color, and," she glanced at the door, "the burn is almost healed."

"Well," there was a pause, "that could complicate things. Do you think he'll shift?"

"I don't know. If he does, I have tranqs, but my biggest concern is that Tomas will find us once this storm clears."

"We're working on that. Gideon is in place at the base of the mountain now. He'll give you a heads up if anyone is sniffing around."

"Okay, good. That erases some tension." It didn't really. The mate issue wasn't going to go away, no matter what.

"Hang on. Illias is going to patch Calum in on the call."

Blaise nodded. Calum Dante would have a plan. From what others told her, he always did.

"Blaise. Kenzo filled me in about the information your prisoner has shared. I talked to Dev about it and we all agree that your…"

"Griffin." She said out of nowhere, "his name is Griffin."

"Right. Griffin's tracker needs to be fried. They're going to come for him if he knows as much as you say."

She nodded. "It's a game changer. The information he wrote down is locations, names, codes, pipelines that transport…"

"Fry the tracker."

She looked at the door. "How?"

"Do you have your taser in your gear?" Kenzo asked.

"Yeah…"

"Not strong enough," Calum interrupted.

Blaise spun around, "I think Raymond has a cattle prod here…"

"Cattle prod?"

Calum chuckled at her boss' tone. "If it's not a lightweight one it could do it. You'll have to apply some pressure right over it."

"This one looks like it could stop a full-grown bear that's having a bad day. How—how do I do that without killing him?" Normally killing someone didn't phase her, but Griffin, he was different. Was it because he was as much a victim as so many others, he was important to the Alliance, or was it because he was her mate? She didn't have time to figure this out.

"One good zap right on top of it should do it." Calum interrupted her thoughts.

"Okay." She had to burn the guy, now shock him. This was not a fun assignment.

"You need to be ready to move, Blaise. If they find him, they're not going to send an announcement."

Blaise nodded. "Got it." She wiped the snow off her face. "Wish me luck. Finding out he *can* shift after I've electrocuted him, isn't going to be a fun time." She jolted, "I left food on the stove. I have to go."

"Message after you do that, and Blaise, maybe have the tranqs ready when you do."

"Will do, boss." She hung up and went back inside.

"I guess the storm hasn't stopped."

She glanced at him and wiped the snow from her head and face. "No. But that's good for us." Stomping the snow off her boots, she went into the kitchen. *Feed him. Electrocute him. Tranq him. Worst assignment ever.*

Chapter Twelve

Griffin paused with the bacon in front of his mouth. Had he ever been this hungry before? He didn't think so. Four bars, a plate of bacon, six eggs, and several pieces of toast and he was still hungry. It was as if his bear had been starved his entire life. He hesitated, chewing slowly, *his bear*. He was a bear, no, not him, or was it him? Balling his hand into a fist, he looked at the muscles in his arm. He wasn't out of shape, exercising was a good way to burn off frustrations and—life, but he'd never had muscles this defined before.

"How are you feeling?"

Licking the grease off his fingers, he shrugged, "not as hungry."

She smirked, "they're always hungry." She motioned to her chest, "the animals." Clearing her throat, she stood there, it wasn't anything obvious, but he could sense she was uneasy. "How's your animal feeling?"

Setting the plate on the floor, he finished chewing the mouthful slowly. He didn't know how his animal was feeling, he hadn't been able to 'get in touch' with him like she'd told him to try. "I don't know." He said it quietly, trying to suss out if he felt anything different inside of him. "There's anger." He was more stating it out loud than talking to her. It was anger, a deep-rooted rage he hadn't ever felt before. He'd never wasted his energy on that emotion. His circumstance of birth wasn't his fault or anything he couldn't fix. "Very angry."

"I get that. If my cat had been suppressed for twenty years, she'd be livid."

"How do you separate what you feel and *she* feels?"

He watched her as she looked him over for a few moments. "You don't really. Your animal is a part of you. Together you're one unit."

That wasn't the revelation he was looking for. "I guess it will take some work." Picking up the plate, he stood up and moved awkwardly toward the door. "Moving too." He glanced down at his legs.

She came over and opened the door and held her hand out for the plate. "Yeah, bulking up without notice has got to be a challenge. Stretches," she shrugged, "might help get you used to your newfound hulkness." She closed the door. "Listen, I called in when I went outside," she looked at the plate for a second, then stiffened before she looked at him. "They want me to fry that tracker in you, so if we have to make a run for it, our movement isn't traced."

"Fry it how?" Was his voice deeper?

"A good jolt of electricity should do it." She spun and went into the kitchen.

Griffin watched for her to return. "A jolt of electricity?" She kept walking without comment and went into the other room with the 'gear'.

When she stepped back out, she was carrying a long rod with a forked end.

"What is that?" His heart accelerated as he watched her examine it.

"An electric prod."

"It looks like it's industrial strength."

She went over and picked up the gun off the table and then turned back to him. "You need to try to control your animal while I do this, so I don't have to tranquilize you." She held up the gun.

Griffin looked from the prod to the gun. "You're going to fry it with *that*?"

She nodded, "you tried to take it out last night." She shrugged, "there's less blood this way.

"More pain, I imagine," Griffin crossed his arms over his chest and then looked down at them. Muscles made that more difficult to do. "So you're going to zap it and that will fry it?"

She nodded again.

"Then I can't be tracked?"

She sent him a hard look. "Don't get any ideas about taking off."

He'd dreamt of being free his entire life, but the reality of it was different, "and go where? I don't know anyone, I have no money, no car..."

"Give me your word that you won't try anything." She moved over and stood outside the door. Her green eyes held his own hostage.

He couldn't have looked away even if he'd wanted to, women didn't look him in the eye.

"You'll trust my word?" He uncrossed his arms because he felt ridiculous with how they rested inches from his body.

"You're a pretty smart guy. Everything you remembered and wrote down," she jerked her chin toward the table where the notebook sat. "I'm sure you understand that I'm your best bet to stay alive if Tomas comes for you."

He hadn't thought of that, not really, but the vibes coming off her were intense and there was something inside of him that trusted she would keep him safe. That was new as well—someone protecting him. Of course, that was saying he survived the jolt he was going to have to get to leave here.

"Okay, you're stuck with me until your Alliance decides what they're doing with me."

The air between them was heavy as she stood there, looking him up and down. "Let's do this." She opened the door, "it will probably be easier if you knelt."

He turned around and dropped to his knees, "oh sure, let's

make it easier for you to zap me."

"Do you want a warning or just do it?"

He hunched forward as he heard the static sound behind him. "Give me a count down." He blew out a breath and rested his balled hands on his knees. Gritting his teeth, he inhaled through his nose.

"Three," his shirt was pulled out of the way, "two."

Every muscle in his body tensed.

"One."

All that registered was the deep guttural sound that came from him. It stung like nothing he'd ever felt where she pushed, and the pains were shooting down his body and up into his head. It felt like every nerve in his body was jumping at the same time. The pain was less alarming than not having control over his own limbs as he twitched. He wasn't sure how long he could stand it and was about to move away when she removed it. He was on his feet fast, grabbing the wand from her and snapped it in two and then stood there frozen, looking down at the mangled item in his hands.

"Take some deep breaths, settle your bear down," her tone was soft and soothing. He dropped the broken prod to the floor as he focused on her tone more than her words.

"Do you think it worked?" He rubbed the area of his neck. His skin still hurt.

"Let's hope. You killed the prod."

Griffin looked down at the pieces by his feet. "Sorry."

Blaise shrugged, an expression close to amusement on her face, "could have been worse."

Griffin nodded, not sure he wanted to know how.

"Look, if you want to stick your head outside for a second, go ahead. It might settle your animal down." She motioned up and down him.

Griffin looked down to see his muscles straining against his shirt and pants fabric. Seeing it caused his heart to speed up again. A strange feeling came over him, if it didn't scare him, he would have paused to explore it further. "Yeah. Fresh air." He stepped out of the cage and then paused. Was he actually free from Aiden tracking him?

"Don't go far, I don't want to have to find you if you get lost in the storm. I'm going to see if Raymond has some clothes here you can borrow."

Clothes that weren't tight would be good. Although most of it was his skin, not the cloth covering it. "I'll just be outside the door." A gust of wind hit him as he stepped outside. He relished the fresh air and sucked it into his body. He was free. As long as Aiden never found him, he might have some kind of life. Once he settled his debt to the Shifter Alliance. A debt he'd earned merely from who his father had been. Griffin wasn't sure what hoops he'd have to jump through to gain their trust, but the first step was that they had the same objective in mind.

Stop Aiden and his associates and free all those being held.

He was free.

Sucking in another breath, he held his hand out in front of him and looked at his arms. He also had a bear inside him. That was going to take a while longer to digest. His entire life he'd pictured what animal his mother may have been. Never once had he thought bear. Rubbing his hand on his chest, he exhaled. "What do you say, bear, we keep it together and not do anything both of us will regret—or get us killed." He waited like he was going to get a response. The anger was till there, but it felt less intense. He'd take that as an answer. Not once in all the years had he ever thought that they'd have to communicate and control their animal side. Actually, he never paused to think about it much, his main concern had been to stay alive and as far out of sight as he would manage with his father, brother, and their human partners.

Chapter Thirteen

Setting the khakis and t-shirt on the table, she blew out a breath. Her whole body was tense, her cat jittery and Blaise didn't know if it was the situation or the new version of Griffin Ballard causing it. Whichever it was, she needed to get her shit together. There was no time for all of this. She had a mission, to keep him alive and safe. Nodding, she went over to her bag and hefted it on the table. She looked at the tranq gun and decided she was keeping it within reach for now. His animal was close and she didn't want to be unprepared if he made and appearance.

She had a feeling in her gut that something was going to happen. She planned to be prepared if it did. Grabbing the notebook and folded map, she tucked them into the waterproof pocket of her bag. Popping open the box that held his items, she placed them inside as well, even his gun and the pills. She left his phone sealed in the electronics bag and stuffed it in too. Pausing, she looked around. If, at some point, they had to make a run for it, she'd need water and protein for him, to appease the bear. Nodding to herself, she went into the kitchen and grabbed a few bottles of water and a pack of bars from the cupboard. Going back out, she put them in her bag and did it up.

Stopping, she looked at the door, went over, and yanked it open. She was relieved he stood right outside it. "You should come in. Clothes on the table."

Turning, he looked down at her. With a slight nod, he stepped back inside. "The air was nice." With long strides, he moved by her, grabbed the clothes, and went to the bathroom. The door closed.

Her cat moved through her, getting her attention. "I'm focused, don't start."

A few minutes later, the door opened. Raymond's clothes fit him. There was room in the pants, which she figured he'd appreciate. The t-shirt was tight fitting and outlined the new body he was driving. She didn't know if he had abs like that before, but they were a thing of beauty. Blaise worked hard to stay in shape, so it was normal to appreciate a toned body. She realized he was staring at her.

"I don't look like myself now."

She gave him an amused look. "That makes it harder for anyone looking for you."

"Good point," he motioned to her bag.

She shrugged, "just making sure I'm prepared."

"For?"

"Bailing if we have to." She put her hands on her hips and leveled him with a serious look. "Can you drive a snowmobile?"

His eyes widened. "I have no idea."

"If we have to go, you take the machine and I'll shift." Her phone buzzed in her pocket, she pulled it out and answered it without checking who it was.

"Blaise, it's Gideon, you have four heading your way, two already went up."

She hated it when her gut proved right about bad things. "Call Kenzo and tell him we're heading across the trail." She hoped the map Illias had sent her was accurate.

"Will do. I'll come up behind them, so don't take me out when you're done with them."

"Delete any you come in contact with." She smirked.

"It will be my pleasure."

She sent a quick message to Kenzo telling him the location was burned and then went over and put it in her phone in her run pack. Taking one gun off her side, she put it in the pack as well. She'd hoped for more time, but this was better than standing here dealing with her cat constantly inhaling the scent of Griffin. Once they were in the clear, she would be having a heart-to-heart with her animal.

"Go see if one of those suits will fit you. We have company coming."

Without a word, he went over and took one of the snowsuits off the hook.

Blaise kicked off her boots and tied them to her bag. "Do you know how to shoot?"

"Yes."

She released her other handgun from the holster and set it on the table. "You might need it. If they get me, you shoot anyone left breathing, grab my phone out of this," she held up her run pack, "and call Kenzo."

He paused, pulling up the suit, "they're not going to get you."

An odd feeling came over her when he said that. That this complete stranger had faith in her like that caused a lump in her throat. She didn't have time for this emotional stuff. "Get ready, I'm going to put the bag on the sled. After I shift, grab my clothes, and you stay behind me. If I stop, you keep going." She paused long enough to see he understood. She motioned around her. "Kill the lights, I'll be right back." It was going to suck going out in that without her boots, but she didn't have time to be sensitive. She needed to get him out of there and make sure he was safe.

Going into the shed, she dropped her bag and grabbed the skis on the sled. Hoping the tank was full enough, she hefted it and moved it over three feet. Repeating the movements until it was aimed out the door, she secured her bag to the back.

Her cat rolled inside her. Blaise froze and inhaled. "I smell them." The ones that had headed up must have been moving fast. She stepped out and checked the wind. It was blowing up the mountain, which was a bonus for her. She'd know before they got here.

The cold registered on her feet. Moving back to the door, she paused and tapped into her cat to see if she could see anything in the snow. Nothing seemed out of place. Going back in, she saw that Griffin had turned off all the lights.

"I can see in the dark now."

She heard the surprise in his tone. "Comes in handy." She picked up her rifle and stood by the window. "The wind is blowing their scents up ahead of them."

"Shouldn't we get going?"

She looked over to see him working his foot into a boot that was probably a lot tighter than it had been a week ago. "No. We'll take out the two that came up ahead, so they can't follow us."

"Okay." He zipped up the suit halfway and picked up gloves, and tucked them into the inside of the suit. He went over, picked up the gun, and then stood in the kitchen archway. She was impressed that he chose a spot that allowed him to see all the windows and anyone stupid enough to try to get him on her watch.

Chapter Fourteen

Griffin had to work hard to clamp down on his emotions. He was being hunted and *this* time he could fight back. No other time in his life had he been able to. He knew it wouldn't be any of the men that tormented him through the years, those ones always stayed close to their enslaver, Aiden—but the ones coming for him now, still deserved to be removed from this life.

He watched Blaise, how she stood motionless and peered out the window. He wasn't going to let anything happen to her. Too many had paid the price when he was younger and tried to go against his father's wishes. No more were going to suffer because he existed. She squatted and opened the window a few inches. He watched her inhale slowly, and duplicated her motion. All he could smell was the flower scent. Did all shifters carry specific scents? He knew it was her he smelled, not some shampoo like she tried to redirect him with. If, no, when they made it out of her, he was going to ask her why she smelled like flowers, and hope she didn't hit him for it.

She jerked her head and looked at him, then motioned with her hand to get closer to the floor. He complied without making a sound, he knelt on one knee and took the safety off the gun. He watched and waited. She had the rifle aimed out the bottom of the window and stayed that way, he couldn't hear if she were even breathing right now. When she lowered it to the floor and moved closer to the door, his heart picked up the pace again.

She was crouched in the middle of the room, a blade in each hand. Before he could register what she was planning to do, the door opened, and a tall man entered. Griffin was more than a little shocked to see he was just wearing pants, no jacket or boots.

He wanted to shoot him, but when Blaise didn't move, he wasn't sure if he should make any kind of movement and draw his attention or not.

The intruder had a long blade in his hand. When he stepped through the doorway, Griffin saw the second man come in behind him. This one held a gun.

"You might as well come out, coward. The boss says it's time to come home, no more running."

Aiden didn't know he'd been taken, they thought he'd run. Before Griffin could decide if that was an advantage, Blaise spun into action. The one with the gun was disarmed and lying on the floor with a blade sticking out of his throat.

The only sound to be heard was him gurgling in his own blood. The other one was halfway across the room, staring Blaise down as she stood, braced for any move he made.

The man chuckled. "You risked your life for a rendezvous? Griffin, the boss is going to love that."

Griffin wanted to shoot him, but Blaise was in the way.

"Settle down, little girl, I have no beef with you."

A low growl filled the room, and a shiver moved over Griffin as he realized it was Blaise making the sound.

"I do hate to kill a frisky woman—"

Whatever else he planned to say was cut off as the second blade Blaise held embedded itself into his throat. He dropped to his knees and then fell to the floor clutching it. When he pulled it out, Griffin winced. Stupidest move to make, now he'd just bleed out faster.

Blaise went over to the first one, retrieved her blade, and

cut free the small pack he'd been wearing, and then to the second man, she placed her foot on his head, removed his pack, and then walked toward Griffin. "Put these in the bag on the sled." She held out the packs. Reaching into her own, she held out something so your head doesn't freeze."

It was the hat she'd had on when she'd walked into the cabin looking like a snowman.

"Tuck my rifle under the bag I tied on." She turned and looked around and then slipped the pack over her head. "Come back in two and grab my clothes." She wiped the blood-covered knives on her jeans and put them in her pack.

Griffin nodded and went outside. He was running on autopilot, unable to think beyond how watching her fall those two men like unwanted trees made him feel. He liked it, which was ridiculous, he hated violence in any form. His body size wasn't the only new thing about him and the sad part was there was no time to think about what else had changed.

After he put the pack in her bag and secured the rifle. He looked at the machine he was going to be driving. Hopefully, it wasn't hard to figure out. A low growl made him pause and look up. A gorgeous dark brown tiger stood outside the door looking at him. Something inside him *moved* and sent a shiver through him. He could only hope it was his animal that he was *supposed* to be able to get in touch with. He wanted to stroke a hand down her back as he moved by her but figured that might have him with only one hand left to drive.

Going in, he grabbed her clothes and rolled them up. He didn't see her small pack. Going back out, he stopped and watched her looking into the storm. The pack was on her. That was genius, he wondered who had designed a pack they could wear in their animal form. He had so much to learn, but as he was running for his life, it would have to wait.

When she turned and looked at him, there was no missing the 'hurry the hell up' expression in her amber cat eyes.

"Sorry," he rushed by her, "you're quite gorgeous, Blaise." He put her clothes in the bag and then sat on the seat of the snowmobile. It took him a second but then it was running, and he glanced at her and nodded. His only thought at this point was he hoped he could control it and not drive off the mountain and die when he crashed into a tree. It would be a short-lived freedom, but at least he'd be free when he died, which was bizarre if not the sadistic dream he'd had most of his life.

Chapter Fifteen

She watched him steer for a minute, making sure he was going to be able to handle it. All she could smell now was that stinky machine. That was bad, she needed to be able to pick up scents. She'd only been able to pick up one signature before the snowmobile started. They were heading away from the cabin, probably searching for guards that they thought might be here with her. She hadn't been able to sense the other. That was the one that worried her the most. She didn't know what clan these jokers were from, she'd killed them too fast that the scent of blood had filled her whole system, so she couldn't pick up a clan signature. Her cat had wanted to gore them, rip them to shreds, which wasn't unusual, but they had been no real threat, so that was odd. Was it because of what he'd said to Griffin? She couldn't be sure but needed to clamp down on that. The last thing she needed was for her animal to feel all possessive and protective of the man that was their *assignment*.

Picking up the pace, she steered her cat back to lead and hoped that she'd be able to pick up the scent of the third one sent to extinguish her and take Griffin back to Aiden Tomas.

It was a bonus that they thought he'd run away. She'd report that to Kenzo as soon as she got him somewhere safe. When they realized he hadn't taken off, there would be a rush at all locations on the chance they got information out of his half-brother. Little did they know that with everything in the notebook, the Alliance would be able to dismantle a lot more than a few houses full of captives.

Her cat tensed, getting her attention. She slowed and inhaled, taking little time to assess what the wind brought her. The one was close.

Stopping, she watched Griffin until he caught up and moved by her at a slower speed. He was looking all around them as he did. Good, at least he was alert. Turning, she perused the mountain, what she could see through the blowing snow. Nothing seemed out of place. This storm was not helpful. It was so much easier to hunt when you could use the forest creatures as allies, but there was nothing out in this weather. Every living creature had taken refuge to wait out the storm.

She wasn't sure which clan she was dealing with, but some of the others said they had hyenas from some other country working for Tomas. What would cause an entire clan to turn on their kind, she didn't know. She'd never killed one, so seeing what it would involve was almost exciting. Her cat seemed interested too. Didn't matter what type of animal, but her sinking her teeth into anything's throat usually ended it fast enough.

The lack of noise from the snowmobile registered. There was no way he had gone so far ahead that she couldn't hear it. Shit, hopefully, he hadn't run out of gas.

Shaking the snow from her coat, she turned to go make sure he was all right.

Her cat reacted before the movement registered. Jumping to the side, an animal landed in the snow where she had been standing. The pale spotted animal looked at her. So that's what they looked like. A little goofy looking, in her opinion. His smaller sharp teeth would hurt enough if he got them into her, but the paws and claws were nothing compared to hers.

Ears flat, she bared her teeth and then emitted a one-time warning growl. Not that he was going to be a challenge, but she felt a warning was necessary. He snapped at her a few times before he charged her. He actually thought he was going to knock her off balance. It was a good strategy, but she outweighed him *a lot*.

He did have the advantage of being smaller, making quick turns easier, but she grew tired of his little game of leapfrog after a few minutes. Straightening, she flicked her tail, daring him to come at her again. She wasn't going to crouch this time. He lunged at her, so she rose on her back legs and caught him in the chest with both front paws, essentially flattening him into the deep snow.

She didn't pause to let him recover, just bit his neck on the side and made sure she had a good grip on it. Out of all the things she liked about her cat, the strength of her bite was one of her favorites. Once she got enough flesh pierced with her teeth, there was no getting free.

He tried to turn and dig his back feet into her side, but her much longer body was a plus as she stepped, so he couldn't reach her. With his front paws, he tried shoving against her face so she would have to let go. Straightening, she backed up and dragged him. He was still for a moment, and just like that, her cat was bored and joined in by shaking her head. She lifted it to check if there was any struggle left. The creature hung from her jaw. Releasing it, she pawed him a few times and there was no response. Fragile little things, these hyenas, she thought. Grabbing the leather strap of his pack, she bit through it.

She smelled gun oil. Spinning around, she crouched down and then saw Griffin standing beside a tree. He was pointing a gun *at her*. Her cat tried to resist, but Blaise overrode her, crouched, and gave him a warning growl. He had about three seconds to lower *her* gun.

Chapter Sixteen

Griffin knew he'd been instructed to keep going and she'd be upset with him for not listening, but when he'd glanced behind and not seen her, something inside him told him to stop. What chance did he have out here on his own? Not much. He had no idea where they were, was really bad at directions, not to mention had no idea how to work this animal inside him. She'd saved his life when he'd fumbled it trying to remove the tracker. She could have just left him there on the floor bleeding out. She could have left him behind too, but she hadn't. He wasn't going without her.

He moved as quietly as he could, with the new body of his. The boots were pinching his feet, but going without them wasn't an option. It was good they were freezing, then he couldn't feel the smaller boots. He tripped over something in the snow, numb feet weren't good for that.

His whole body tensed when he saw her squaring off with a large hyena. Raising the gun, he aimed. He'd never shot something that was moving before. There was no way for him to take the shot without possible injury to her. When the other animal lunged for her, Blaise rose and batted him down, pouncing with her large paws. She had her teeth sunk into the animal's neck before the idiot with his face planted in the snow could recover,

The hyena twisted and struggled against her grip. Griffin would have shaken his head at the stupidity of all the movement when teeth were the only thing blocking him from bleeding out, but he didn't want to take his eyes off the sight of the gun. He doubted she would need the help, but he would be ready if she did.

Blaise dragged the animal five feet and then shook her head, and the other shifter stopped moving. Had she broken his neck? Or maybe she'd bit through all major arteries in its neck he couldn't be sure. He watched her large cat paw at the body a few times, and when she was sure it wasn't getting up, she used her strong bite to rip the pack off the motionless body.

Griffin was about to lower the gun when she turned and looked right at him. Clearly, he hadn't been as silent as he thought. He was about to lower it when movement behind her had him retake aim. She crouched down and emitted a low growl. Did she think he was aiming at her? He didn't have time to ponder the absurdity of that. The wind gusted and then cleared, allowing him to catch a glimpse of the creature again. It was inching its way silently up behind her. Sucking in a breath, he squeezed the trigger, and it dropped into the snow.

Blaise spun around and looked at the animal behind her. Dropping the pack, she took cautious steps toward it and then straightened and walked over. She ripped the pack off it.

Griffin hurried over to pick it up when she came over and dropped the other one at his feet. "Was that all of them?" She made a sound and looked around. He had no idea if that meant yes or no. "Do we keep going?" He knew it was a stupid question as soon as it left his mouth. Of course, they couldn't go back. Aiden knew where he'd been and would send others after him.

Turning around, he went back to where he'd left the snowmobile. Tucking the packs under her bag, he got on and turned around to see Blaise was not behind him. It took him a minute more to find her in the trees, she was lifting her head and scenting the air. He mimicked her and then rolled his eyes at his stupidity; all he could smell was the stench of the snowmobile.

When she turned and looked in his direction, he put the gun inside the suit and started the machine. He had about a thousand questions at this point but getting somewhere out of the weather probably made more sense than talking to a woman who, in her current state of body couldn't talk back to answer him—or he couldn't understand. Both applied.

Chapter Seventeen

Blaise hefted her pack over her shoulder and exited the bathroom. She had no idea where they were. She was great with directions on a normal day, but with the storm and most recent events, today wasn't anywhere in the realm of normal.

Once they had gotten off the mountain, they'd found a small town that looked like it was closed due to the weather. It had been pure luck that the gas station was open. Most likely for the snow removal trucks, she imagined. The one elderly man behind the counter was nodding off, which had been to their advantage, otherwise seeing a tiger go into the bathroom would have had him question his sanity, and others his sobriety.

Griffin was standing beside the sled, glancing over his shoulder every three seconds. At least he was alert, that was good. She still couldn't believe he'd dropped the one she hadn't even known was there. In her defense, all she could taste and smell at that moment was blood. Later, she'd have to do a little soul-searching. She'd believed he was going to kill her and take off, but instead, he saved her hide. He'd done well driving through this. He had to be half frozen by now.

He turned and saw her, "sorry about the mixed messages, I don't speak cat." He hadn't understood when she'd wanted him to put her stuff in the bathroom and open the door for her.

Her mouth quirked, then she sobered. "You caught on fast enough." Securing the bag to the back of the sled, she looked around. "I need to figure out where we are."

"I think we should get some fuel."

She nodded, "yeah."

"Uh," he took off her hat and held it out to her, "I don't know how to do it." His expression changed to disappointment, "I've never been allowed to fuel anything."

That reminded her of who he was and what kind of life he'd had. "I'll show you. I just want to touch base with my boss and let him know we made it down."

"Do you think more are following?"

Blaise looked at the mountain. "I don't know how soon he'll send more, I don't think he'll stop." She glanced back at him, "get the sled over to the pumps."

He studied her for a moment and then turned back to the machine.

Jamming her hat on, that was wet, but warm from him, she pulled her phone out of her pack. There was one message, *are you dead?* She smirked at Kenzo's message. Hitting the call button, she watched Griffin look at the gas pump. He really had been locked up all of his life.

"Dead people don't make phone calls, so this is a good sign."

"We're in some little sleepy town at the bottom of the mountain. I have no idea which side or where we are. We had to weave our way down with the snowmobile, so I couldn't go in a straight line."

"Hold on. I'll get Illias to find you."

She waited until she heard someone answer him.

"How many did you take out?"

"Two at the cabin, and two following," she looked over at Griffin, "actually, Griffin shot the second one just before they got the drop on me."

"You gave him a gun? Did you tag the bodies?"

Blaise shrugged, "he knows he's dead if they get him—they thought he'd just taken off, boss. They had no idea we got him." She squeezed her eyes shut, "I did not tag them, sorry."

"That's okay, Gideon is still there. I'll send him on a search run."

"Sorry, boss."

"No. You did right, getting out of there. It's just if the bodies are found in the spring—have you ever seen an x-ray of our skeletal structure? Looks like a jigsaw puzzle."

Blaise didn't know that and had never thought about it much. It made sense that a human two-leg form shifting into an animal had to have an unusual skeletal system.

"Did you say they think he took off?"

"Yeah."

"Really? That's good for us. We're breaching two more locations in a few hours."

She looked up at the sky, "in daylight?"

"The storm is working in our favor; they'll figure we're holed up riding out the storm."

"True. Did you get enough of the teams to go in?"

"A few more on route should be here in time." There was a pause, "okay, Illias knows where you are. Hang on."

She could hear muffled speaking and wondered who he was talking to that he covered the phone.

"Blaise."

"Yeah."

"Devin says you're close to his sister, Raquel's place. Illias will send you the coordinates. Get there without pause."

The prince's sister? "Okay." What was that going to be like? A mutt and a half-breed pulling up to the princess's place?

"According to Illias, it's about a forty-five-minute ride. Can you get fuel?"

"We're at a gas station."

"Perfect. How's his animal?"

She turned to see Griffin lowering the nozzle to the gas tank. He must have figured it out. "He seems to be fine."

"Keep an eye on him, we don't need any incidents on the

way."

"Will do."

"Are you—uh, all right?"

She smirked at his awkwardness. "I'm aces, boss." Except *I've found my mate.*

"Good. Get moving."

"Yes, sir." She hung up and checked the battery before putting it in her pack. Pulling out some cash, she started to go over to Griffin when her phone buzzed. She opened the message to see coordinates and the message saying, *you are here,* with a smiley face. *You are going here,* and more coordinates. Smirking, she pulled out her map and went over to make sure Griffin didn't spill fuel all over the machine.

"Everything good?" He asked her without looking up from what he was doing.

"Yeah. We have a safe location to go to."

He released the trigger on the pump and looked at her. She could see the doubt in his eyes.

"Prince's sister's place," she shrugged, "probably a fortress with a lot of guards."

The doubt turned to apprehension, "Good." His tone didn't reflect that he was happy about it.

She'd get him there, where he'd be safe and then she was moving onto the next assignment. Her cat let her know she was unhappy with that thought, but Blaise ignored it and found their location on the map.

He had enough going against him being related to Aiden Tomas and a half-breed. Nothing was going to come out of staying around him. If anything, just being with a mixed breed was going to make his life more complicated.

Chapter Eighteen

Blaise couldn't get off the sled fast enough, she almost landed face-first in the snow. When they'd left the gas station, she was driving but had to admit to freezing about twenty minutes later. She hadn't paused long enough to grab a snowsuit for herself.

Griffin had taken over driving, using his body as a shield from the wind. It had sounded great in theory. Allowing her to watch for anyone following them, but with her bag on the back, she was mashed up against his back with no air between them. She'd been warmer, but also had to sit there and breathe in his scent for twenty-five minutes. Her cat was losing her mind and Blaise wasn't far behind her. Sucking in the cold air, she tried to purge his taste from her tongue.

"This has to be it."

She spun back around and looked at Griffin, then at the tall wooden gate in front of the sled. She hadn't even looked around when he'd stopped, just bailed to get away from him. The gate started to open slowly, and Blaise pulled her gun and side-stepped to put herself between it and the man she was responsible for.

With four feet of space between the gates, a man in his shirt sleeves, no coat, stepped into view. He was huge, and his aura screamed, 'give up now'. In his hand was a rifl; he had it aimed at the ground in front of her. "Blaise Morgan?"

She nodded, "Yes. Devin sent us."

He nodded, giving Griffin a quick once over. "I'm Boone Weaver. Pull the machine inside, and we'll go get the two of you warmed up."

Blaise lowered the gun but kept it in her hand as Griffin started the sled and pulled it behind the fence. She turned to peruse the road and noted Boone was checking the trees.

"Let's get inside." He stepped back and motioned in the gate.

As she moved by him, she caught his scent and had to bite her tongue not to vocalize her analysis of it. He was pure one-form. Completely human. What was he doing guarding the princess? Going over, she undid her bag and didn't scoff when Griffin slung it over his shoulder. She was okay with having both hands free until she figured out what was going on. Griffin gave her a quick look; his expression was asking if she was okay. She didn't know how he knew what a look from a man she didn't know meant, but she did. She nodded and jerked her head telling him to stay behind her while they followed Boone up what looked like a long, tree-lined laneway.

She lost all feeling in her feet by the time they reached the house. It was more of a log cabin retreat than the fortress she'd pictured. The door flew open and a tiny woman with brown hair stood in it. She was the very definition of cute and it wasn't until they were closer, and Blaise saw the pale blue eyes that she realized it was the princess.

Blaise started to bow her head when the woman stopped her.

"I'm not royalty now." She stated it in a lighthearted tone, which confused Blaise even more. The confusion on her face must have been evident, when Raquel chuckled, "I'll explain later, come in and get warm."

Blaise motioned for Griffin to go in first and then she moved by Boone with quick steps. She hated having strangers at her back. Where were the other guards? She couldn't see any.

The heat inside made her cheeks sting, but she'd take it.

"You guys must be freezing. Coffee or tea drinkers?"

"Coffee." Griffin and Blaise answered in unison.

Raquel smirked, "hot coffee coming up. I have some cinnamon buns in the oven too, they'll be done in a few minutes."

Blaise watched her go in a doorway, and then looked around. The princess who wasn't royalty had only one guard and baked. This was not what she'd expected.

"Just toss your stuff over the rack, and go in and sit by the fireplace," Boone said, turning and disappearing through the same door Raquel had gone.

Griffin leaned closer, "how is royalty not royal anymore?"

Blaise looked up at him as she pulled her hat off. "I have no clue." The warmth of the fireplace was amazing, but Blaise was on edge now. Her plan to leave Griffin here with guards was gone out the window now. She moved over to stand on the other side of the room.

Raquel came in and smiled at her. "You have questions."

Blaise glanced over her shoulder to see the two men sitting by the fire still. "Yeah."

"I chose to marry Boone and step down from the Alliance's royal family."

Blaise blinked and processed what she said once more to make sure she hadn't heard her wrong. "You're married to," she frowned and looked down at the cup again.

"The heart wants what it wants, isn't that the saying?" Raquel smirked.

Blaise didn't know what her heart wanted, so she couldn't say. "I-I guess." She studied her for a moment. "I didn't know such a thing was an option."

"It's not, well, it wasn't." She rolled her eyes, "there was a big to-do over it of course, especially because Dev was off brooding on his own and refusing to accept he was going to be king," she smirked, "I knew there would be no way the Alliance was progressive enough to have a Queen as the leader, so," she shrugged, "I followed my heart."

Blaise leaned forward, "what happens if you meet your…"

"Unless he runs up to the front door waging his fluffy tail, there's not much chance of that happening." She frowned for a moment, "I'm sure it has before, but I chose Boone and I'll never change my mind."

"I thought he was a guard."

"He's part of the RCMP emergency response team, so he may as well be a guard when he's home."

Blaise opened her mouth and then closed it again, "I've never heard of a mixed marriage with our kind before."

"What team are you with?"

"Special operations."

Raquel smirked, "so you only see the worse case scenarios in our world."

Blaise shrugged, "I guess." Her phone buzzing on the table startled her. She was usually more together than this. She answered it without pause. "Yeah."

"Blaise, it's Illias. Kenzo is a little busy, so he asked me to call and fill you in. Devin is on his way to you."

"Alone?" She stood up.

"No. I don't think he's ever allowed to be alone, well, except maybe," he cleared his throat, "he's safe."

"Okay. What's the plan for when he gets here? Are we moving Griffin to another location?"

"Yes. Where I don't know yet."

She nodded, "Okay, when is he due to arrive?"

"By morning is the best I can do right now."

She glanced around, not sure how comfortable she was here. Not only were there no guards, but she was also going to have Griffin *and* the prince of the Alliance here. She set her phone down and looked at Raquel. "Your brother will be here in the morning."

Raquel smirked, "good, I can bow to him, he hates that." She went over to Boone and Griffin.

It made Blaise realize she hadn't seen her own brother, or family for that matter for a few years. It wasn't that she didn't love them, or them her—in their own way. She just couldn't handle how her own family never accepted that she was different. It was better this way for everyone. They weren't embarrassed and she didn't hate them.

Chapter Nineteen

Griffin's heart pounded hard when three men stepped into the room. He stood up because Blaise did with quick movements. He watched her incline her head to the man standing in front of the other two. He had to be their prince; he was too young to be a king. He wasn't what he'd pictured as a prince, with his shaggy brown hair and casual clothes.

"We don't need formalities," the prince told her.

"Dev." Raquel went over and hugged her brother.

Griffin looked away from the tender scene. Love within a family he never understood. Come to think of it, he didn't understand love in any other form. The one man with the prince looked so familiar, his pale eyes and white hair, he thought for a second it was Lindon and then realized he was too young to be.

"I'm not him," he said in a low tone.

"I-I, sorry, the resemblance—"

"He's dead."

Griffin felt his shoulders go slack, "good." There was nothing else to say. That man not being in the world was a good thing, plain and simple.

As the prince introduced the man to his sister, Griffin glanced at the other man that stood there in a stiff pose, his awkwardness was very clear in his expression. When his amber eyes turned to look at Griffin, his heart felt like it jumped into his throat. He never thought he'd ever see those anguish-filled eyes again. "You got away." It came out in a whisper, and he couldn't stop the smile that followed.

"You know each other?" Blaise stood between them, looking from one to the other waiting for an answer.

"We do." Griffin nodded but didn't look at her. He couldn't believe he was standing here, a free man. "We spent a year at the camp together." Noah was here. "Watching each other's back and trying to stay alive."

Noah's blank look cleared, and he turned to the blond man. "He looked after me when," he inhaled a deep breath, "when I got my scars."

Griffin nodded his head quickly, "as a punishment so I could see what happens if you disobey."

"Can I go take Aiden out? I'm a good shot."

The prince barely glanced at the man asking, "not yet, Blair, we have to shut it all down, the head of the snake won't stop it, that are too many nests."

Noah moved with stiff motions across the room and stopped right in front of Griffin. "I would have died if it weren't for you."

Griffin tried not to see the images of his bloodied body and failed. "I never would have survived the camp without you, so we're even."

The rest of the room faded until it was just them standing a few feet apart watching the memories flash behind the other's eyes. Noah's expression softened for a split second before he grasped Griffin's shoulder in a tight grip. "You've gotten bigger."

Griffin smirked and smacked his arm, "so have you."

"A bear huh?"

"So I'm told." He still hadn't accepted that fact.

"What's that like?"

Griffin blew out a breath, "I don't know, we haven't figured out the communication part."

Noah snorted, "be happy about that, they don't shut up once you do."

"I'm sorry, but is Noah showing actual emotion?"

Noah dropped his hand away and glanced at Blair, "it happens."

Blair smirked, "oh, I know, but it's usually your beastie thing, not happiness, or whatever this is."

"Noah, you've helped the alliance a lot this past year."

Griffin watched Noah stiffen again as he turned to face the prince.

The royal man motioned to Griffin, "do we need to worry?"

Noah turned back to him, and Griffin held his gaze, unable to prevent the response to the pain he could see his childhood friend's eyes, his only friend of this lifetime, and he felt his own water under the appraisal.

"No," Noah finally said in a voice that was much deeper than moments before. "All we ever wanted, even at our reunion when I lay bleeding out at his feet was to get away and pay back all those that had destroyed us."

His heart was trying to beat out of his chest and then it wasn't. Without him doing anything it started beating slowly, gently, and steadily. The fear and memories were suddenly not there, and peaceful anger filled him instead.

"Griffin."

He felt a light touch on his arm and looked down at Blaise.

"Breathe it away."

He frowned, not sure what she was talking about. He felt fine.

"Your bear," she squeezed his arm and he looked down to see the muscle in it was pulsing in a strange way.

His bear. He blinked wondering why things looked so vivid and different.

"Hey." Noah stepped over and cupped the back of his head and held it, "which ones are yours?" His friend's voice was more like an animal growl.

Griffin sucked in a breath, "Mylar, Davison, and Aiden." His half-sibling's name was spat from his mouth. "Yours?" He held Noah's look and didn't blink, even though his eyes were no longer that of his friend but were now animal eyes.

"Roger, Al, and that little prick Mario." Noah released his neck and held up his hand.

The thick scar in the center of his palm took Griffin back fifteen years to the two of them huddled in the darkness, whispering their pact to one another. He looked down at his hand to see the mirrored scar on his own palm. He slapped his hand into Noah's light grip.

"Great. Now we have two that do the scary beastie."

Noah released his hand and then turned to Blair, "jealous?"

Blair grinned. "No, maybe." He quirked an eyebrow, "What was that?"

Noah stepped back, "something that used to get us through the tough times."

"Like a blood pact?"

Griffin looked at his palm, "or as close as we could do with a dull fork to cut our palms." He glanced around to see Blaise looked angry, more than her normal cold look, and Raquel was hugging Boone, tears running down her cheek.

Devin rolled his shoulders and blew out a breath. "As much as I'd like to see a Kermode bear up close, can you try not to have it happen indoors?"

Griffin looked to see his arm was normal size again. His new normal size. "I have no idea what I'm doing."

Blair chuckled, "my life's moto lately."

Devin pulled out his phone and looked at it. "Our reinforcements will be here in three hours, and then we're moving to another location and having some discussions." He studied Griffin for a moment. He expected to see animosity on the other man's face when he looked at him, but that wasn't what he saw.

Recognition clicked in Griffin's brain. "I've seen you in photos," all movement in the room paused, "Aiden has photos of you—with Rayne."

Devin glanced at Blair and then looked back at him. "Where?"

Griffin shook his head, "I don't know. Somewhere outdoors, a lot of trees in them." He cleared his throat. "I'm glad she got away from him. She would have been his pet, not his wife."

Devin's expression hardened to the point where he looked like a man that wanted vengeance. He spun around and looked at Blaise. "Where is that information he gave you?"

Griffin watched Blaise go over to her bag and get out the details he'd written down. He cleared his throat, "I just," he motioned to the door, "need some air."

Devin paused and looked him up and down, then glanced at Blair.

"I've got him," Blaise handed the map and notepad to her prince.

Chapter Twenty

Griffin walked quietly into the kitchen and looked out the window. He hadn't been able to sleep and if he moved around much more in there, he was going to wake the others. He had so much going through his head he couldn't turn it off.

Movement from the darkened room caught his attention. It was Noah. He had his boots in his hands and was moving quickly toward the door. The look on his face told Griffin that he was running from a nightmare. He knew the ones that haunted his friend and if there was anything he could have done to help him, he would have.

"He'll be all right."

The soft words from behind him startled him. He turned to see the prince standing in the far corner of the kitchen. "None of us are sleeping much lately." He held up a cup and motioned to the coffee maker on the counter.

Griffin nodded.

The prince got a cup out of the cupboard, set it beside the machine, and then moved by him to close the kitchen door. "I've been going over your notes."

Going over, Griffin picked up the cup and poured some of the hot liquid into it. When he turned around, the other man was sitting at the table with the maps and notes he'd written in front of him.

"If only half of this is accurate, it's so much more than we've had this far."

Griffin slipped into the chair across from him, "Prince…"

He looked up at him, "Devin."

"Devin, I just want to stop what's been happening."

"We're on the same page there." He sat back and blew out a breath, "I was—off the grid for a few years and had no idea how bad this was." He shrugged a shoulder, "that's on me for not doing something sooner…"

"I doubt you alone could have stopped it." Griffin leaned on the table, "they've had help for more years than we've been alive."

Devin studied him for a moment, "it's going to be rough, for you especially." He glanced out the window for a moment, "Aiden Tomas isn't going to stop looking for you. Ever."

"He can't when he's dead."

The prince smirked, "that was my thought too."

"I'm glad Rayne got away from him and has you now."

The other man's pale eyes locked on Griffin's face and he was barely able to breath under the scrutiny. "She said I was to be nice to you," he rolled his eyes, "that your parentage wasn't your fault."

Griffin didn't know if there was anything he could say to that, so he picked up the cup and took a small sip.

"I agree with her." Leaning forward, Devin flipped the page on the notepad, "this list," he nodded, "we never would have looked in any of these places." He looked up at him. "Thank you."

He was more than shocked that the prince of all the shifters was thanking him. "I just—want it stopped."

"Well, it's going to happen much faster now."

"Your people respect you." He blurted it out. "Aiden's fear him."

Devin held his look.

"What I mean is it's going to be easier to shut it all down because they're doing it out of fear. If they're given an out, most will take it."

He watched the other man pick up his cup and take a sip before he spoke. "I hope you're right but doing it out of fear doesn't excuse them."

"No. I know it doesn't." He studied the liquid in his cup for a moment, "I can't think of anyone—that I know of that's been helping that deserves a full pardon."

"Even yourself."

Griffin took a deep breath, "I've done things I'm not proud of."

"We're they your choice?"

He shook his head, "no, well, I could have chosen to die instead or worse." He knew he didn't have to explain what was worse than death.

"Noah. Rayne and Blaise all vouch for you, so that's good enough for dad and me."

Griffin knew Noah did, but he had no idea that Rayne and Blaise had. "I won't let any of you down."

Before he could say anything else, Noah came into the kitchen. The haunted look was still in his eyes.

"You call Emersyn?"

Noah nodded and then went and got a cup out of the cupboard.

Devin gathered up the items on the table and put them in a pile. "I don't even know how I breathed before Rayne." He pulled his phone out. "I'm going to go call her just to hear her mumble to me about coffee." He grinned and went to the door.

Noah stiffened.

"Relax, I'll stand on the doorstep."

Noah nodded, "or you could kick Blair and make him stand outside with you."

Devin grinned, "that's an idea." He left the room.

Noah looked Griffin up and down, "are you okay?"

Griffin blew out a breath, "just dandy. It's a little hard to sleep when I know there are hundreds of bodies out there hoping to get the kill shot on me."

"We won't let that happen." Instead of sitting down, he

picked up his cup and leaned back against the counter.

The door opened, and Blair stuck his head in, "I'll get even." He sent Noah a hard look.

Noah shrugged and then sipped his coffee.

Griffin watched him for a moment, "you've settled well."

Noah snorted softly, "as much as I think I ever will."

Blaise came in. Griffin noted her hair was a mess, and she wasn't adorned in weapons. "Oh good, you're with him. I'm going for a run; check the perimeter."

Noah nodded. "Blair is out there with Devin."

She looked out the window. "I guess we're all on edge." She glanced at Griffin, "are you all right?"

Griffin nodded, "yes, I never sleep well."

"With a lunatic controlling your life, that's understandable." She turned on her heel and went back out the door.

Griffin stared at the door.

"I'm glad there's someone for you too."

Turning he looked back at him, "not that I have the first clue what to do about it."

Noah smiled, "I feel that. I'm still figuring it out."

Griffin's gaze went to the mark on his neck, "you're miles ahead of me."

"Today." Noah toasted him with the cup and then went over and looked out the window.

Griffin looked down at his cup like that coffee was going to give him the answers. He doubted anyone had the answers he needed. He was a prisoner. Had been his whole life, the only difference was the ones responsible for him now weren't cruel and demented. "I'm going to try sleep again." He stood up and watched Noah for a response. He barely moved his head. Setting the cup in the sink, he went back out to the main area.

Chapter Twenty-One

Blaise studied him as he stared into the trees. What was he thinking about? "You were in a camp with Noah?"

His shoulders stiffened as he turned just his head to look at her. "To learn what my life would be if I didn't listen to my father."

"You were there for a year." What kind of human could do that to their own child? Half-breed or not.

"I had a problem with obedience." He said the last word with exaggerated enunciation.

"Thank you." She cringed that it just popped out of her mouth. "For looking after him after he found Emersyn." The confusion was clear in his eyes. "When they beat him because he found his mate." He made no comment. "They're together now." She realized he had no idea. "Noah found her at one of the houses we," she paused, unsure of what word to use when discussing it with him, "liberated."

He turned toward her, "really?"

"Yeah. It's uh," she motioned her hand in the air, not sure how to describe anything pertaining to mates, "not exactly a normal mating, but they have each other now and her little girl," she glanced at the house, "we found Lindon's clan and freed them too."

His expression darkened, "I thought Blair was Lindon for a second."

"Yeah, well, Blair killed big brother, and now he's alpha to a very large clan of tigers."

"Are you part of that clan?"

She shook her head, "no, I'm still part of my family's that came over."

"I don't understand about mates."

She snorted, "neither do I. I actually never thought," she scowled at the ground, "had hoped I'd never find mine."

"Past tense." He tilted his head and held her in place with a hard look, "you have a mate?"

Blaise took a step back and realized she just trapped herself by flapping her mouth. "Uh, yeah it looks that way, but it's even more complicated than Noah and Emersyn."

"My bear," he frowned, "animal seems to be angry at the thought," he rolled his eyes, "it's all anger, but now it's…"

"About that," she cleared her throat. Did she want to have this conversation with him? No, yet he was, for the first time in his life, finding his animal, and after the intense display in the house, she didn't want him to struggle with his own animal side, "I think it's you."

"What is? My bear is angry because of me?"

There was a reason she didn't have lengthy conversations with others, she sucked at it. "I think, okay, my cat *knows* you're our mate."

The silence as he stood there just looking at her was painful.

"I don't understand. If I'm," he waved a hand around, "some kind of bear species—you're a tiger." His brow creased further, "is that common? Different," he motioned between them.

Blaise blew out a breath, "I have no idea. I don't know shit about mating and this cosmic fate crap." She huffed out another breath, "I guess it's because we're both mixed."

"Mixed?"

She pinned him in place with a 'duh' look, "half human, half bear, and," she stabbed a finger into her own chest, "two tiger flavors."

He just stood there like a statue as he digested that. She had no idea what now and hoped he wasn't looking at her for answers.

"What-what does this mean?"

She lifted her hands and let them drop. "I don't," she realized he was holding his breath, "I don't know." She motioned between them, "aside from the mixed part, it's not like we met at a social gathering of clans for games, and of course, the underlying reason—the hope to stumble across your fated mate."

"Right." His expression blanked, "I'm from the enemy team."

"But you're not." Her mouth needed to stop with the free-flowing words. What was wrong with her? "The enemy? Are you?" She pointed to the house, "with the information you've given us, you'll have gained a lot of favor at the Alliance."

"Is that what I need to do? Gain favor, earn my freedom?" He looked her up and down, and she hated that her cat was all but purring inside her from his attention.

"I don't know, maybe." She backed up another step. Her cat wanted to rub up against him and there would be none of *that* happening. "Maybe go meet your clan."

Surprise filled his eyes. "And do what, be a half-bear member of a clan I know nothing about?"

"You have to have a clan, or you're a rogue. The Alliance doesn't protect rogues."

He ran a hand through his hair, leaving it messy and she thought for one fool-hardy second that it suited him more than the flattened, neatly parted hair did. "There are so many rules. I know nothing about any of this. I know nothing about what is considered normal life in either world I'm a part of."

The anxiety coming off him made her tense. "You don't have to learn it all in a day." She glanced at the house, hoping like a coward that someone would come out soon and interrupt this conversation she didn't want to have.

"I've never been with a woman and now I have a mate."

Blaise blinked, wishing she hadn't heard that, "don't expect me to do anything about that."

"I didn't mean…"

"Good." She crossed her arms over her chest. "Just," just what? "Focus on helping us shut down Tomas—that is my *only* priority right now."

His expression either changed to disbelief or relief; she wasn't sure.

"Right. Aiden needs to not be breathing before I can be anything but a vastly hunted liability to your Alliance."

"You'll be safe," she'd smack herself later for saying it, "I'll make sure of it."

"Blaise."

She turned to see Noah standing by the outside door.

"Devin needs to talk to you."

Nodding, she gave Griffin a quick look and went toward the door.

"I'll stay out here with him," Noah stepped aside when she reached the door.

Blaise went in and then glanced back to see them both looking at her. Noah looked pleased, and Griffin was unsure. She closed the door, and the next thing they'd do is high-five each other or something equally lame. *Yay, bro, you found your woman.* She groaned out loud and kicked off her boots. Men were ridiculous creatures.

Chapter Twenty-Two

Griffin stood with the cup in his hand and watched the coffee pot fill. They'd moved to a hotel, that as far as he could tell was filled with various shifters from the Alliance. He had no idea where he was, but regardless of how many warriors were lurking near the prince, he didn't feel safe. He would probably never be safe until Aiden and his associates were all dead. From conversations he'd overheard, they didn't plan on incarcerating any in the top levels of the sadistic groups, the ones imprisoning shifters on the merit that they were different.

He'd come to understand one more thing in the last two days, humans, or one-forms as they were referred to, were the cruel, maniacal animals, not the shifters. These people he'd met in the past few days were nicer than any of the ones he'd been around all his life.

"You just going to stare at it, or were you going to get some?"

He was jolted out of his head and turned to see Blair smirking at him with a cup in his hand. "Sorry, my mind wandered away." He grabbed the coffee pot.

"Yeah, that happens." Blair snorted, "in your case, I'm surprised you can function at all."

Griffin held out the pot, offering to fill his cup. "How do

you mean?”

Blair nodded when the cup was filled to his liking. “With being away from Tomas and getting in touch with your bear for the first time ever,” he set the cup down and opened the cupboard, “and the mate thing is always a mind fuck, so how you’re not a babbling lunatic or tearing wall out, with your bare hands, I have no idea.”

Griffin glanced at Blaise as she leaned over the map and discussed things with Noah. “Well,” he turned back to the other man, “I believe I was told *that* wasn’t happening.” He shrugged, “not that I have a clue about any of it.”

Blair grinned, “yeah, they say that.” He lifted his cup to his mouth, “until they don’t.” Taking a small sip, he glanced at the table, “you ready to look at some pictures?”

“Of?”

“Men we’ve freed, men we’ve captured, and people that work *for* the Alliance that we haven’t cleared.”

“Is that a lot of pictures?”

“Hundreds,” Blair toasted him again and then went to the laptop.

Griffin looked over at Blaise again, she was watching him. She did that a lot, he’d noticed. He couldn’t read her expressions though, so he had no idea what she was thinking about. *Until they don’t.* What the hell did that mean? Deciding less thought about that would be better for his state of mind, he went over and sat down in the chair in front of the laptop.

Devin stood beside him. “The Alliance has been gathering intel and photos for several years.” He glanced at Noah, “we haven’t shared them with anyone, not even you or Rayne. She’s in some of the older ones.” His pale blue eyes flicked to Griffin, “but it’s time for names if you know them.”

Griffin nodded, “I’ll do what I can. I was a background decoration for a lot of meetings. Don’t move. Don’t speak kind of deal.”

Devin nodded to Blair, who tapped a button on the keyboard.

~

How long had passed? He couldn't be sure, but his leg was cramped, and his cup had been empty for a long time. So far, he'd identified his half-brother, four of Aiden's top dogs, a few ambassadors, and one captive that had Devin on the phone to someone so fast that Griffin had to wonder where he was that he moved that fast.

"Let's take a break." Blair stood up and patted him on the back. "You've made me a *very* happy man, Griffin, I have so many targets now that I won't need to work out for years."

"When do you work out?" Noah pushed away from the wall and came over.

"I could," Blair shrugged, "If I ever had thirty seconds to myself." His phone chimed, "see." Answering it, he wandered into the kitchenette area.

"That will be Kobie with an update about the chaos back home."

"Chaos?" Griffin got up and winced at the stiffness of his muscles.

"I can't even describe it, teen boys, teen girls, young ones—it's never-ending motion."

"Do you live with them?"

Noah shook his head, "no, I have my own house of crazy." He smirked briefly, "I should go call Coop and Emersyn and see how things are."

"What's it like?"

Noah gave him a confused look, "the house of crazy?"

"No, having a mate?"

Noah blew out a breath, "it's like—I can't," he huffed out a breath, "hard to explain, and my mating isn't exactly normal, but the best I can describe it is your mate is the person who helps you learn many lessons—about yourself and they accept you regardless of your own opinion of yourself."

"That's—" he wasn't even sure.

"Yeah." Noah turned on his heel and walked toward the door.

"Hey," he turned to see Devin lower his phone, "do you know where the hyenas working for Tomas are from?"

Griffin ran his hand through his hair, "somewhere in Europe, their accents vary."

Devin held his look for a second and then nodded and put the phone back to his ear.

Griffin went over and opened the cupboard that the protein bars were in. He wasn't really hungry but had discovered in the last day that if he stuffed one in his body, often, his bear seemed more content. Still mad but not raging. As soon as everyone was off their phones, he would see if he was allowed to go outside. He needed fresh air as much as he need to snack.

Glancing over at Blaise, he wondered who she was talking to; her facial expression was less, 'I want to kill everyone', so he was curious who could take that look off her face, even for a few minutes.

Taking another bite, he chewed the dry bar. They should get these in beef flavor or something a little more appetizing. He looked at the wrapper, it said blueberry, but the taste in his mouth was not any sort of berry.

Chapter Twenty-Three

Blaise flicked her gaze over to see Griffin was looking at her *again*. Getting up, she went into the bedroom and closed the door. That was a mistake, it was the one Griffin had slept in and the entire space was drenched with his scent. She sighed into the phone.

"What's going on?" Emersyn asked her, "I know you call a few times a week, but you haven't said five words this time just listen to me rattle on about Aspyn and the other kids."

She needed to *tell* someone, and it wasn't like she even had girl talks with any of her family. "Griffin, the half-brother of Aiden Tomas is," she bit her lip, then softly breathed, "my mate."

"Okay. Is that good or bad, because from your tone, I can't be sure?"

"I don't know." It was the truth, she wasn't sure because her own feelings and emotions were changing multiple times each hour. "He's a half-breed." She scowled at her own words. It felt wrong even to say that after what she'd been through in her life. She knew better than to use a label.

"I don't think he had any choice in that."

Blaise crossed her arm over her chest and rested her other elbow on it, "no, I get that."

"Is he a bad person?"

Leave it to Emersyn to ask the questions no one else would think of. "No. I don't get that vibe. Sure, he's done some bad things to survive, but overall," she looked at the door, "he might be boy-scout material."

"Is *that* bad? I'm not sure what that means."

"He's given us a lot of intel, and I mean game-changing information that will help us stop Tomas and all those that work with him."

"Bless him. That's great. So, he wants to stop them then."

"Yeah, but—" but what? "I have to go; we're just taking a short break, and I'm sure Noah will want to check in with you."

"Oh, okay. Blaise, I know I don't understand a great deal, but I'm always here if you need someone to talk to."

"I know. I appreciate that."

"Are you okay? Or as okay as possible right now?"

Blaise smiled and then nodded, "I'm all aces, Em."

She heard the soft laugh, "I can't believe you still say that aces thing. That was a lifetime ago."

"It was, but it still stands. I'll talk to you soon." She hung up as soon as her friend said goodbye and then looked at her phone. Emersyn was probably her only friend. Others she worked with, she rarely socialized with. All she had in her life was work. Going from assignment to assignment and carrying out orders.

Going back out, she saw that Blair and Devin were going over the notes and map again. Griffin had really come through with viable information. She turned to see he stood by the window staring out it. His shoulders lifted and dropped a few times. She knew the signs of feeling confined indoors all too well. "Grab your jacket, and we'll go out for some air."

He turned, and she saw him exhale. "Yes."

"Comm up, report anything off," Devin told her.

She nodded and picked up two of the earbuds sitting on the charger.

Blair came over and grabbed one, and put it in his ear. "Blaise and Griffin are coming out for some air." He stated.

She held out the other one to Griffin, who frowned at it, but put it in his ear anyway.

Blaise wasn't sure who was nearby. She'd caught sight of a few she recognized in the last few days but didn't know them by name, just that they were on one Alliance team or another.

She imagined Griffin wouldn't be without hidden guards for a long time. He'd always had guards, only this time, they were here to protect him, not imprison him.

"Copy," a voice she didn't recognize said in her ear.

Slipping her boots on, she motioned for Griffin to go out after her. He stepped aside, happy to comply. Blaise wasn't sure of their exact location, but the air was so clean and pure, she didn't care. It was so much better than being in the city. How did shifters even tolerate breathing in toxins every day? She would never be a city dweller.

"Think we can go for a short walk?" Griffin spoke from behind her.

She held up her hand and then depressed the comm button. "We clear for a walk?" She scanned the area.

"Nothing seems out of place." The unknown male informed her.

"Don't go too far," Blair's voice she knew.

"Will do." She responded and then motioned for Griffin to lead the way. She was more comfortable following.

They walked in silence for a few minutes, she was okay with the quiet. A rabbit darted out of the trees, and Blaise had her hand over the gun strapped to her side. She left it there to see if it was just one and not something in the snow-covered bush that was causing the critter to evacuate in such a hurry. After a moment, she confirmed it was just the one.

"I don't think Aiden is aware."

She looked at him when he paused so she was beside him. "Aware?"

"That he's been watched all these years." He started to walk again. "He seems to think your kind—"

"Our kind." He was, just as much as her.

"*Our* kind are addle-minded."

"That's an advantage for us."

"It is." He rolled his shoulders, "I'm exhausted. With each face or detail, I have to live through the memory to go with it."

"I can't even imagine that." She had her own memories that haunted her, but her childhood issues couldn't compare with thirty years of being a prisoner of circumstance.

"This new version of my body cramps up so easily." He paused and stretched.

She smirked, "yeah, the animal inside isn't calm and relaxed often. You'll get used to it. Runs and stretching help a lot— and communication."

He looked down at her, "I don't think we're talking yet."

"I would probably be crabby if I'd been trapped for the last fifteen years too."

"Fifteen years?"

"Yeah," she motioned to walk, "our animals are dormant for fifteen years, roughly—mostly males, females are a bit longer." She turned down a road, figuring they would circle back around in a few minutes. "Yours has been forced to sleep for the last fifteen years."

"Guess I see his point with the anger, but he could give a guy a break. Trying to function when your leg muscle is rock hard, or arms don't bend all the way because of muscle expansion—isn't pleasant."

Blaise grinned, "hopefully, you get used to it soon." She looked him up and down, and then looked away before her cat got any ideas she didn't need to think about.

"Do you think I'll ever shift?"

"Hard to say." She tensed when she heard a vehicle coming up on them. Turning she saw it was an old stake truck with crates on it, the tarp was falling off. She started walking again. "I don't think you'll shift all of a sudden without warning if that's what you're afraid of."

"That's—" he collapsed on the ground beside her.

"Griffin?" She dropped down and then felt a pinch in her neck. Quickly she pushed the comm button, "stake truck, yellow—" everything blurred.

"I'll find you, Blaise."
She blinked, was that Tripp? Tripp was here.

Chapter Twenty-Four

Her head was pounding. Had she taken a hit? She didn't remember fighting. Why did it feel like she was sleeping in a moving car? She never slept in a vehicle, too many things could go wrong if you weren't alert all the time. Stretching her arm, she froze when it touched cold metal. Opening her eyes, she blinked, it was pitch black. She squeezed them shut again so she could tap into her cat and use her vision in the dark. "What the—" She turned her head to see Griffin beside her, almost on top of her, and he was out cold.

He had fallen on the ground… "Shit." Someone had gotten the drop on them. Her, mostly her. It was her job to keep him safe, and she'd failed. She reached over and checked his pulse. It was strong enough. "Griffin." She shook his shoulder, "come on, fight through it." How did tranqs affect half-breeds? His bear should be burning it off fast like her cat was. She closed her eyes to check on her animal. Oh yeah, she was there and very much looking forward to finding the soon-to-be-dead person that had tranq'd her. Blaise checked and confirmed that her guns and knives were gone. "Shit."

"Blaise? She should be awake by now."

They hadn't taken her comm. Probably thought they were just out for a stroll. Alliance teams were always on guard.

Pushing the comm, she swallowed the bile down, "I'm here."

"Took you long enough." It was Tripp Carson. "We're following the tracks."

We? "The prince?"

"Is back at the hotel with Blair and two others."

"Kay." Her mouth was so dry.

Griffin jolted awake and tried to sit up. Whatever they had them in wasn't big enough for much movement. He dropped back down and held his hand over his forehead. "Where are we?" He groaned.

"Metal can." She had no answers for him other than that.

"We're moving."

"Tripp is tracking us."

"Good. Tell him to hurry. As soon as I don't want to puke, I'm going to freak out. I don't do small, dark spaces."

"Talk to your bear, Griffin. Shifting could crush Blaise."

He lowered his hand, "how do I—" he pointed to his ear.

"They can hear you through mine because we're mushed in here so close."

"I don't know *how* to talk to my bear, Noah, or I'd already have communicated we need to get out of here."

"Just breathe through any thought of rage," Noah advised.

"Yeah," Griffin didn't sound pleased, "I'll work on that."

"We've stopped." Blaise put her hand against the metal to check for vibrations. There weren't any.

"We're still miles behind you. It took us a few to scramble to come after you."

Blaise grimaced at that news, "move fast if they—"

"Shh, I'm trying to hear."

She looked at Griffin, "shifter hearing is good, but—"

"I know. I've always had it." Was his response.

Blaise closed her eyes and held her breath, trying to see if she could hear anything. She couldn't. "I don't—"

"Tripp, can *you* hear me?" Griffin glared at her as he spoke.

"Uh, yeah."

"Okay." He turned his head, "so she can as well."

Someone chuckled into the comms.

"There's nothing to hear." She seriously doubted he could hear something if she couldn't. All she could hear was their breathing.

"As much as I love your voice, you need to refrain from using it for a moment. They're talking about whether to leave us until the others arrive or let us out, and I'd like to know the outcome of the discussion."

Blaise frowned and looked at him. Did all bear clans have hearing like this? Who did she know that was one? She had questions.

"Best *refrain*, Blaise." Tripp sounded too amused. Being mated had given him a sick sense of humor or something.

"They're leaving us in here." Griffin's voice was much deeper than it had been. "How much room do you have?"

"Uh," she attempted to turn and couldn't, "I'm almost curled into a ball."

"Make yourself as compact as possible. I am *not* staying in this." There was a low growl in his voice.

She pulled her legs up and watched him run his hands along the corner of the box. Shifting he pulled off his boot and then awkwardly reached the other and took it off too. With each movement, she felt like she was pinned against the cold surface.

"Griffin…"

"I have to get out of here." He growled. "I can't deal with small spaces. Darkness closes in on me and then the memories swamp me. *And* every time I breathe you in, I want to slay dragons and kill something."

Blaise was stunned, she had no words. It may have been the nicest and most bizarre thing anyone had said to her.

"Would you slay dragons for me?" A female's voice came through the comms.

"Unicorns too, babe, but focus on driving, we need to get there, or we'll miss the bloody parts," Tripp answered. The woman had to be Amari.

Griffin's breathing became louder and then she heard the metal creaking against the pressure from his legs.

She pressed her back into the metal, giving him more room to move. She wasn't sure if he was able to do it. Her cat sure as hell couldn't get them out of this, but from the sounds of the box, his bear was determined.

"I can hear what he's doing to the metal from here. Go team bear." Tripp said, "give it all you've got before they hear you."

A low growl came from Griffin, causing the hair on the back of her neck to stand up. A shiver went through her and Blaise realized it was her *cat* responding to his *bear*. How messed up was her world?

A snapping sound told her that the seams of the crate had given way to his brute strength. He slid out of the box so fast, she was crushed into the side of it in the process. A large hand reached in and grabbed her ankle and pulled her free of the cold box.

Squinting, she tried to adjust the bright light. A movement out of the corner of her eye, had her grab for a gun that wasn't there. "Watch out." She slid off the truck to the ground, ready to take on the man that was rushing at them.

Griffin spun around and caught the assailant by the throat as he launched himself at them.

Blaise paused and noticed that he was much larger, even more so than when they had been at Raquel's when he'd gotten upset.

The man struggled against the hold, then dangled in mid-air, his body swinging like a ragdoll as Griffin walked toward a tree. When he reached it, he slammed the guy back against it, once, twice, and then released him. The man dropped to the ground and didn't move.

"One down," she reported.

"Good work," Tripp answered.

"Save some for us, please," Amari pleaded.

"I didn't do it, Griffin just beat him against a tree." She smirked. It was entertaining and beyond what she could ever hope to do.

"Griffin, keep the bear in check. We don't have time for a run through the bush to find you." Noah's tone was emotionless.

"Mmm," was the only reply Griffin gave.

Blaise looked around, "small cabin, no other cars," she reported. "I don't know how many more there are."

"Two," Griffin growled and then started walking toward the cabin.

"Well, shit," Blaise took off after him. He wasn't even wearing his boots. "Uh, we're going in the cabin after the other two." She looked around as she went for anything she could use as a weapon. If he burst in and they tranq'd him, she'd be on her own against the other two.

"Drop me here, and I'll keep watch for company," Noah said.

That meant they had to be close. If they got her too, at least Tripp and his mate would storm in and save them both from being dragged off—again.

Griffin ripped the door right off the cabin and went inside.

As she reached it, she heard a large crash and darted into the building ready to fight. Griffin stood holding a wooden table in two hands and the men lay on the floor unconscious.

"That's one way to do it." She hurried over. "Go grab the other one; we'll tie them up. Tripp find out what we're doing with them."

He chortled, "standing order is to put them down if they're a threat."

Blaise grabbed the curtain; maybe she could tie them up with it. "they're not much of a threat right now. We should tag this location, so Illias can find out who it belongs to."

"We can do that," Tripp told her.

"We don't want to know how they knew where we were?" She had no qualms about putting them down for good, but she wanted answers too.

"Same rats that have been betraying us all along, I imagine," Amari said in a venomous tone.

Blaise paused to check out the one's face. It was swollen and bleeding. All of it. "I think you smashed this one's face in, Griffin."

"What did he hit him with?" Tripp sounded like he was running now.

Blaise glanced at the table on the floor on its side. "A table."

"Oh damn."

Griffin came through the door dragging the other one by the back of his jacket and dropped him beside the other two.

Blaise lifted coats to see if any of them wore a belt. "I think we need to take one back and find out how they found us."

"Since when are you the voice of reason? How are we looking, Noah?"

"All clear so far," Noah replied. "What if they have trackers in them?"

Blaise looked to see Griffin standing looking out the door. He still hadn't grabbed his boots. He was going to want them once his anger settled and his animal wasn't pumping out the heat. "They tranq'd me, I want to know." She answered.

"Well, you are *much* bigger than last we saw you. Love the white streaks, they're a statement."

Blaise looked up at Amari's words, then moved over to the window to see Tripp and Amari standing outside the cabin, both with guns in their hands but not pointed at Griffin. Yet.

She hurried over and skirted around his large frame to look up at him. "They're on the same side you're on now, Griffin."

"We're the good guys," Tripp said with a smirk.

"Breathe through it, Griffin, they got you out of Aiden's prison." Noah reminded.

Blaise put her hand on his chest and patted it a few times. "Why don't you go find your boots and look in the truck for my stuff."

His chest rose and fell a few more times before he finally nodded and stepped around her.

Amari and Tripp stepped back and turned their whole bodies to follow the direction he went, guns still in their hands.

When he was far enough away, Blaise pointed to her ear and then pressed the comm button, so anything she said wouldn't be broadcasted to the others. Griffin could probably hear them, but she was sure he knew a lot more than he'd ever share.

Tripp and Amari both turned off the mic on their comms.

"Damn," Tripp gave her a gobsmacked look, then glanced in the direction that Griffin had gone. "What did you feed him?"

Blaise rolled her eyes at that, "they had him taking meds to suppress his animal all these years."

"Does he shift?" Amari scanned the treeline, moving just her eyes.

"Does he need to? He just took out two guys with a dining room table. I don't think I want to see his bear if the man is that size." Tripp checked all around them.

"Devin says tag it, grab ID and phones, and put them down. Disable the truck, then get back to the hotel; we're moving out." Noah stated over the comms.

Amari grinned and walked toward the cabin. "I got this."

Tripp had the expression of a besotted idiot on his face as he watched her walk away.

"What did you guys drive here? Will all of us fit?" She had no problem shifting and running all the way back.

Tripped jerked his head to look back at her, "just as long as the bear doesn't get any ideas, we will fit."

"The bear has a lot of ideas," Griffin said in a more normal voice as he walked toward them, his boots in his hand. He wasn't as large now, but the expression on his face said he was barely containing the need to go inside and tear those men into tiny bite-size pieces.

"As long as they're for our side, have at it." Tripp saluted him and then went into the cabin.

"Thanks for getting us out of there." Blaise had no problem thanking a person when they saved her hide.

Griffin shrugged, "apparently, my bear is part superman." He smirked briefly and then looked down at his boots. "I need bigger boots."

Chapter Twenty-Five

Blaise looked at her phone and then put it back to her ear again. "That's the plan? Why not take him to the Alliance or—" she stopped, they couldn't do that, they still had no idea who they could or couldn't trust. She glanced over to see Devin watching her, if she wasn't mistaken, he looked apologetic.

"We bounced ideas around, but your place is the only one that's completely off the grid."

She scowled, there was a reason for that. It was *her* place, and she liked the privacy and simplicity of it. It was where she went when she needed to be alone and battle her demons.

"We need someone to watch him at all times, and with all the information leaks, we can't risk taking him anywhere else right now—if Tomas gets him, it's game over. We can't send him anywhere else we have other, because it will freak out any that were rescued when they see him."

Blaise dropped into the chair and looked out the window. There was no hiding the guards now, three of them were in plain sight.

"Fine, but I'll need—"

"Your truck is on the way to you."

She quirked an eyebrow and wondered who jacked her ride because she knew the only existing keys were in her run pack.

"Uri is bringing it. He'll be your overwatch until you get home too, so keep that in mind when you want to drive faster than he can fly."

The surveillance team leader was bringing her truck and was going to be her escort. It made sense, Griffin was an important key to ending all the torment.

"Don't worry, his owl can haul ass," Kenzo assured her.

She blew out a breath. "How did the ops go?" She'd almost forgotten about them. The snow had stopped where they were, but she didn't know if that was the same everywhere.

He chuckled, "it got a little hairy, hitting so many with smaller teams, but all were a success. Bad guys are in pens with Raymond and—" he huffed out a breath, "I don't have all the numbers right now, but a lot were liberated."

She grinned, "that's great. Sorry I missed it." Nothing was more gratifying than freeing their kind that had been imprisoned for so many years. She glanced at Griffin. He had been too.

"I hear you had your own adventures."

She watched Griffin nod to something Blair said and then lean across the table and tap the map. "It's been interesting."

"Mmm, I heard about the half-breed—"

"Griffin." She corrected. "I think he's done enough to warrant his name being used."

Kenzo cleared his throat, "right. You're right. Just keep your tranq gun handy at all times, Tripp told me how big he gets."

"Yeah. He busted us out of a metal can."

"If he shifts—"

"I know, boss. I don't know if he will fully; wouldn't he have by now?" His animal was close enough.

"Anything is possible. The research team has been gathering data, and many that were held or medicated only do partially, *but* being careful is never wrong."

"Got it." She leaned back and looked at the ceiling, "when will Uri be here?"

"I'll check," he chuckled, "looking forward to a few days at home."

"Teams are heading home now?"

"While the information your—Griffin gave us is gone through. I'm told it's a lot." He clicked his teeth together, "I only hope it gets us close to someone in charge."

She opened her eyes and sat forward. "We can only hope." She looked at Griffin again, "he's got his own hit list, boss."

Kenzo laughed, "I have no doubt his life couldn't have been good at all. Three hours. Uri will be there in three hours. Grab a nap, so you can get there with as few stops as possible."

She nodded, "will do, boss."

"I know it's a big ask, Blaise; everyone appreciates it."

"Don't worry about me, boss, I'm aces."

"Always are." He cleared his throat, "just between you and I, the king and Raymond have been working on a new *unofficial* location for Alliance operations."

"Really? That's great. No rate and—"

"We can get down to business without all the cloak and dagger shit. Message me when you're leaving."

"Yup." She hung up without waiting to see if he had any more to say. She was anything but aces right now. She had to take the most sought-after man that ever existed in their world to her private home—and do what then? It wasn't like she had a mansion or even five rooms. She had three. A kitchen, bathroom, and main area, which was her bedroom, den, and whatever else she needed. Might as well have stayed smushed in the tin can with the man.

She glanced at him, the man that was a very large bear inside and her mate.

Her mate. She didn't even know what to do about *that* mess. Currently, she was just trying to outrun it. She knew it was impossible, but still had to try. Once they were stuck in her ride alone, it would be harder to do. She couldn't even think about being confined at her place with him. All she could hope for right now was they would find somewhere safe for him to be.

Chapter Twenty-Six

Griffin was thankful she turned the radio up, making the silence less awkward. Blaise drove with her hand occasionally taping against the steering wheel in time to the song playing. He glanced out the window to look at the owl flying above them. His mind was still stuck on the fact that the large grey owl was a man. He'd met the man, and the fact that he was as big as he was and then turned into a bird, even as large as it was, well, it flabbergasted him. He'd never heard any talk of bird shifters from Aiden or any of his associates, so he wondered if they knew. Or was it that catching them was a lot more difficult?

He looked down at his hand and turned it over, flexing it. He'd picked up a man by the throat and carried him with that hand. Griffin wasn't a weak man, he stayed in shape working out to fill long hours of being held at his apartment, but to pick up a man with one hand—that was beyond any strength he had. How had he done it? His animal had given him a new body and apparently god-like strength with it. He didn't feel one bit of remorse that he'd hurt those three men. They would take him back to Aiden, and that was *never* happening.

Taking a deep breath, he smirked fleetingly. Blaise's scent seemed to be the key to his animal communicating. Like right now, inhaling her scent calmed his animal, yet she was also why other things had happened. His only thought hadn't been of being dragged back to his half-brother. His biggest worry, when trapped in that can, was of Blaise. He'd seen what female shifters went through at the hands of Aiden and his associates, and he wasn't going to let that happen. The fact that she was a mix of two clans made it worse, and if Aiden knew she couldn't have children—her life would have been forfeit. Tomas' associates had no use for female captives who couldn't multiply their business and wallets by procreating more shifters.

That was how he'd found the strength to break them out of a giant welded box and why he'd had no care in what happened to the three men that had put them there.

He discovered a new feeling when it came to her. Protectiveness. In a way he'd never experienced before. Sure, he'd wanted to do something to help those being held against their will, but he'd never done anything to try and prevent what was bound to happen to them. How could he? He was incarcerated right along with them. The only difference was that he had nicer clothes and a private apartment, whereas they had cages, dirty, overcrowded, rundown houses, or infested camps. His skin still crawled when he thought of his time at the camp.

He glanced over at Blaise again. She was completely focused on the road, which he was thankful for. The roads had been cleared after the storm, mostly, but the blowing snow was making some spots a guessing game as to where the road was.

Her truck wasn't what he pictured she'd drive, but he was glad for it. The last thing they needed was to be stranded somewhere. He didn't know how Aiden had found them the last time, but he knew there were many people he used that shared information, so he had his doubts that wherever they were going would be safe. He needed to go through those pictures again and maybe ask if the ones they trusted could be added because someone in the inner circle was sharing with Aiden. He knew they'd found out that Aiden's people had breached their computer network, the temper tantrum from his so-called blood relative had been of epic proportions when they'd been shut down, but maybe there was another way they weren't thinking of.

The truck slowed down, and Griffin immediately looked in the mirror to see if someone was behind them. He looked around. Why were they stopping? There was nothing here.

Blaise turned down the radio, "I'll be right back." She reached into the backseat, pulled out Uri's backpack, and hopped out of the truck. She stood in front of the truck and looked up.

Griffin watched the large owl glide and land on the truck's hood. Blaise pointed and then held up the backpack. He was in awe when Uri took flight and clutched the bag in his talons, and then flew away. Griffin leaned forward and watched with his mouth hanging open.

Blaise got back in and closed the door.

"He'll just fly home carrying a backpack?"

She grinned, "he might, but he'll probably shift and call for backup to come and get him. His team is all over the place all the time; they must have something set up." She put the truck into gear, "you might want to hang onto something."

Griffin was about to ask why when she stomped on the accelerator and headed straight for the snowbank. They hit it hard, and snow flew over the hood, but she kept going.

"I haven't been home to clear the road."

Griffin grabbed the handle near his door and tried to hold himself still as the truck shifted over the rough ground. He was bounced against the window a few times. Blaise didn't let up on the gas, just kept making a trail through it. When it leveled out, he was going to ask how much further they had to go through it when she turned suddenly and went up a hill. The rev of the engine told him the truck was struggling and he felt at that moment that his silence would be better appreciated than interrupting her focus.

The truck stopped.

"That was something." She patted her hand on the dash,

"good girl." She turned it off. "Grab the grocery sacks." She hopped out and opened the back door, and picked up her bag.

Griffin looked around. Grab them and go where? There wasn't a building in sight, just trees.

Blaise walked by him, not caring that the snow was up to her knees. Grabbing his few clothes and the cloth bags, he grit his teeth as the snow filled his boots. Closing the door, he hurried to catch up to her. She walked into the trees, and he stopped and stood there as she went upstairs. There were stairs in the middle of the trees. He lifted his head and looked above them. There was a building *in* the trees. "You live in a treehouse?" Did people even do that?

She glanced over his shoulder, a look of amusement on her face, "it's not *in* the trees, just surrounded by them.

He turned around in a slow circle and noticed the tall pillars that blended in with a natural-looking tree. Shaking his head, he followed her up the stairs.

"I'll have to get everything going and clear the panels off, but the batteries should have enough juice to get the heat going. The water line might be frozen if the heat cables haven't had any power for too long, but it won't take long to thaw."

Griffin went in the door she held open and then just stood there.

"Just give me a second," she opened a panel that blended into the wood and pressed a few switches, "wouldn't want you getting electrocuted for touching a window or door." She unlocked the second door and motioned for him to go in.

Electrocuted? That was a harsh security system she had. Kicking the snow from his boots, he stepped in and then slipped his feet out. Looking down, he saw his socks were caked with snow.

"Just put those in the kitchen," she pointed to the doorway across from where they stood.

"You use solar power, I take it?"

She dropped her bag and went to a large panel on the wall. "I couldn't get any electrical lines run out here, so I found another way." She flipped a few breakers and pushed a button.

"Batteries were fully charged when the storm hit." She looked down at her feet, "I'll go do the panels now, so I don't have to go back out."

Griffin could only nod. He didn't know much about solar power or what it took to maintain it. He went into the kitchen and set the bags on the counter. It was a large space, but it was organized and spotless. In the corner was a small fridge, which he imagined was more than adequate for one person. He'd never done his own shopping, so he had no idea the thought that went into purchasing and storage. His fridge had always had a moderate amount of food in it.

He couldn't believe her home was built in the trees or among them. Going over to the window, he pulled the curtain aside. The view was something. He could see for miles, and the snow covering things from this vantage looked pristine and pure. Was that why she'd chosen this spot? For the peaceful views? It was better than looking out and seeing endless buildings, cars, and far too many people, which is what he was used to. He doubted the beauty of this wore off.

Griffin wasn't sure if he should put the groceries away or just stand here and wait for her to return. Going back out, he went over to the other side where they'd come in and pulled the curtain back. It was a snow-covered deck. Movement on the ground had him lean closer. It was Blaise; she was using a narrow brush on a pole. After a few more minutes of observation and he concluded she was clearing off her solar panels. They were on platforms about five feet off the ground, and at least ten were lined up facing one direction He released the curtain and stepped back when she paused and looked up at him stepped back.

He turned around slowly to check out the room. It was a large area. He grinned; the fact that he hadn't noticed the building until he was standing under it made him shake his head would never have thought to look up for her home. He had a lot to learn about life outside Aiden's grasp and part of him was anxious to begin, while the other part, the knots in his stomach part, told him he had a long road ahead of him.

Chapter Twenty-Seven

She'd cleaned the panels, shoveled a path to them, cleared the road with the snowblower, cleared the deck, and checked the battery storage—twice. She'd even stalled by taking a long hot shower and now she was out of things to do to avoid sitting here looking at Griffin.

He had saved that happening a short while ago by asking if he could make dinner. He liked cooking. Blaise was happy not to have to come up with a meal for them. Feeding him when he was in a cage was one thing, but preparing a meal now felt too intimate—or something close to that.

She couldn't get his words out of her head, what he'd said about slaying dragons when they'd been in that metal box. What did that even mean? He breathed her in and wanted to kill things. Her cat rubbed against her to get her attention. Blaise ignored it and went over to check that everything was charging properly. Her animal crushing on Griffin was not something she wanted to deal with.

When she turned around, he was standing outside the kitchen.

"It will be a few minutes yet." He ran his hand through his hair, was it thicker now? "You don't have a lot of spices, so I had to improvise."

"I'm sure it will be fine." She wasn't a picky eater. Food as long as it was edible, worked for her.

"You don't live with your clan."

She went over and looked out the window to see if there was any movement below. "No, I don't."

"Is that safe? Shouldn't clan live close?"

Instead of turning around and looking at him, she kept her eyes on the vast whiteness outside, seeing if anything or one was out there. "Most clans do, but you don't have to."

"I didn't know that, but every clan has an Alpha and a second family, I think it's called."

She glanced at him, "yeah, that's how it works." She looked back outside again. A few birds took flight, she kept her eyes trained on the spot they'd flown from to see if there was a reason on the ground that spooked them.

"I heard clans were locked down. What does that mean?"

A fox came running out of the trees, a small fury victim in its mouth. Turning, she went over to the other window. "Travel is restricted. The kids are doing online schooling until the Alliance is certain there are no information leaks."

"Smart. It pissed Aiden off."

She saw him grin, very pleased by the fact that his one-form brother was upset. "How did you hear that?"

"A conversation between Aiden and someone on the phone."

"How long ago?" She crossed her arms over her chest and leaned back against the windowsill.

"A few months at least."

She nodded, "good, so not since we shut down his access to our systems."

"Yeah, that *really* pissed him off."

Blaise smirked.

"What do they do now for money? Don't they have jobs?"

She knew he wasn't pumping her for information, he looked too sincere, but she wished for quiet. Looking out the window, she scanned the treeline for any trails in the snow. "Those that can still work safely do."

"What team are you on with the Alliance?"

Blowing out a breath, she went over to the table and checked her phone. Kenzo needed to message soon with a new game plan. This one was going to drive her crazy. "Special operations." She could feel his eyes on her back and knew he'd stand there staring at her until she answered.

"How many teams are there?"

She bit her lip briefly, trying not to lose her patience with the chatty one. "Ten, maybe twelve, I'm not sure. I mostly interact with the four main ones." Turning, slowly, she gave him a look asking if that was all.

"Sorry," he glanced into the kitchen, "I know nothing of *normal* life and even less about how a clan unit functions."

"I guess it's an adjustment."

"It is, but this is the most freedom I've ever had, which considering I was captured, is saying a lot."

She could only nod. What was she supposed to say to that?

"The two that got me—"

"Tripp and Amari."

"Yeah. They're mates?"

"That's what I'm told."

"They seem like a good match."

She smirked, "they're both a little out of control if that's what you mean."

"Are they on the same team as you?"

She shook her head, "Tripp is, Amari is on the co-ord team."

"Co-ord?"

"Clan co-ordination," she shrugged, "I don't know their exact job."

"Your team's tasks are usually violent?" He motioned to the knives attached to her.

Just the way I like it. "We go in when it's the last resort most times. Lately, all teams are working to free those from your brother—"

"Please don't call him that." His expression darkened, "we may share a bit of blood, but there are no positive feelings on either end for each other."

"Fair enough."

"Hold on, I think it's done. We can talk more while we eat."

Blaise looked at the small table in the corner. She had two chairs, only because the table came with two. She didn't want to sit face-to-face with him while they ate. She went into the kitchen and watched him heap a plate with food. It was some sort of casserole, and it smelled amazing. He motioned for her to take the plate and filled a second one. She thought it was good she had two plates as she grabbed a fork. "Thanks." Picking up the plate, she went out and sat on the couch. He was free to sit wherever he wanted.

When she sat on the couch, she looked down at it. This was also her bed. She had no idea where they were sleeping.

Griffin came out, looked at her, and then went and sat down at the table. He looked even larger sitting in the small chair.

She took a bite and then nodded and gave a thumbs up. It burned her tongue, but she didn't care. She couldn't remember the last time she had anything that wasn't from a package or takeout. It was good. Why did food you didn't have to make always taste better?

He ate in silence for a few minutes, and she thought it would continue that way for the duration of the meal.

"Where's your family live? With your clan?"

She swallowed the food in her mouth and then pointed, "on the Manitoba border, with our clan." She got up, went to the kitchen, and grabbed a bottle of water out of the case on the floor. Sighing, she picked up a second one and went back out. Without comment, she set it on the table and returned to the couch.

"Thanks." He opened it and took a drink. "Your teams, they're doing good. At least they were before I was captured."

"They still are." She sat back and looked at him, "we should have done more sooner," she snorted, "years ago. If we had, then some clans would still be around."

"I don't understand." He set the fork down and turned in the chair, giving her his full attention.

He was so schooled in manners it made her feel awkward. "Twenty-five clans," she looked at the bottle in her hand, "it could be more now, but at last count, twenty-five entire clans are completely gone." She looked back at him, "vanished, their lands abandoned."

His brows creased. "They didn't just relocate?"

She shook her head.

"I didn't know that." His chest rose and fell as he took a deep breath, "I mean, I knew it was bad—that my father and Aiden were acquiring large numbers, but I didn't know it was that bad."

"Well, it is. One clan was down to one member, and then we found a bunch of them at those houses."

His expression lightened slightly, "I'm glad they were found."

Blaise studied him for a moment, "how did you manage to survive it? You don't hide your emotions very well."

Amusement filled his eyes, "with you. Standing in a room with Aiden and five of his lackeys," he shrugged, "trust me, I'm completely emotionless. I had to be."

"I'm happy," she motioned at him, "that you survived it." She nodded, "you're the ace we needed to bring it all down."

He smirked, "last time I checked, one ace isn't a very good hand."

Blaise couldn't help the smile on her face, "it's a good start though."

Griffin nodded, "hopefully, the information I shared will lead you to a few more aces, so you can have a strong hand."

Blaise picked up her fork, "don't worry about that; we've been annihilating all the lower deck, and now we can work on the higher cards."

He held up his bottle in a toast, "here's to watching Aiden fall off his tower of blood and concrete."

She laughed, "and go spligack at the bottom." He gave her a strange look, and she shrugged, "that's like a splat, only messier."

Griffin smiled, "I like it. Spligack."

Chapter Twenty-Eight

Day two. Blaise glared at the coffee in her cup. She'd barely survived the day before and now she had to do it all over again.

Griffin had accepted sleeping on the couch after she said that she needed to keep watch. And she had for the most part of the night but seemed to watch him more than out the windows. The longer she was around him and his scent, the worse it seemed to be getting. She could even smell him over the gun oil when she was cleaning hers. It was crazy, but she thought she could even taste his scent—how did that work?

Right now, he was in the shower and she was standing there trying not to think about *that*. Her cat had no problem thinking about him naked. She set the cup down with a clunk on the counter. She needed to go for a run, but then he'd be left here alone. Her cat was perfectly content here, with him and she didn't need an instruction manual for her animal to know it had nothing to do with his safety. The creature wanted to bite him. What was she supposed to do with that?

Blaise decided she would shift and do a couple of laps around the perimeter, she just needed to get her lusty cat to agree. It was weird her animal was so interested in someone, usually, except in her cycle, she could care less about males.

Grabbing her run pack off the hook, she headed for the

door.

Griffin stepped out of the bathroom with a towel wrapped around his waist. He held his clothes bunched up in his hand, "I forgot to take the change of clothes Blair gave me in with me."

Blaise stood there; no words would form on her tongue. How did a man that was confined to an apartment have such a toned body? Her eyes tracked the water dripping from his hair onto his shoulder. It rolled down over the muscle and then deviated to the center of his chest to continue its journey. "Uh, I'll grab them." She almost tripped over her feet turning around to grab the bag in the corner.

When she turned, he held up the clothes, "can we wash these or give them a rinse?" His arm flexed with the motion, and she felt her mouth fill with salvia.

Swallowing it, she nodded, "yeah, then we can, uh, hang them on the rack to dry."

He grinned, "thanks." He bunched them up under his arm and held his other hand out for the bag she forgot she was holding.

She lurched forward and held it out. "I can give those a rinse," she pointed to the clothes under his arm. What? Since when did she volunteer to do someone else's wash? She *really* needed to go for a run and clear her head.

He gave her a surprised look and handed her the clothes.

When the bathroom door closed, she looked at the clothes she held. Turning abruptly, she hurried to the kitchen and dropped them in the sink—before she followed through with the thought of sniffing them, because that was just weird, smelling a man's dirty clothes. She wanted to set fire to them and fill her nostrils with the rancid smell of burning fabric, so she could stop acting so strange. This mating stuff was going to kill her. Flipping the tap on, she pulled out her phone and checked for messages. None.

Huffing out a breath, she text Kenzo and asked if there was any news. She was tempted to just send 123 to make him call, but that was her team's version of 911 and she wasn't ready to sink that low.

Turning the tap off, she spun around, she needed to check the power levels, her systems were set up for one person, not two.

"These will take some time to get used to."

She glanced at him and then looked away quickly. Blair had given him some jeans and they hugged all the right parts perfectly. She cleared her throat, "once things settle down, I'm sure someone can take you shopping," she opened the panel on the wall, but couldn't focus on the numbers in front of her, "buy what you'd prefer to wear."

"My father didn't think jeans were appropriate to wear."

She blinked, "Oh." His father was very wrong.

"Is everything all right?"

She hesitantly looked back at him, hoping her thoughts weren't clear on her face. He motioned to the panel, "uh," she turned away, "yeah, just checking how things are holding up with two of us using the hot water and power."

"Is it? Holding up?"

She stared at the numbers, willing her brain to function. "As long as no storms roll in, we should be okay." She glanced at the box in the corner. Closing the panel, she motioned to it, "I have a backup power supply, I've been meaning to set up." She went over and opened it and pulled out the cables. "I haven't been home long enough to get it done."

"I can help you do it." He came over and looked in the box, "I don't know what it is, but I follow instructions very well."

She turned to answer him to find with him looking down at her, they were face to face. She dropped the cables and stepped back. "Sure. Yeah. That would save me running up and down the stairs."

He grinned, "so what is it?"

"Oh, backup generator." She glanced at it, "a little one, in case the storms are bad this year." She smirked, "I sat here with no power for two days last year."

"How did you stay warm?"

She shrugged, "our animals have built-in heat."

"That explains why I feel hot when I should be cold."

She looked down at his bare feet, "or stomp around without your boots on and smack people off trees."

His smile was slow, "I did that."

"Yes, you did." She quirked an eyebrow at him, "do you regret it?"

He sobered, "no."

"I need to thank you again for breaking us out of that tin can."

"Staying in it wasn't an option, and what would happen if we had, also wasn't an option."

She nodded slowly, "I agree with that."

They stood there looking at each other and not even realizing it was happening.

He cleared his throat, "so how do we set this up?"

She blinked, "oh, I'm going to set it up at the bottom, there's a storage space under the first section of stairs, so I don't have to haul gas up here."

He nodded, "what can I do?"

Chapter Twenty-Nine

Blaise was happy to be doing something other than being stuck in a small space with Griffin. They had the generator set up in the storage area, a hole for the cables and now had them run halfway up the stairs. Outside was good, the cold air diluted the smell of Griffin. The least he could do was try to stink bad instead of smelling like something she needed to sniff him, and lick him and more—

She smacked the stapler on the step. "It's jammed," she looked up at him, "go grab me a screwdriver."

He nodded and carefully set the two coils of cable on the step.

If he weren't here, she would have had to run one at a time. Popping the cartridge out, she scowled at it. The temperatures were dropping and holding the metal stapler was freezing her hand. Snapping it back in, she aimed it away from her body and smiled when a staple flew out. "Perfect."

Grabbing a clip from the box, she lined it up over the cable and secured it to the side of the step. Moving up one, she pulled a bit more of the black cable, it caught the roll of red and then proceeded to slide off the edge.

"Crap." Leaning over, she pulled enough back up so she could get the clip over it and staple it in place. As she leaned down to pull some up, strong hands lifted her up under her arms.

Griffin set her back from the edge. "You take a dive off these and I'm on my own," he tilted his head, "and I wouldn't want you to damage your lovely face."

The rant about how she didn't need to be coddled and was perfectly capable of looking after herself died on her tongue. Lovely? He thought her face was lovely. In her entire life, no one had thought her face was anything other than something to avoid staring at. She didn't know what to say.

"Give me a second, I'll roll them back up." He held out the screwdriver.

Taking it, she stood there watching him roll up the cables. Her phone buzzing in her back pocket almost made her drop the stapler. It was Kenzo. "Hey boss," she hoped it was good news, like the kind that would have her taking Griffin somewhere else.

"Blaise. How are you doing? Any problems?"

She looked down at Griffin on one knee. Other than being here with him. "No. All quiet here."

"Good. I need you to go to wherever you get good receptions, there's a group call being set up in an hour."

"Okay. The team?" It wasn't uncommon for him to call the whole team at once.

"No. A much larger group, around twenty."

She raised an eyebrow and glanced at Griffin. "Is it something my guest can hear because I don't exactly have a room I can hide in?" She wasn't going to sit in her bathroom for a group call.

"That's fine. Part of it pertains to him, so Shepard says he can be included."

The King was going to be on a call she was. "Okay. Anything I should know before it?"

Kenzo snorted, "yeah, good luck if you want to get a word in, most of them are team leaders."

"Oh." She looked at the distance to the top of the stairs, "I'll finish up what I'm doing and get set up for the call."

"Sounds good."

She hung up and looked at the phone before putting it back in her pocket.

"Everything all right?" He stood up, once again holding the two rolls of cable.

"Yeah. There's a big group call in about an hour."

He looked up the stairs, "we'll have it finished by then."

Nodding, she went up a few steps and waited for him to unravel enough wiring.

"Is it a good call?"

She grabbed the box of clips and set them a few steps ahead of her before taking one out. "I'm not sure, but it must be important because the king is part of it."

"Shepard Addison."

She paused and looked at him.

He shrugged, "I listened in on a lot of conversations."

She secured the clip to the cable and then stapled it. "Your——Aiden isn't very intelligent. He completely underestimated you."

"I'm a half-breed, the shifter DNA cancels out the other half according to him."

She gave him a dumbfounded look, "I guess he's going to find out the hard way how wrong he is."

Griffin grinned, "I can only hope to be there when he does."

Blaise smiled back and grabbed another clip.

Griffin cleared his throat, "did your boss happen to tell you of my fate?"

Moving up a few more steps, she waited for him to unroll the wire. "No, he said you can be part of it because some of it is about you."

"Mmm, I wonder if that's good for me or otherwise."

Blaise shrugged, "I don't know, but we need to get this done before the call."

That spurred him into action again. She studied his face as he untangled a section of the wire so it would lay flat. His brows were drawn, and small creases surrounded his mouth. His expression was very grim. She wanted to reassure him that everything was going to work out, but none of that was in her control. Her current task was to keep him safe until she was told otherwise that's what she was going to do. It had to be weighing on him though, where his life was headed.

All she knew for sure was that until Aiden Tomas was gone, Griffin would have to live under guard. Was his life better than it had been before? She wasn't sure. She knew was she couldn't have lived as he had. She needed her freedom. Keeping her head down, she stapled the next few clips. None of it compared to those that had been abducted thoughts. What they went through made her see red. Her cat stirred and then she noticed her vision was shifting back and forth between hers and her animal.

"Blaise," Griffin put his hand on her shoulder. He'd sensed the conflict in her. She looked up at him and watched him pause to study her eyes. "I can finish this, why don't you go for a run or whatever it is full shifters do when their animal is too close."

She stood up slowly, watching the compassionate expression in his eyes. "Yeah," she handed him the stapler. "I'll go run the perimeter before the call."

He nodded and offered her no further words.

Turning, she ran down the stairs.

Chapter Thirty

Griffin carried the two mugs of coffee out. Blaise was at the table, a map and notepad in front of her. "Expecting a trip?"

She tapped her phone and looked at it. "I like to see where places are if they're mentioned," she shrugged, "easier to volunteer for things if I know what's involved."

"Smart." He set a cup in front of her and then sat in the other chair. "You seem more settled after a run." It was the first time he knew something was being conveyed by his inner bear when he'd felt panic and anxiety, but knew it wasn't his own. When she'd looked up at him, her eyes had been more cat than a woman.

Blaise blew on the liquid in her cup, "it helps. A run." She took a small sip, "how are you doing with your bear?"

He gave her an exaggerated expression trying to relay his frustration, "I'm not sure. I know when he doesn't want something, but we're still not communicating."

She smirked, "it takes time."

Setting his cup down, he flipped his hands open toward her, "good thing I have a lot of that right now."

The phone rang, ending any further conversation.

"Blaise, it's Illias, two secs and I'll put you through to the others."

"Sounds good, Illias," she set the phone down and tapped the speaker button.

"Okay, that's everyone for now." The same man said.

"Blaise?"

She leaned forward, "I'm here, Kenzo."

Griffin knew that was her boss.

"I'm sorry for the short notice, everyone, but time is not in our favor right now, so I needed to get all of you involved right from the start."

Griffin gave her a curious look, she held her hand over her head and made a circle, telling him it was the King's voice they were hearing.

"Who is everyone?" A woman with a deep voice asked.

"I was just about to tell everyone, Wynter." The King told her.

"Sounds good, sir."

He saw Blaise smirk. She glanced at him and then wrote something on the notepad and slid it over. She had written *Incursion team leader.* He nodded.

"Joining us is my son and his mate."

Blaise wrote Devin and Rayne for him. Griffin was happy that Rayne had a life now. He'd always wondered how she ended up with Aiden, then again, her choices weren't many when his father had shielded her after her parent's *mysterious* death.

"Calum Dante and his mate, our best medical advisor currently." The King continued.

She wrote down *Shae*, so he knew the mate's name.

"Alpha Blair Elden and his mate, our best tracker, Kobie Sorum."

Someone laughed quietly and he wondered why that was entertaining.

"Leader of our coordination team, Jesse Pruitt, and his talented mate."

"Evanna is here with me." A male informed them.

Griffin glanced at Blaise, she wrote quickly and leaned back. *She has a split personality. Leah and Evanna.* He gave her a surprised look and she shrugged.

"Noah is also here, his insight on matters with the Tomas organization is always welcome."

Griffin nodded, it was good that Noah had found his place in life and was included. He could only hope that he did in the future.

"Head of surveillance, Uri Welton, from our Tech team, Nate Howe," the King continued, "as well as Raymond, head of security," Griffin would never forget that huge man, "Konner Flores, who is bringing the offer of more help to the table today."

Blaise glanced at the phone and he wondered why that part interested her so much.

"We also have Blaise Morgan from Kenzo's team with us and Griffin Ballard, who has brought us thirty years of knowledge from inside the Tomas organization."

The line went quiet.

"Heard you had the misfortune of being related to Tomas, Mister Ballard," he recognized the leader of the incursion's team voice, "I say we let him stick the knife in that Aiden's heart at the end of this—sir."

Blaise smirked and Griffin was shocked. This Wynter woman was very blunt.

"I'll take that into consideration, Wynter," Shepard said in a light tone. "I'll try not to take up too much of your time today," he continued, "Konner has some contacts in other countries that he's been utilizing to transport our kind under the wire, so to speak." No one commented.

Griffin glanced at Blaise; she had a hard look on her face making him wonder why it was personal for her. He wanted to know more of her story, but the few times she'd inadvertently told him something about herself, she'd gone cold afterward.

"Konner has asked these men, once they're finished assisting on their side of borders if they'd like to become part of the Alliance."

"What was the outcome of that, Shep?"

Blaise wrote down Calum.

"They've agreed, Calum. Only a few of them will be left over there after the others' families are safely moved to the appropriate clans here."

"That's good news, sir. That their families will be safe." A voice he'd never forget said. It was the large man in charge of security. Raymond Hardy.

"It is, Raymond. To facilitate things on this end, we have one working with Konner to set up safe routes and assist our teams with transport. Is Mister Steele with us, Illias?"

"He will be in a few secs, sir."

There was a soft click on the line.

"Taggart Steele here, sir." Griffin looked at the phone, he understood his name was Taggart, but it sounded more like Tegarrt with the man's accent.

"Taggart, I was just explaining to our team leaders that you are going to be heading up our new team that will be handling ambassadors gone astray."

"Ja, it will be my pleasure, sir. To toss out the rotten apples."

With the way he enunciated his o's and r's, Griffin thought he must be from the Northern European region. He'd watched a lot of documentaries to kill time and his accent was either Dutch or German, or somewhere close to those.

Blaise was grinning at him, and he couldn't be sure if it was the man's words or that he was going to be tossing out rotten apples.

"The records with the sales listed has not been very useful for us to locate which ports the most bodies flowing through." Griffin noticed him speaking carefully and wondered how long he had been working on his English. Most of the words he was doing good using the American dialect.

"We have new information to sort through as well, so there may be even more opportunities for your people to help."

"I brought four of my men with me, sir, we are happy to jump in the action if we are needed."

"We're going to need a few more working on surveillance right now, watching the addresses and people that have been given to us.”

Blaise lurched forward and wrote Uri on the notepad. At least Griffin knew that one.

“We can do that. We are very good at not being seen.”

Blaise raised an eyebrow and then wrote *mercenaries?* on the paper. Griffin lifted a shoulder in reply, he couldn’t be sure.

“With this new information, we may be able to close down the main connection here.” The King said.

“That would be a great thing, sir.”

“I’m unable to contact Cecil about your sister and you joining their clan right now, Taggart. We’re still filtering through associates of each clan for possible information leaks, but as soon as we can, it will be done. Until that time, you and your sister are under my protection.

“Ja, I understand. My sister is happy to be help at the campground. Arcadia, I believe it is called.”

“She’s been a great help.” A woman told him.

“Thank you, princess. I am just happy she is out of there.”

Griffin glanced at Blaise and then mouthed, ‘Rayne’. She nodded. He used to love her gentle voice; it was a nice break from all the brainless goons his brother kept himself surrounded with.

“I am going to half to go, sir, one of my men just arrived, and I need to go over his trip with him.”

“I understand, Taggart. Thank you again for joining us.”

“I am just happy to be doing something about it on the bigger scale. I will be in touch with all of your team leaders in the next week to see how I can help with their transports inside the border.”

“Thank you, Taggart.” There was a short pause and then a click.

“That’s some great news,” Wynter said.

“It is, Wynter. I’d like to discuss some of the information Griffin has given us now.”

Griffin sat straighter and watched the phone like something would come out of it for him.

“We have a few more spies weeded out with his help.

They've been dealt with. There are more files we'll have him go through, so we can finally go about things more normally."

"Were there a lot? On the inside?" Uri asked.

"Even one is too many, there should never have been any."

"I agree, Nate. We're going to ask Griffin to go through the sales records recovered from Lindon Eldon as well, see if he can't fit a few more pieces together for us."

Griffin frowned. "I'm sorry, Lindon kept records of his *transactions*?" He shook his head.

"Dates, how many, sometimes the clan and the amount are the only part that's been translated." He recognized Blair's voice.

"One of mine, with the help of Nate's team, figured out that so far, we're just not sure about the rest."

He glanced at Blaise, not recognizing the voice. She wrote Konner on the paper. "Would I be able to look at these records? I know places, ports, companies, and names for many areas that were used, maybe I can figure out more." He wanted to try. At this point, he'd do anything to stop Aiden—before Aiden found him.

"I was going to speak with you about that, Griffin," the King said quietly, "I'm sure you understand we can't just let you roam around…"

Griffin snorted, "I have nowhere to roam, sir, no way to roam," he looked down at the jeans he wore, "I don't even have clothes of my own."

"The clothes we can remedy; however, until things are resolved with the Tomas organization, you will be required to stay with one of our team members or a secure location."

He knew a secure location was a polite way of saying locked up. "I understand." He glanced at Blaise, who, for whatever reason, looked offended.

"Bring him here," Blair said, "well, not here-here. We have too many children to risk that, but he could go to Ed's, it's probably one of the safest areas to be in with my place and Noah's close by."

"I wouldn't mind doing blood tests and seeing how the data

measures after taking the medication for as long as he did."

Eyebrows raised; he watched Blaise circle Shae's name on the paper.

Someone spoke quietly away from their phone for a moment.

"I guess we're going to Ed's too," Blaise tapped the pen the paper over the name Calum, "Blair isn't wrong, Shep; there will be more than enough to keep him out of Tomas' reach."

As much as Griffin wanted to help, he didn't feel there would be any safe place out of reach of Aiden.

"I trust you to keep an eye on things, Calum." The King agreed.

Blaise leaned over the map and looked at it for a moment. "I'm looking at two days, maybe longer to get there, depending on how well the roads have been cleared."

"Do you need anyone to accompany you, Blaise?" Shepard Addison asked.

Blaise glanced at the phone, "no, I'll be fine on my own."

"You keep me on speed dial, Blaise."

She smirked, "yes, boss."

"I'd just like to say if Griffin can help us shut this down, I am all for whatever he needs to get it done."

"I agree with Kaid." Wynter stated, "you need any backup, Blaise, you call, and I'll have the team there in no time."

"Thanks, Wynter." Blaise grinned.

"Any idea when we're setting up some more ops?" Kenzo said in a quiet tone.

"We're watching the locations Griffin gave us right now, but don't get too comfortable at home when we confirm we'll be moving fast," Devin informed all listening.

Blaise gave the phone a thumbs up.

"If that's everything, I'll end the call here." Shepard paused for a moment, "you've all been doing excellent work under trying circumstances. I know in the near future; all of our kind will be freed."

The line was quiet.

"Thanks, dad," it seemed odd to hear Devin call the King

dad, "I need Blair, Calum, Kenzo, and Blaise to stay on the line."

"That's our cue to hang up," Wynter said. "Call if we're needed."

There were a few other goodbye remarks, and Illias said, "everyone else is gone."

"Thanks, Illias." He wondered why Devin needed just these people on the call. "Blair, you need to read Ed in, and Coop, make sure patrols are diligent."

"I will, I'm not worried. We have so many tigers around here, we can patrol in five directions at the same time."

"Okay, good. Get Gage in on the patrol at Ed's, just to be sure."

"Will do."

"How soon can you get to Ed's, Cal?"

"We're heading to Konner's to check on the twins, I'm sure he can fly us there now that the storm is over. We'll be there before Blaise." This Calum sounded too calm and easygoing. Griffin wondered if he really was.

"Good. Kenzo, I need more of yours on a few sights that we're watching. There's been no movement and the guys posted there can't stay awake forever."

"Text me the details, I can get someone there. I'll go myself if I have to. Do we expect movement?" Blaise was the most interested in her boss speaking, Griffin could see she had an immense amount of respect for the man with the expression on her face.

"We're hoping. They're locations Griffin gave us and important ones, we just need them to emerge so we can get counts and intel."

"All right, I'll get more eyes on it."

"Blaise, take what you need and bring extra in case that weather circles back, don't kill yourself trying to get there fast, just get there in one piece."

Blaise smirked, "bad weather isn't a problem for me."

"Keep your phone in sight at all times, and if anything feels off, you let us know. Illias, I want her movement tracked until she's surrounded by Blair's tigers."

Someone chuckled, "got it."

"Okay. We'll see you all soon."

"What do you mean we?" Calum didn't sound so relaxed now.

"We don't trust sending everything over lines, so I'm bringing a laptop of all of it that has no online capability and can't be traced." Devin chuckled, "I'm not staying, so don't worry. Rayne and I are heading back to Arcadia to check on everything since the storm."

"Okay, good. We have enough to worry about with Griffin being there. We don't need to be watching your back the whole time too."

"I miss you too, Cal." Devin sounded amused. "If that's all…"

"Can I make one stop to get Griffin some clothes that fit his new size?" Blaise asked abruptly.

"Yes. Make it fast though."

"No worries, sir, I'm not big on shopping." Blaise glanced at him for a second and smirked.

Chapter Thirty-One

The first day of the drive had been pretty relaxed, Griffin took turns between napping, snacking, and staring at the scenery, which was mainly trees and some rocks, and the odd frozen lake that was visible. She'd realized then that he'd been kept in the city his entire life. From that point, she became a tour guide, telling him odd facts about the areas they drove through. Blaise wasn't a chatty person, and from what she'd seen about him, neither was he, yet they'd had a few conversations that hadn't been awkward or uncomfortable.

She'd taken him into a small store in a mediocre town to grab some jeans and a few sweaters. He didn't have a clue what he was doing. Griffin had no idea what size he was in anything, even his old size. A few times Blaise wanted to go over and bite the clerk for the odd looks she was giving them. It wasn't his fault he'd never been shopping.

It wasn't until four in the morning that she'd needed to stop for a short nap that she realized he was scared. She hadn't picked up on it until that point. As she settled back in her seat, she watched him sit completely board straight in the seat, the gun white-knuckled in his hand, and he was turning his head non-stop, checking all around them. For a few minutes, she debated on just getting up and continuing to drive, but he'd noticed her still awake and assured her she could sleep. She had to admire that he was willing to sit through his fears so she could rest. His fear was justified, if Aiden Tomas got his hands on him again, she doubted he'd live through it.

It was day two, and he'd been silent since his early morning watch. She glanced over at him again, he just looked out the window, offering no conversation. Her phone ringing startled them both. She tapped the screen and answered.

"Blaise, it's Devin. Illias told me where you are, and I need you to stop and do something quick for me."

Eyebrows raised, she looked at the phone, "okay." Wasn't the plan to drive with as few stops as possible?

"One of the clans near your location isn't responding to communication, I just need you to stop in and make sure everything is all right with them."

She sat straighter, "of course. Have Illias send me a location." She glanced at Griffin, who was also staring at the phone, "when was the last contact with them?"

"A few weeks ago, but we just want to make sure all is well."

Blaise nodded and then tapped her phone when a message notification popped up. It was from Illias. "I have the location."

"Be careful, don't take any chances. Your main priority is to get Griffin to Ed's."

"I will. I'll call after we get there."

"Okay." He hung up.

Griffin looked over at her, "is that unusual?"

"Not really, but with the discovery of missing clans, we check out any that haven't been in touch or we can't reach."

"You'll know if something isn't right?"

Checking the message from Illias again, she glanced around them; they weren't that far at all. "I'm sure everything is fine; they're probably busy digging out after the storm."

"I didn't think of that."

Her cat stirred, sensing he was nervous. "It will be fine; this is what I do." She offered him a reassuring smile, "I'm not normally a babysitter."

He looked at her for a few seconds and then smiled back.

It never reached his eyes though.

~

Blaise walked out of the Alpha's house and pulled out her phone. She opened Illias' message and typed; *power is down from the storm. They should have it back up by tonight. All is good here.* Tucking it back in her pocket, she started walking toward her truck. Griffin had done as he was told and stayed inside it. She noticed that when he agreed, he pulled the gun out of the side of the door where it had ridden for the entire drive.

A group of four young males stood in front of the truck, watching her walk back toward it. She knew the look well, the one that said, 'what is wrong with your face?' Tucking her hands into her jacket pockets, she kept her head down so she wouldn't rest them on her gun and be tempted to shoot them in the face. After this long, you would think she would be able to ignore it, but it still took her back to when she was a kid and the teasing and ignorance of others in her own clan.

She heard the hushed talk and snickers and kept going. Griffin got out on the other side as she opened the door to get in the truck.

"Can I help you with something?" He growled and walked to the front of the truck.

Closing the door, she rushed over, "let it go, Griffin." She stopped in front of him and looked up, noticing how close his bear was. "It's fine."

He looked down at her; his expression was pure anger. "It's not fine. They're being disrespectful."

She patted his chest. "I'm used to it." Turning, she looked at the others, making sure her chin was high, and they could see the darkened side of her face, "you guys better move along." They looked from her and then back to Griffin, before stepping back and turning in unison to go down the path she'd just come up. Blowing out a breath, she turned back around and looked up at him. "I'm used to it."

His brows furrowed as he searched her face, "you shouldn't have to get used to something like that. There's nothing wrong with how you look, or your cat—who you should let out to smack them in the head a few times."

She couldn't help but grin but sobered quickly. Besides Emersyn when they were kids, she couldn't remember anyone sticking up for her. "Hey," she grabbed the side of his face and reached up and kissed him. "Thank you." Her cat moved inside her, jolting her back to reality. What was going on with her? She'd just kissed the man. It may have been a fleeting smack of lips, but since when did she go around kissing people? She stepped back and motioned to the truck, "we should get back on the road."

Griffin stood there and looked at her instead of getting in the truck; with his long arm span, he cupped the back of her neck and brought her closer in one fast move she hadn't seen coming. He kissed her mouth firmly and then looked down at her. "No need to thank me." Releasing her, he turned and got back in the truck.

What just happened? Shaking her head, she scowled at the ground, stomped over, and opened the door. Yanking her phone out of her pocket, she climbed in and put it in the holder. Without looking in his direction, she started the truck and put it in reverse. She needed to eat up as many miles as she could and try to get them to Ed's by tonight. It would be pushing it, but she needed out of this small space with his scent swallowing her. She licked her lips and then regretted it. She could taste him on her lips.

"Was that wrong?"

She stared out the windshield. Not talking about it would have been better. "It was unnecessary." Was she talking about the kiss or the whole scene? She wasn't sure. Right now, she just needed him to drop it and leave it alone.

"I disagree."

She could feel him watching her and wasn't going to look at him right now. Her cat wanted her to gawk at him too. "We're just going to have to disagree then." She pulled out onto the main road and then reached over and turned up the radio, ending any chance of the conversation continuing.

Chapter Thirty-Two

He'd never kissed anyone before, ever. Griffin wasn't sure what possessed him to grab her and kiss her. Yes, she had kissed him first, and he'd been shocked, then decided without thought he needed to do it again.

Griffin licked his lips; her taste was gone, which wasn't surprising; he had probably run his tongue over his mouth thirty times in the first few minutes after it.

She'd turned the radio down but hadn't so much as looked at him in the last four hours.

Her phone rang, dragging him out of his head.

"Hello."

"Blaise, it's Sloane Travis."

Blaise grinned, "hey, Sloane, what's up?"

"Kenzo told me you're about twenty minutes from my location. I may need an assist."

Blaise frowned, "what's going on?"

"I was heading home to recoup from my injury…"

"Injury?"

"I was at Benny's clan, some young cub was illegally trying to take Alpha from Benny," she blew out a breath into the mouthpiece, "damn lions are insanely strong, my arm got busted up a bit. Nothing too bad, a week of no shifting until it repairs enough that I can."

"Damn. All good at Benny's now?"

Sloane snorted, "I beat the cub upside the head with the butt of my gun after his stunt, so he's chill now."

"Better you than me, I would have shot him."

"I won't lie, the thought crossed my mind. Drives me crazy. I don't care if it's a clan of squirrels, we shouldn't be fighting each other right now, not when our own are being picked off like flies being swatted."

"What do you mean?"

"Four boys were shot last week. Outright shot, not taken, or mugged or anything, just erased."

"I hadn't heard about that."

"We've all been a little busy lately for catching up."

"Did they get who did it?"

"Yeah, they got Calder and Jett into it, and they tracked them, just before the storms came in."

"Who was it?"

"Stupidity, that's what it was, rogues. Our own taking out kids."

Blaise shook her head. "We don't have time for crap like that right now."

"Tell that to the rogues."

"So, what are you doing now?"

Blaise glanced at him finally, and he could see the concern on her face. Was that concern for the woman on the phone, her situation, or taking him somewhere else again? He needed to find out more about rogues.

"More stupidity to check in on." He heard a door slam. "I'll hold up here until you're here. I don't know what I'm walking into and I'm not taking a chance with only one arm. A group from Maxine's clan broke off on their own, some internal beef or something, and they moved down into Ontario."

Blaise squinted at the windshield, "wolverines?"

Griffin's eyebrows went up; there were wolverine clans?

"Yeah. The King asked Wynter to send someone to check in on them."

"Did they declare a new clan with Alpha?"

"Yes and no, don't ask me for details, that's all I got. I'm just checking in on them and making sure they know to report to the Alliance office with numbers and names and all that."

"Yeah, text me your location and we'll be there asap."

"We? Kenzo didn't tell me you were riding with someone. Perfect, more backup."

Blaise glanced at him again, "I'm taking Griffin to Ed's clan to do some things for the King," she lifted one shoulder and let it drop, "for the whole Alliance, I guess."

"Griffin. Aiden Tomas' half-brother?"

"Yes." She smirked. "I guess that news made its rounds."

"With many cheers and toasting, with coffee, but still toasting, these ops are exhausting." There was a short pause, "I hear we will have many more, thanks to Griffin."

"We will."

"I look forward to meeting him. Okay, I'll text you the address before you've already driven by."

"See you shortly." She tapped the screen and hung up the phone. A Second later, it buzzed, and she checked the screen.

Griffin stared at his hand trying to process what he'd just heard.

"What?"

He looked over at her, "nothing, just—" He lifted his hand and let it drop. "That's not the reaction I expected." He tipped his head back and looked at the ceiling, blowing out a breath he dropped it and shook it. "None of it. I thought I would live in a cage for the rest of my life."

"You could have been, but then you did the smart thing and gave us the information we needed."

"I didn't," he reached and cracked the window an inch for some air, "I didn't think what I was sharing was all that important, most of it was just little things I remembered."

Blaise snorted, "little things that tell us how it all works, who is involved, and," she stopped so he looked over to see her leveling him with a serious look, "who the rats are that have been sabotaging us for a long time." Her expression lightened, "that's pretty important, Griffin."

"I just want it done. I want Aiden—all the others to be sitting in a cage so they know what it feels like, I want the clan members they've abducted and bred, forced to live like," he waved a hand around, "*animals* to be able to make their own decisions, have a life."

"All of that *will* happen, thanks to you."

He took a deep breath and blew it out in one loud one, saying, "I hope it's enough."

"Hey," she reached over and put her hand on his arm. He looked over at her, "we'll make it enough. We're not going to stop until it's done. Trust me on that. When you meet some of the ones we pulled out of those houses and worse, that camp Lindon had his clan at, you're going to see that it *is* happening." She turned back to watch the road.

"Where am I meeting them?" He was going to come face to face with those he'd had to watch suffer. No, that couldn't happen.

"Blair's, Noah's…"

"They are not going to want to see me." He shook his head.

Blaise smirked, "I don't know if you've looked in a mirror, but you don't exactly resemble that scrawny, neat, and tidy man that Tripp tranq'd."

Rubbing his hand over his hair, "but I'll know."

"Well, know this too, you're helping end it. And," she gave him a quick look, "if anyone says any different, I'll clue them in." She gripped the steering wheel a few times, "if you don't want to, it's okay."

He quirked an eyebrow at her, "so you're allowed to stand up for me, but not the other way around?"

She stiffened in the seat, "we have about eight minutes to discuss this and then it's done."

Griffin leaned back and crossed his arms over his chest. He would never get used to his arms being too big to do this comfortably. "Okay, talk."

"I appreciate what you did, I really do." She flexed her hands on the steering wheel a few times, "people don't bother defending that I look different, that I'm…"

"Lovely?"

She glared at him, "no, different. I," she jerked her chin and held her head higher, "I kissed you because I was touched that you did." He watched her clench her jaw a few times.

"And you didn't like that. *Feeling*." He was rewarded with another glare. "I get it that you have to be this tough woman and that you've had a rough life. I understand. I've spent my whole life observing others, and I know when someone had to build a wall or shell themselves in to survive, and that you have." He dropped his arms because he felt ridiculous with them crossed, "but I don't care if I'm technically a prisoner, I'm not going to stand back and watch anyone be mistreated again. I've had a lifetime of swallowing down the bitterness of seeing it and being able to do nothing about it—and I'm not going to anymore, so deal with that."

Blaise looked at him and then back to the road, only to glance his way again. "I get that. Just don't think we're going to be kissing each other every time something *nice* happens."

Griffin grinned, he knew he probably shouldn't, but he couldn't help it. "I guess we can't have that, *nice* moments."

"Shut up." She jerked her chin toward the windshield, "we're here."

Checking the clock on the dash, he sighed, "that was a short eight minutes, what did you do speed up?"

"Maybe you just said too many words." She pulled over and put it into park, then looked him up and down. "I don't want to leave you sitting here. You'll have to come with us, but hang back, I don't know what we're walking into."

"I didn't know there were wolverine clans."

She opened the door and then turned to look at him, "I'll get you a list of clans, how's that?" She hopped down and then looked back in the door at him, "if you just promise to go back to that guy with the internal dialogue and stop chatting at me."

Griffin opened the door and got out, then smirked at her, "with you," he pointed to her, "you chat back." He closed the door, leaving her standing there scowling at it. He felt pretty good, overall. He'd enjoyed talking. He's also liked having the last word for the first time in his life.

Chapter Thirty-Three

Blaise didn't like any of it. The atmosphere was all wrong at this new clan. As far as she could tell, there were only a dozen members of it, and all had shady vibes. This was Sloane's gig, so she let her take the lead, but she stayed alert and her hand didn't stray far from the gun at her side. Griffin stayed back as she'd requested, and now she was second-guessing that maybe she should have told him to stay in the truck. It was a helluva spot to be in, keep him close and safe or out of sight and hope he was safe.

"I'm here on behalf of the Alliance and King, I need to speak to your Alpha."

Bonus points for Sloane, she didn't say Alpha with the sarcasm that Blaise was thinking as she looked around.

After the one she spoke to gave her a good up-and-down look, he pointed to the biggest house in the four that could be seen. They were run down, and she had to wonder who they belonged to before this clan took them over. Many out-of-province clans had small areas set up, for gatherings and meetings, but she didn't see Maxine just handing clan property to them. Were they even here legally or were they squatters?

She moved over to see who came out the door and keep an eye on the others lurking around watching them with great intent. Glancing at Griffin, she motioned with her head for him to stand at her back so she knew he was close. Without hesitation, he did.

The door opened and a short man, she'd peg somewhere in his thirties came out. He gave Sloane a cold look and barely glanced at Blaise, but Griffin definitely caught his attention. That didn't surprise her—all males would be seen as a possible challenger.

"The Alliance sent us to check in." Sloane kept her tone polite and courteous. Blaise would never be a great ambassador or coordinator; she didn't do the fake voice or intentions well at all.

"Check in for what?" The fake Alpha asked.

"Part of the agreement made with the Alliance was you would be in touch with names in your clan and other details once you were completely settled." Sloane looked around, "you need to get in touch with a representative."

"You're here, you see we're here, so that's done." He crossed his arms and stared at her.

"I believe you were given a number; you'll need to call and speak with them."

"I lost my phone." He replied too quickly.

Blaise watched Sloane's spin stiffen. Her first reaction was to rest her hand on her gun and be ready.

"You're going to have to get a phone, get in touch, or you will be marked as rogues and the next Alliance reps that come to visit won't be so friendly."

Blaise saw the two that had been standing nearby, move to block the path they'd taken to the small building. Her cat was right there with her when the warning bells started to go off in her head. She didn't want a confrontation, but she had no problem resolving one if it came to that.

"I don't answer to anyone now," he motioned his hand in the air, "around here I'm in charge."

"Not with me." Sloane's tone wasn't as polite and friendly now. "I only take orders from three people, my Alpha, my team leader, and the King."

"Well have him come see me and I'll report directly to him."

Sloane looked over at Blaise, she gave a slight shrug, letting her know that she had her back, however, she wanted to play it. She saw Sloane take a deep breath and try to keep her composure. "That's not how it works. We're part of the Alliance teams and this visit is just a courtesy before you're reported as a non-response and tagged as rogue."

Blaise had to hand it to her, she was definitely trying to get through to the jerk.

Sloane glanced around at a few others, "if you're not part of an official clan, you are rogue and not protected by the Alliance…"

"Protected?" One of them snarled. "Where was that protection when our clan was on lockdown and not allowed to do anything? If the Alliance were doing its job, none of that would have happened."

"These guys are assholes," Griffin whispered behind her. Blaise smirked but didn't reply. It amazed her that some were so ignorant when it came to the battle everyone in the shifter community was fighting. If they lost, worst case, extinction, and sadly that was also the best outcome because anything between now and that happening was no way to live.

"Restrictions were for safety." Sloane rested her hand on her gun, and Blaise hoped it was her good hand, because the way things were going, they would need it. "It wasn't convenient for anyone, but it was necessary."

"You seem to have the freedom to travel around."

"I'm on official…"

"Look, lady," the Alpha stepped off the step and got in her face, "we'll contact the Alliance when we're ready. They're not out here helping us. We're on our own and don't have to follow all those rules."

"You do if you want to…"

"Be protected by the Alliance, yeah, I caught that. Thanks, but no thanks."

Sloane stood there, nodding her head slowly, and Blaise wasn't sure which way she was going to go with this until she saw her pull out her phone. "I just have to report to my boss that I did my part." She shrugged and held up her phone.

"Whatever, just do it somewhere else." The Alpha turned and opened the door. Glancing over his shoulder, he jerked his chin to the males that were blocking the path.

Blaise glanced back at Griffin, "stay on my hip all the way to the truck." He nodded his head once, letting her know he understood.

Sloane took a few steps back, then turned so her back was to Blaise and not the strangers. She saw her typing into her phone, holding it with her bad arm, and still keeping the other one free to do anything required. When she finished, she tucked the phone in her pocket, put her hand on her gun, and began walking. "Someone will be in touch." Her voice was so pleasant you would have thought she was a customer service rep in a store instead of part of the Alliance's incursion team.

Blaise wanted to walk backward and keep an eye on them, her cat wanted the same, but she decided it was better just to walk away and not incite anything by snarling at the people watching them leave. Griffin bumped into her; she'd have to explain later that 'on her hip' wasn't meant to be literal.

By the time a gunshot registered in her head, she already had her gun pulled and spun around. The blood drops in the white snow took her a little longer to process. She felt no pain, so Blaise knew it wasn't from her. Griffin was hunched forward, but still standing. The blood was landing at his feet. She wanted to look at him, but her sight was focused on the man behind them holding a gun.

Sloane stepped between them, her phone in the hand of the arm she shouldn't be using and her gun in the other aimed at the man.

She knew Sloane was speaking, but no words registered in her ears. Blaise moved over to Griffin and placed her body in front of his, without taking her eyes off the man still stupid enough to be standing there aiming his gun at them. He had about three seconds to lower it before Blaise laid him to rest permanently.

The Alpha bolted out of his shack and went over to the man

Sloane was facing off with. He grabbed the man's gun and forced him to his knees.

When Sloane looked at her, she knew it was safe to look away. With her gun still up, Blaise turned to look at Griffin. From the placement of the blood spot expanding on his jacket, he'd take a bullet to his right shoulder. "Get the jacket off." He'd been shot while his back was turned. She felt the color drain from her face when she realized he'd nudged her over and taken a shot meant for her.

He struggled with one arm, so she grabbed the material and jerked it down. "Did it go all the way through?" She tugged his shirt up and hissed when she saw the blood rolling down his back.

"Here."

She turned to see a young woman holding out some white material. Grabbing it, she pressed it against his shoulder.

"Blood on the front," Griffin grunted.

"Straight through."

"Eddy didn't mean it," the woman said.

Blaise leaned on the clothe and glanced back to see the Alpha holding Eddy by the back of his neck. "*Eddy*," Blaise looked at her, "will have to tell that to the security when they get here." She didn't like how fast the white clothe was turning red, "Sloane," she waited for her to look at her, "I have to get him back to the truck. My med bag is there."

Sloane nodded, "backup will be here in twenty." She looked at the Alpha, "seems cooperation is going to happen now."

Blaise wanted to shoot the Alpha in the head, and everyone else that watched them. "I'll patch him up and be right back."

Sloane put a comm piece in her ear and grimaced as she used her bad arm to put her phone in her pocket, "I've got Pasha on the line, she and Tait are closest."

"Tell Illias to patch me in, my comm bud is in the truck."

She nodded and turned back to the man, her gun ready if anyone else stepped out of line.

Keeping her gun in her hand, Blaise motioned for Griffin to start walking.

"Are you okay?" He asked in a breathless voice.

Blaise looked up at him, he was very pale. It was probably the first time he'd been shot. "You're the one leaving a trail in the snow, and you want to know if *I'm* okay?"

"I turned and saw him with the gun—" he groaned.

She needed him to get to the truck before he passed out. "Just focus on not face-planting on the ground. I don't think I'd get you up. We'll discuss your hero badge later."

He made a sound that was either from pain or a snort, she wasn't sure. "You have a mouth on you." He smiled at her, but she could see the pain in his eyes.

Blaise shook her head, "its part of my charm."

Her phone rang as they reached the truck, she answered it and hit the speaker, and set it on the floor mat while she got him to perch in the open door.

"Blaise?"

"I'm here, Kenzo."

"What the hell is going on?"

The whole front of his shirt was red now, "Griffin got shot."

"I got that part. How bad?"

She yanked his shirt over his shoulder until the material ripped and gave way. "Right shoulder, straight through."

"I thought Sloane was just doing a check-in."

"Hostile, uncooperative, newly proclaimed Alpha." She knelt by the seat, grabbed her med bag, and dragged it to the floor mat beside her phone.

"The Alpha shot him?"

"I don't know who the hell the jerk was—" she sucked in a breath and willed herself to stay calm, "they were aiming for *my* back, and Griffin had a chivalrous moment."

"Is the situation under control?"

Blaise dosed the back of his shoulder with an antibacterial wash and then paused when he hissed out a breath. "Sorry." She poured some over the front. "The Alpha found his senses and holds the shooter until Pasha arrives." Something Blaise wanted to see, but she couldn't stick around too long.

"Wynter was on a call with Raymond when Sloane called in."

Ripping the bandage package, she slapped it over the entry point and then did the same with the front. Her cat was going absolutely crazy inside her. Their mate was hurt. She wanted revenge. It took all Blaise had to keep her under control. Going around, she opened the back door and took out a juice from the cooler. She reassured her cat that his care was the priority, and retribution would have to wait. Hurrying around, she handed it to him. "I'm going to hang here until they arrive."

"Is Griffin all right?"

She pulled the bunched-up jacket from his hand and helped him get his other arm in. "I just patched him up. I'll leave him in the truck and move to the trail where I can see him and if Sloane is having any trouble.

"Set up with your rifle." He growled, "if anyone even looks at each other the wrong way, lay them down. Not permanently, just to keep them down until backup is there. I'll call Shaelan and have her ready for your arrival."

"Okay. Get Illias to patch me in on the call with Sloane and Pasha." She helped Griffin get up into the passenger seat. His coloring was not looking good. She heard Kenzo hang up. If she knew him there would be some yelling and snarling in the next few moments.

Opening the backdoor, she pulled out her rifle case and grabbed a few protein bars. Handing the bars to Griffin, she opened the glove box and got her earbud out. Jamming it in her ear, she picked up her phone and waited for the call. "I'll be right over there," She pointed to a downed tree at the end of the path to the buildings.

"Don't shoot them all." He closed his eyes for a second, then shifted in the seat and got the gun out of the door. Resting it on his lap, he nodded. "Don't sneak up on me in case I nod off."

"*Try* to stay awake." She looked around, "watch my back." She didn't need him to, but if it was motivation to keep him conscious, she'd use it.

"Okay."

Her phone rang as she was closing the door. "Yeah," she tucked it in her pocket and pressed the com button.

"We're breaking records getting there." Pasha informed her, "how's the injured?"

"He's patched up for now," she went over to a stump and opened the case.

"Everyone still behaving, Sloane?" She recognized Tait's voice. Later she'd ask why an Alliance Security and Surveillance team members were together.

Resting her rifle on the case, Blaise dropped to one knee and found the group standing with Sloane.

"We're good so far," Blaise saw her turn and look in her direction, "Blaise is on the rifle now in case anyone gets any ideas. Is Griffin okay, Blaise?"

Blaise left her comm switch on whenever she was using her rifle, so she wouldn't have to refocus after moving. "It went straight through, back to front, right shoulder. He'll be good for a bit more before I get him to Shaelan."

"Wait, *the* Griffin?" Pasha sounded upset.

"Yeah." Blaise chanced a quick glance to check on him. He was still upright in the seat, so she took that as a good sign.

"Why the hell would they shoot him?" Tait asked.

Checking the group through her scope to make sure none had stupid ideas, she exhaled slowly. "They were aiming for *my* back and Griffin nudged me out of the way."

"Shooter isn't going to have a good time with my boss," Pasha chuckled, "Raymond has been in overdrive since he got the information from this Griffin, hell, I might even kiss him if his helping means a win for us across the board."

Blaise had to clamp down on her cat at the idea of Pasha kissing Griffin. "May not want to stir up anything with him, Pasha," did she sound nonchalant, she was trying to, "he's struggling with his bear that's been suppressed for fifteen years."

"Oh. Damn, poor guy—yeah, no lip action for sure. I don't want to meet his bear unannounced."

Blaise sneered, that had done it.

"Tait just got word, the whole clan is being brought in." Pasha laughed, "as I said, the boss doesn't want anything happening to our golden goose, or bear, in this case, I guess."

"I'll wait and let you tell them the good news," Sloane was still standing steadfast, gun aimed at Eddy.

"Transport is already on the way." Pasha reported, "see you in five."

Chapter Thirty-Four

Shaelan came out of the other room and into the kitchen. Blaise stood up and tried to gauge if the expression was good or bad.

"He's going to heal fast, but not like if he could shift." She walked over to the sink, turned on the tap, and began washing her hands, "the trick is going to be to keep his animal from getting too close and popping those stitches."

Blaise went around the table and leaned on the counter, "he can't communicate with him very well and when his bear is close, he bulks up *a lot*."

Drying her hands, Shaelan folded the towel neatly and hung it over the edge of the sink again, "I guess we'll have to keep him distracted."

Blaise nodded, "he's got a lot of information to go through."

Noah came in the door and stomped the snow from his boots, he didn't take them off. "How is he?"

Shaelan offered him a nice smile, "he'll be fine."

Noah nodded his head slowly, and then looked at Blaise, "we were going to put him in the bunkhouse, but if he's injured, maybe he should stay in here."

Shaelan nodded, "Beth has already said he can use the room

downstairs," she glanced at Blaise, "you can have Kelsey's old room, Calum and I will be staying over at Noah's."

Blaise nodded, she didn't care where she slept, just that she got what she was here to do done, so she could go home or better yet, back out on ops.

Noah looked at her again, "Emersyn is hoping you'll come over for a visit while you're here."

Blaise grinned, "I can do that." She waved her hand around, "there's plenty of large males around to keep a watch." Anything to get out of here. By the time they'd got here, it had taken three of them to get Griffin into the house. Since that moment, she'd paced, sat, and worried, and then paced some more. A little distance was a very welcomed thing right now.

~

"I didn't want a mate—I mean, I'm a mixed breed, who wants that? And then I find him and he's a half-breed," Blaise laughed because it was either that or cry, "fate had herself a jolly chuckle with this *match*. More of a mismatch." She sobered, "He stuck up for me when people were staring and whispering," she motioned to the darker side of her face like it wasn't obvious, and Emersyn had never seen it, "then he goes and does this heroic shit, and gets himself shot. What do I do with that?"

"I saw him a few times."

Blaise frowned.

"Griffin, I didn't know who he was, just thought he was another there against their will." Emersyn looked at her hands as she clasped them together, "he wasn't like the others."

"What others?"

"The ones that enjoyed imprisoning women to those houses, even though they were shifters too." She folded her arms over her chest, "he always looked sad, a little lost in all of it."

"He was a pet to his father." Blaise sat down and leaned onto her knees, "he spent time in the camp too."

"I think he's always been alone." Emersyn took a deep, ragged breath and raised her chin, "the rest of us had each other, even if it was only for short times, we were in the same house, I think Griffin was always alone. No real family or the love of a family. No friends because he was related to the ones holding all of us." She glanced out the window, checking on the kids, "and the one-forms treated him worse because he wasn't pure." She turned back to her, "you could see it when they looked at him. He was beneath them, maybe even more than the shifters they held."

Blaise hadn't thought of what it would mean, not in detail. He had a private apartment prison and wasn't forced to wear a collar, but the way Emersyn was describing it, she was sure she was right. He'd been alone for his entire life, with no allies, no friends, just him. She blew out a breath, "I don't know what's going to happen."

"With the mission to save everyone taken?"

Blaise jerked her head roughly, "that too, but no, I meant with Griffin, I don't know if he's going to be in a glorified cell and under guard for the rest of his life or what."

Emersyn gave her a compassionate look, "I think only time will answer that. Noah said he wasn't safe until his brother was stopped or dead."

"Yeah, he's not safe. That Aiden jerk wants him back in a bad way." She was on her feet again, she couldn't just lounge and think of all of this, she needed action, something to do.

"You don't think Aiden will cut his losses and move on?"

Blaise shook her head, "I don't think he'll ever stop looking for him. He's a real special edition that one, there's so much wrong with that guy."

Emersyn gave her a soft smile, "then it's good that Griffin is helping."

She couldn't argue that, "with the information he's already given us, we can shut down transport, border points, and companies that help, not to mention we know what Tomas' top people look like now."

"That's wonderful. So many lives will be saved too when he's stopped."

Blaise bit her lip, so she wouldn't start blurting out

information she knew wasn't supposed to leave the teams. How much did Noah tell his mate? He didn't seem like a chatty type. Did the others tell their mates? The level of sharing between mates was even beyond her understanding right now.

"I think it's a good thing that Griffin is helping and that he has you to keep him safe and," she shrugged, "explain the way clan life works." She chuckled, "I'm still trying to figure that out, and Noah doesn't know much more than I do there."

"But you guys are doing okay?"

Emersyn nodded, her expression was pure joy, which was good to see. "Yes. I miss him when he's away, but it's good he still goes. We can't jump into this after what we've been through, but yes, it's good, and we're very happy."

Someone cleared their throat from the doorway.

Blaise turned to see Noah standing there, "I didn't mean to interrupt."

"No biggie, it's your place." Blaise nodded, "we were just catching up." She turned to see the look Emersyn had on her face as she looked at him, it was happiness, not fake or anything in between.

"The kids never seem to get cold," he motioned to the window.

Emersyn got up and glanced outside, "I can only stay out for a few minutes at a time," she huffed out a breath, "Shaelan says that will get better as my health does."

Noah met her halfway across the room, leaned down, and kissed her mouth. He touched her cheek and just looked down at her for what felt like hours.

Blaise felt like she was intruding on something so deeply intimate that it felt wrong. "I should, uh, get back to Ed's and see how Griffin is making out."

Noah turned and looked at her, "he's annoyed and frustrated but really smart." He gave her a lopsided grin, "he's figured out another piece of the code that Lindon used, so now we're waiting on Illias and some of those brainy ones at HQ to finish the list."

"List?" Blaise felt her heart speed up.

He nodded, "some ports and drop-off points." His expression was grim, "he figured out the system, and they're running it through databases or whatever they do to give us the names of the places."

Blaise's heart kicked up speed, "so we'll be able to go shut them down?"

Noah shrugged, "I don't know, Devin is talking to his father, who's talking to other people, and then at some point they'll give us a location and we do our thing."

Blaise grinned, "that works for me." She jerked her chin toward the door, "how's his shoulder doing?"

"He's healing fast." Noah went over to the counter to the coffee maker, "his bear may never come out, but it's there." He glanced over his shoulder, "his scent is definitely a big scary bear."

Blaise rolled her eyes, "he does that puffed-out half-shift thing you do too," she couldn't feel bad about that, it had gotten them out of the metal box. "Any tips on how he can control it more?" She bit her lip, "like whenever he's angry or emotional, it happens."

Noah put his hands on his hips and looked at the floor for a minute, "I don't," he looked up at her, "I don't have answers for that. I *can* communicate with my cat, but if he can't get through to his animal, I don't know."

"You should talk to Shaelan," Emersyn went over and nudged Noah out of the way and put a filter in the coffee maker, "she could ask the medical people, they might know." She glanced at her, "I'm sure it's not the first time someone can't communicate with their animal," she offered a small smile, "just as I'm sure there have been cases where they can't shift."

Blaise nodded, "that's a good idea." She glanced around, still feeling awkward with the looks they were giving each other. She wasn't bitter, they both deserved it, she just wasn't a cozy homey kind of gal. "I'm going to head back over now." She turned to go.

"Blaise," stopping she looked back at Noah, "I keep

wanting to ask someone, but don't know how to go about it."

She frowned.

"Asking about what's going to happen to Griffin now." He waved his hand around, "he might have a clan that was his mothers' but they're not his, so where does that leave him?"

She gnawed on her lip for a moment, "yeah, I've wondered too." She nodded slowly, "I can ask Kenzo and see if he can get some answers."

"Okay," he motioned to her, "I just thought you should know what's going on with him being your mate."

Blaise opened her mouth and then shut it, unsure of what to say.

He shrugged, "Just give it time." He shrugged and then glanced lovingly at Emersyn, "it has a way of figuring itself out." He turned back to her and smirked, "and whatever you do, do not ask Blair for advice. His sucks."

Blaise could only nod. She needed to get out of there. Now. This talk just made her feel way too much and then nothing at the same time. "Got it." She nodded her head once to Emersyn and then turned to go find the door asap.

Chapter Thirty-Five

He could feel her eyes staring at him. Anytime he glanced up from the screen, she was looking at him. Griffin turned in the chair and checked, she was doing it again. Why was she looking at him? "I'm trying to concentrate here, and you're boring a hole in the back of my head."

Her brows furrowed, and then she pushed away from the counter and stomped across the room. She looked mad, maybe he shouldn't have said something. When she was right in front of him, she looked down at him, fiery temper very plain in her eyes. She grabbed his face and kissed him. Not a quick contact of lips, but a kiss that reached his soul and several levels deeper, if that were possible. She broke the kiss off just as he was going to reach for her.

"Get it done." Turning on her heel, she stomped to the door and left.

Griffin looked at the closed door and then at Blair. He was smirking. Noah was too.

"I thought she was going to punch you." Blair grinned.

Noah nodded, "I don't understand women."

Blair snorted, "None of us do. The trick is to fake it and hope it's in the right way, so they don't gut you."

Griffin licked his lips which were Blaise flavored now.

"That doesn't seem like sound advice."

Blair looked up from the page he held, "it's not, but it's all I can offer."

"I don't think she's happy with the match." He sat back and motioned to his chest, "half-breed, born on the wrong side of the fight and related to the tyrant that's destroyed so many lives."

Blair put the papers down and rested his hands on the table, "mates have a way of working things out, with or without your cooperation."

His doubt must have been plain to see because Blair grinned.

"I was head over heels for someone else, nursing a broken heart," he motioned to the door, "Kobie had lost her whole clan and resented everything that males stood for because they'd walked right by her all of her life," he shrugged, "it was rocky, but we got there."

Griffin ran his hand through his hair, it seemed like it was thicker and longer every time he touched it. His bear must have some shaggy coat. "I don't see me having freedom anytime soon, so it will be a lot more than rocky."

Noah smirked, "you don't even know rocky when it comes to mates. My mating is the most unmate-like mating in history."

Blair glanced at him, "but it works for you, right? What Kobie and I have works for us," he motioned around the table, "that's what I'm saying, it works out for each couple."

Noah rolled his eyes, "you don't even know what you're saying." He held out a few more pages, "get back to reading this and stop trying to be a counselor."

Blair glared at him, "I have to be everything as an Alpha. I don't know what I'm doing, I keep telling people that, but no one believes me."

"You excel at faking it," Noah mumbled.

"I do, don't I?" Blair smiled and picked up more pages.

Chapter Thirty-Six

Griffin picked up the cup and then realized it was empty. Getting up, he went over to the coffee maker, only to find it empty too. Turning, he saw that there was no one in the room now. When had everyone left? Setting the cup down, he walked into the large living room area, to see bodies sprawled on the couch, chair, and even the floor.

"We left you to it when you started matching up faces to places and names."

Calum spoke from the corner by the front door. Griffin hadn't even seen him standing there. He didn't know what kind of shifter he was, but he also wasn't sure he wanted to see him in that form. His every move screamed predator and he was so silent for such a big man. "I'm done."

He pushed away from the corner, "all of them?"

Griffin nodded, "I've gone through every face on the computer and made notes."

Calum raised an eyebrow as he nonchalantly kicked Blair's feet where he was slumped back on the couch.

"What?" Blair bolted up. "Oh." He glared at Calum.

"He's done."

"Done?" Blair stood up and then blinked a few times. "All of them?"

Calum nodded and started to walk out of the room, "all two

thousand."

Griffin followed him.

"I'm surprised your eyes haven't dried up and fallen out of your face," Blair mumbled as he went over to the coffee maker and then groaned at it. Picking up the pot, he filled it, "do we call Devin now or wait until," he looked at the clock and scowled, "it's actual daylight morning time."

Calum grinned, "oh, I think now is good."

Blair poured the water into the machine and then waved the empty pot at Calum, "you know someday he'll be king and you will be running all the awful errands for him."

Calum grinned, "he can try."

"What's going on?" Blaise came out and then yawned.

Griffin stared at her, she looked disarmed when she was half asleep. The hard look that usually filled her eyes wasn't there right now.

"Boy scout finished all the pictures," Blair said and then turned back to the machine.

"All of them?" Blaise went over and looked at the notepad sitting on top of scattered pages of information. "So now what?" She looked at Calum.

"I'm calling Devin." He pulled out his phone.

"At four in the morning?" She went over and took a cup out of the sink and gave it a quick rinse.

"Absolutely, he's a prince. It's his job to serve."

"Serve you up on a platter with an apple in your mouth, maybe," Blair said teasingly, pulling out his phone and looking at it.

Blaise looked at him, and Griffin waited to see if she was angry or just annoyed because it was usually one or the other, "I can't believe you have checked every picture of every shifter in the Alliance or been found by the Alliance."

"If we can take out the ones working with Aiden, then it's just a matter of time before we get all those following him." Griffin went over and flipped back a few pages, "there's two here that are in and out of his office a dozen times a week, they coordinate for him."

"Coordinate what?" Blaise glanced at Blair briefly before looking back at him.

"Transporting to camps, from camps to houses and outside buyers."

"As in those being sold off across the map?" Blair leaned back against the counter and crossed his arms over his chest.

"Yes." Griffin straightened up because the ache in his arm registered. "Maybe when the people that are working on the sales records are done, we can connect them."

Blair snorted, "to hell with connecting them, I say we shut them all down."

Calum came back in, grinning, "Devin will be calling us shortly, he's waking the others up."

"You enjoyed waking him, didn't you?" Blair checked the coffee maker's progress.

"I did."

"He never sleeps," Shaelan came into the kitchen, went over to him, and wrapped her arms around his waist.

Calum wrapped his arms around her, leaned down, and kissed her head. "If you're working on something, you never sleep either."

Griffin had never been around couples before, and it caused an ache beside him every time he witnessed something tender between them. He glanced at Blaise, who flicked just her eyes to him. Was she feeling it too? That empty ache that had never been present before being around all these mated couples.

With the coffee brewed, they lined up to fill their cups, leaving none left by the time Blair went to fill his. "We need to buy those industrial-size catering things for coffee."

Kobie came out into the room and smiled at him, "I'll get your coffee; go sit."

"You are the most beautiful creature that ever lived." He kissed her as she went to the sink to fill the pot again.

Griffin looked at Blaise again; her expression was basically telling him not to even go there. He lowered his head, so no one would see the smirk on his face, especially her. He sat down, and then realized how tired he was.

Someone's phone rang. Calum set his on the table and tapped speaker, "Devin."

"Yeah. Illias will have Raymond and Dad on the line in a minute." There was mumbling in the background. "Rayne won't be joining us until she has coffee."

Calum grinned, "understandable."

"Okay, Illias messaged, the call will reconnect with Dad and Raymond." The line clicked.

"Good morning, everyone."

Griffin looked at the phone; the King didn't sound like he was just woken up.

"Dad, Griffin has finished going through the pictures and information."

"Nate called about a half hour ago and says they have also finished the list."

"So we'll be going out soon?" Blair asked, sounding more awake now.

"How many were identified?" Griffin recognized Raymond Hardy's voice.

Calum moved over and picked up the notebook. He flipped through the pages, "a lot." He leaned down and tapped the laptop, so the screen saver went off, opened the photo file, and clicked on one. Griffin watched him click on a few more. "Several are faces we look at all the time."

"I'm going to need that list," Raymond said.

"I uh," Griffin cleared his throat, "I listed them by the photo number."

"I don't care how they're listed, just as long as they are."

"How are we doing with the locations under surveillance?" The King inquired.

"Uri says there hasn't been any movement. We thought it was because of the storm, everyone was staying close to home, but now we're not sure what's happening. We haven't been able to confirm much."

Blair and Calum exchanged a look.

"And Mister Tomas, what has he been up to?"

"Not much movement there either, sir, we're not sure

what's happening."

"He's regrouping." Griffin glanced around as the others looked at him, "he'll hole up in his office and get in touch with all of his contacts and work on finding new holding houses," he shrugged, "with all the raids or whatever you're calling them that has happened in the last few weeks, he's going to be coming up with a new plan."

"There has to be a way to get him moving again. We can't breach locations if they're all on lockdown." Devin sounded annoyed, and Griffin felt that he wanted them to succeed.

"I presume Aiden's office building is being watched." Griffin stood up, "right now."

"Of course, it is," Raymond answered.

He rubbed his hand over his hair, "how bad do you want him to jump into action?"

"We need to confirm numbers and see what we're up against, we can't go in anywhere if we don't know this."

Griffin nodded to what Raymond said. "Let me call him."

Everyone in the room looked at him. Blaise glared at him for a second, then came over, grabbed his good arm, and pulled him over by the door.

"Are you insane? He'll just send more out to look for you."

"I just want to help."

She shook her head, "so write down more information."

Griffin heaved out a breath, "I don't have anymore. I could write names but don't know the details that go with them. I've given every location I know." He looked over at Blair, "they need to panic and move," he shrugged, "well after he's done screaming and smashing things, he'll panic and move."

"He's right." Rayne was on the call now. "Aiden will scream at his men, and then everyone will scramble to please him."

Calum looked across the room at Blaise, "if we can isolate even a few of his top gophers, it's a big win for us. Taking out those that make things happen is the only to slow things down," he turned and glanced at Blair, "until we get networks set up overseas and at more borders to stop them."

Blaise put her hands on her hips, "it's ridiculous; it's like painting a neon target on his back saying 'come and get me'."

"I'm good at my job," Illias drawled, "they won't know where he is."

"You don't think you can protect him?" The King asked.

Blaise scowled at the phone, "I didn't say that, but if he does call, we can't stay here after the call; there are too many in this area."

"We can arrange for you to stay on the move, Blaise. Griffin will be safe." The King stated in a matter-of-fact tone. "Jesse had to do that for a while to make sure he couldn't be tracked with Leah. We have many locations not on any public record or in any name that could trace back to anyone connected with the Alliance."

"We're going to need him to be mobile anyway," Devin interrupted, "to be nearby when we go in places. If he can see who we're bringing out, we have a better shot at not putting any more moles into the Alliance."

Everyone turned and looked at Blaise, himself included. Griffin didn't know what was going to be involved in staying on the move, but if this is what needed to be done to get things moving and shut Aiden down, he wanted to do it.

Blaise blew out a breath, "okay, give him a secure phone, and I'm going to need supplies."

Chapter Thirty-Six

Griffin picked up the cup and then realized it was empty. Getting up, he went over to the coffee maker, only to find it empty too. Turning, he saw that there was no one in the room now. When had everyone left? Setting the cup down, he walked into the large living room area, to see bodies sprawled on the couch, chair, and even the floor.

"We left you to it when you started matching up faces to places and names."

Calum spoke from the corner by the front door. Griffin hadn't even seen him standing there. He didn't know what kind of shifter he was, but he also wasn't sure he wanted to see him in that form. His every move screamed predator and he was so silent for such a big man. "I'm done."

He pushed away from the corner, "all of them?"

Griffin nodded, "I've gone through every face on the computer and made notes."

Calum raised an eyebrow as he nonchalantly kicked Blair's feet where he was slumped back on the couch.

"What?" Blair bolted up. "Oh." He glared at Calum.

"He's done."

"Done?" Blair stood up and then blinked a few times. "All of them?"

Calum nodded and started to walk out of the room, "all two

thousand."

Griffin followed him.

"I'm surprised your eyes haven't dried up and fallen out of your face," Blair mumbled as he went over to the coffee maker and then groaned at it. Picking up the pot, he filled it, "do we call Devin now or wait until," he looked at the clock and scowled, "it's actual daylight morning time."

Calum grinned, "oh, I think now is good."

Blair poured the water into the machine and then waved the empty pot at Calum, "you know someday he'll be king and you will be running all the awful errands for him."

Calum grinned, "he can try."

"What's going on?" Blaise came out and then yawned.

Griffin stared at her, she looked disarmed when she was half asleep. The hard look that usually filled her eyes wasn't there right now.

"Boy scout finished all the pictures," Blair said and then turned back to the machine.

"All of them?" Blaise went over and looked at the notepad sitting on top of scattered pages of information. "So now what?" She looked at Calum.

"I'm calling Devin." He pulled out his phone.

"At four in the morning?" She went over and took a cup out of the sink and gave it a quick rinse.

"Absolutely, he's a prince. It's his job to serve."

"Serve you up on a platter with an apple in your mouth, maybe," Blair said teasingly, pulling out his phone and looking at it.

Blaise looked at him, and Griffin waited to see if she was angry or just annoyed because it was usually one or the other, "I can't believe you have checked every picture of every shifter in the Alliance or been found by the Alliance."

"If we can take out the ones working with Aiden, then it's just a matter of time before we get all those following him." Griffin went over and flipped back a few pages, "there's two here that are in and out of his office a dozen times a week, they coordinate for him."

"Coordinate what?" Blaise glanced at Blair briefly before looking back at him.

"Transporting to camps, from camps to houses and outside buyers."

"As in those being sold off across the map?" Blair leaned back against the counter and crossed his arms over his chest.

"Yes." Griffin straightened up because the ache in his arm registered. "Maybe when the people that are working on the sales records are done, we can connect them."

Blair snorted, "to hell with connecting them, I say we shut them all down."

Calum came back in, grinning, "Devin will be calling us shortly, he's waking the others up."

"You enjoyed waking him, didn't you?" Blair checked the coffee maker's progress.

"I did."

"He never sleeps," Shaelan came into the kitchen, went over to him, and wrapped her arms around his waist.

Calum wrapped his arms around her, leaned down, and kissed her head. "If you're working on something, you never sleep either."

Griffin had never been around couples before, and it caused an ache beside him every time he witnessed something tender between them. He glanced at Blaise, who flicked just her eyes to him. Was she feeling it too? That empty ache that had never been present before being around all these mated couples.

With the coffee brewed, they lined up to fill their cups, leaving none left by the time Blair went to fill his. "We need to buy those industrial-size catering things for coffee."

Kobie came out into the room and smiled at him, "I'll get your coffee; go sit."

"You are the most beautiful creature that ever lived." He kissed her as she went to the sink to fill the pot again.

Griffin looked at Blaise again; her expression was basically telling him not to even go there. He lowered his head, so no one would see the smirk on his face, especially her. He sat down, and then realized how tired he was.

Someone's phone rang. Calum set his on the table and tapped speaker, "Devin."

"Yeah. Illias will have Raymond and Dad on the line in a minute." There was mumbling in the background. "Rayne won't be joining us until she has coffee."

Calum grinned, "understandable."

"Okay, Illias messaged, the call will reconnect with Dad and Raymond." The line clicked.

"Good morning, everyone."

Griffin looked at the phone; the King didn't sound like he was just woken up.

"Dad, Griffin has finished going through the pictures and information."

"Nate called about a half hour ago and says they have also finished the list."

"So we'll be going out soon?" Blair asked, sounding more awake now.

"How many were identified?" Griffin recognized Raymond Hardy's voice.

Calum moved over and picked up the notebook. He flipped through the pages, "a lot." He leaned down and tapped the laptop, so the screen saver went off, opened the photo file, and clicked on one. Griffin watched him click on a few more. "Several are faces we look at all the time."

"I'm going to need that list," Raymond said.

"I uh," Griffin cleared his throat, "I listed them by the photo number."

"I don't care how they're listed, just as long as they are."

"How are we doing with the locations under surveillance?" The King inquired.

"Uri says there hasn't been any movement. We thought it was because of the storm, everyone was staying close to home, but now we're not sure what's happening. We haven't been able to confirm much."

Blair and Calum exchanged a look.

"And Mister Tomas, what has he been up to?"

"Not much movement there either, sir, we're not sure

what's happening."

"He's regrouping." Griffin glanced around as the others looked at him, "he'll hole up in his office and get in touch with all of his contacts and work on finding new holding houses," he shrugged, "with all the raids or whatever you're calling them that has happened in the last few weeks, he's going to be coming up with a new plan."

"There has to be a way to get him moving again. We can't breach locations if they're all on lockdown." Devin sounded annoyed, and Griffin felt that he wanted them to succeed.

"I presume Aiden's office building is being watched." Griffin stood up, "right now."

"Of course, it is," Raymond answered.

He rubbed his hand over his hair, "how bad do you want him to jump into action?"

"We need to confirm numbers and see what we're up against, we can't go in anywhere if we don't know this."

Griffin nodded to what Raymond said. "Let me call him."

Everyone in the room looked at him. Blaise glared at him for a second, then came over, grabbed his good arm, and pulled him over by the door.

"Are you insane? He'll just send more out to look for you."

"I just want to help."

She shook her head, "so write down more information."

Griffin heaved out a breath, "I don't have anymore. I could write names but don't know the details that go with them. I've given every location I know." He looked over at Blair, "they need to panic and move," he shrugged, "well after he's done screaming and smashing things, he'll panic and move."

"He's right." Rayne was on the call now. "Aiden will scream at his men, and then everyone will scramble to please him."

Calum looked across the room at Blaise, "if we can isolate even a few of his top gophers, it's a big win for us. Taking out those that make things happen is the only to slow things down," he turned and glanced at Blair, "until we get networks set up overseas and at more borders to stop them."

Blaise put her hands on her hips, "it's ridiculous; it's like painting a neon target on his back saying 'come and get me'."

"I'm good at my job," Illias drawled, "they won't know where he is."

"You don't think you can protect him?" The King asked.

Blaise scowled at the phone, "I didn't say that, but if he does call, we can't stay here after the call; there are too many in this area."

"We can arrange for you to stay on the move, Blaise. Griffin will be safe." The King stated in a matter-of-fact tone. "Jesse had to do that for a while to make sure he couldn't be tracked with Leah. We have many locations not on any public record or in any name that could trace back to anyone connected with the Alliance."

"We're going to need him to be mobile anyway," Devin interrupted, "to be nearby when we go in places. If he can see who we're bringing out, we have a better shot at not putting any more moles into the Alliance."

Everyone turned and looked at Blaise, himself included. Griffin didn't know what was going to be involved in staying on the move, but if this is what needed to be done to get things moving and shut Aiden down, he wanted to do it.

Blaise blew out a breath, "okay, give him a secure phone, and I'm going to need supplies."

Chapter Thirty-Seven

Blaise typed the last few items she was going to need if they were to become road runners and stay off all radars. Hitting send, she sent it off to a guy named Zain. Calum assured her would get all of it and probably extras too. She didn't know where they were going to go; the list of places hadn't been given to her yet.

Tucking her phone back in her pocket, she looked around, there were more bodies in the kitchen, but Griffin wasn't one of them. She glanced into the other room, he wasn't there either. Panic filled her, even though she knew he wouldn't take off. He was too important by too many to leave her sight. Her cat rolled through her, reminding her there were other reasons too. Blaise wasn't ready to admit that to the animal inside her. She pushed through the door and stepped out onto the deck. Griffin stood near the end, leaning on the railing. Noah was beside him.

Noah inclined his head to her as he walked down the steps, "I can't hear this." He said quietly, "I'll be in the shop with Jake if I'm needed."

She watched him walk along a narrow drive and could see the large building on the other end of it. Turning back, she walked toward Griffin, "second thoughts?" She could only hope he had.

He glanced at her, shook his head, and then looked across the yard. "More like composing my thoughts to make sense when I speak to him." He straightened up and faced her, "Do you know I've always had to watch every word I said to him, so I didn't *offend* him?" He tapped his hand on the side of his head, "I have so much I want to say to that sick bastard, I don't even know where to start."

Blaise crossed her arms over her chest, "you don't have any problems with words; you'll figure it out."

He smirked, "I hope your faith in my ability to talk isn't misplaced."

"See, just spew some of that fancy stuff at him, and he won't know what to say."

Griffin smiled at her, "I'll do that." He rubbed his hand over his injured shoulder, "thank you, by the way, for agreeing to drive me around for an unknown amount of time, I know you'd rather be helping your team."

She leaned back against the railing and looked over at him, "I'm helping all the teams and every clan in the Alliance by keeping you whole," she shrugged, "sure, I'll miss out on kicking some teeth in, but it's a fair trade."

He stood there for a moment, searching her face, "what did they mean by having me close to see who they find at these various sites?"

Blaise shrugged, "I have no idea. I just do what I'm told. The clan coordinator team's office guy is rounding up all the supplies and gear we'll need. It could be remote, or we'll be on the scene, we won't know until they tell us, and they're not likely to advertise it in advance."

He looked around, "this place is nice. All the fresh air a body could want."

Blaise nodded, "it is." She motioned to the road, "but there are too many bodies in this area for my taste."

"I guess you're not big on the city life then."

"No. Too many buildings, people, it smells bad, and there are not enough trees."

"Griffin," we turned to see Blair standing at the door, "they have all the surveillance guys on standby now."

Griffin nodded, and Blair went back inside.

Blaise huffed out a breath and moved closer, she put her hand on his chest and looked up at him. "You know him better than anyone, say whatever you need to say to get all the parts moving so we can track every last one of them."

"And then we ride off into the sunset." He smirked and glanced around, "sunrise." He yawned.

"You can nap on the road. Get in there and get us some action."

"Yes, 'mam." He touched the side of her face with a gentle touch. "Just think of all the time we'll have to talk."

Blaise hissed out a breath, "go." She stepped back so his hand would drop away.

When she returned, she moved to the counter area, across from where Griffin had sat down. She didn't know how he could sit there. She'd have to pace and move around if it were her making such an important phone call.

"Is everyone on the line?" Calum leaned on the table over a phone.

"They are." Illias answered, "I have all of them muted, so they can listen and not be heard." He chuckled, "I like that power."

Calum shook his head, "just be ready to reroute calls when the surveillance teams start reporting back."

"I'm on it," Illias said.

Griffin lifted his hand, "I don't know Aiden's number..."

Illias snorted, "I have *all* the numbers. Just tell me when you pick up the phone and I'll do the rest."

"Okay." Griffin looked at the other phone sitting on the table. He didn't turn and look at anyone else, just lifted his eyes and held Blaise's look for a moment. She nodded her head, telling him to go ahead.

It was such a sappy thing, that something like that made her feel important. He was in a room with Alpha's and important people and yet looked to her for that last boost of confidence to make the call.

Griffin exhaled a deep breath and picked up the phone. "I have the phone." He said quietly.

"Great. Hang on two seconds," we could all hear the keys tapping in the background as Illias did whatever magic he did.

Chapter Thirty-Eight

The room was so quiet Blaise was afraid to breathe. The desire to lean closer to the table made her grab the counter on either side of her and stay where she was. There was enough crowding around him right now.

"Yes?"

She watched Griffin's spine straighten, "hello, little brother." His voice was steady.

There was a long pause. "How many times have I told you not to call me that?"

"Many." Griffin looked amused.

"I'm actually shocked you had to balls to call me after taking off. What, do you need rescuing? Don't like it out there in the big world?"

"Hardly. I just thought I'd see if you were missing me at all."

"You do know I will find you and then…"

"No, you won't." Griffin glanced around the room, "I have the entire Shifter Alliance looking out for me."

The pause was so long it was almost awkward. "You ran to them? You fucking coward, after everything I did to give you a normal life instead of being some freak that was ogled and…"

Griffin laughed, and Blaise couldn't be sure if it was put on or real, "*normal* life? How does keeping me under guard in a sparse apartment fall into the normal category?"

"I told father you should have been treated just like the others…" The calm tone Aiden had been using was gone now.

"Your father didn't consider your opinion important. Do you know why you inherited the businesses? Because he had no other legitimate heirs. If he had a daughter, he surely would have chosen her over you."

Another long pause, this time motion in the background could be heard, and then a slamming door. "I will use every resource I have to hunt you down, Griffin, and when I do…"

"Did I mention my chats with the King of the Alliance? He's a very intelligent and calm man. I have a great deal of respect for what he does."

"You've been talking to them? What have you told them?" The words were hissed in a quieter tone.

Griffin rubbed his hand over his head, "not as much verbally as you'd assume," he paused and looked at Calum when he pulled out his phone. After glancing at it, Calum nodded to Griffin. Blaise didn't know who had messaged him, but calling Aiden must be working.

"What does that mean? Don't use fancy talk, just say what you mean."

Blaise couldn't help the grin; it was clear which sibling got the brains.

"I just did. I have not had many in-depth conversations with members of the Alliance." Griffin looked at the papers on the table. "I have jotted down many details of things I remember."

"What things?" The sound of something crashing made Griffin look even more amused. Then there were muffled sounds like someone had covered the phone's mouthpiece. "What have you told them, Griffin?"

Griffin shrugged, "places I've been, people I've seen, some conversations I've overheard."

"I swear if you…"

"If I what?" He stood up, the chair scraping along the floor, "what are you going to do, Aiden? Lock me in a room again? Put a collar around my neck?" Griffin snarled, and Blaise's cat moved inside her. "Do you know what happens when you stop taking that medication that was forced on me for the last fifteen years?"

"You-you shift now?"

Aiden didn't sound so sure of himself now. "Let's just say my bear…"

"You shift into a bear? A bear?" Other voices could be heard in the background now. Blaise hoped Illias and the other techy ones were recording it at least, so it could be played back later.

Calum gave him a thumbs up, and Blaise could only assume that meant all the pieces that had been staying so stationary this past week were now on the move.

"I have one question: why didn't you lock me in a cage in the last five years? Father wasn't there to stop you."

Aiden snorted, "cages are for those that need breaking or are a threat." He scoffed, "Dad put it in his will that you were live out your natural life without harm. You wouldn't be alive right now if it weren't for that."

Had his father actually cared about him? There was more commotion in the background of the call. "It sounds like you're busy. I won't keep you. I just wanted to call to tell you that you had better run far and fast, little brother, because I will find you, and when I do, I plan to seek retribution for your depravity. You could have stopped when *our* father died, but instead, you took it to the extreme and destroyed so many more lives than he ever did." Griffin glanced at Blaise; she could see the solemn promise in his eyes. "Run, little brother." His tone was so low that it made all the hair stand up on the back of her neck. He hung up the phone, set it on the table, and then stepped back.

The room was silent for a minute, and then Blair started clapping.

"Well done, Griffin." The king's voice came over the other phone. "They are moving now."

Griffin nodded but didn't speak. His heart was beating so fast. He'd actually done that.

"I suggest you get ready to move, Miss Morgan."

Blaise jolted, "yes, sir."

"I'll message you the safe locations," Illias said.

Blaise nodded and went over and grabbed her jacket. She needed to get her bags into the truck. When she turned, she saw Blair grip Griffin's shoulder and nod to him. A lump formed in her throat. Griffin was accepted.

Chapter Thirty-Nine

Griffin couldn't believe he'd done it. His entire life he'd waited to speak however he wanted, to Aiden especially and he'd finally done it.

The door opened behind him, he turned to see Blair and Calum coming out, with big grins on their faces. The call must have gone well after he left for some air. Both smiled at him as they went down the steps. Genuine grins, not stiff, polite ones. How often had anyone ever smiled at him—without malice intent? Never that he could recall.

Blaise and Kobie came outside, "we're going for a quick run before we all head out." Kobie informed him.

Blaise paused and glanced back at the house.

"I'll stay with him." Noah came walking across the yard.

"Thanks." Blaise glanced briefly at Griffin and then ran down the steps to catch up to Kobie.

Griffin motioned to the path everyone was taking, "you can go, I don't..."

"No." Noah kicked the snow off the step, "you're not going to be left alone at this point," he looked over at his shoulder in the direction they went, "and I'm good." He shrugged and turned back to him, "sometimes it's better if I don't let my cat out," he tapped the side of his head, "if things are bad up here, it's best if I stay on two feet."

Griffin crossed his arms over his chest, sighed at their bulkiness, and jammed his hands in his pockets instead, "I don't know how any of that works," he rolled his eyes, "my inside animal and I still aren't communicating well."

Noah smirked, then sobered quickly, "you know, the collar," he tugged at the collar of his jacket, "when you're in it for so long, your animal is—" he scowled at the ground, "unsure if they can trust coming out or not."

Griffin nodded but didn't actually understand. "But you shift now."

Noah nodded slowly, "I do, not even completely sometimes, just," he motioned to his arms, "parts of me like you do." His gaze connected with him, and Griffin could see the anxiety in the man's eyes. "But if I'm having internal struggles," Noah snorted, "which is every minute of every day really, its best if I stay in this form. My cat has never yet taken complete control, and I'm afraid to see what happens if he does."

Griffin blew out a loud breath, "oddly that makes me feel better." He sent him an apologetic look, "that I don't shift. I have enough issues controlling the part that does happen."

"It will get better with time," he turned his head suddenly just as a large black jaguar came out of the trees, "or so I'm told."

Griffin could only look at the animal; with his predatory movement, he knew without question it was Calum. Before he could process that, a huge white tiger came bounding out of the trees and lept over him. Griffin smirked; it could only be Blair. Right on his tail was a gorgeous black tiger, and he'd be lying if he said he wasn't in awe of being this close to 'free' shifters in their animal forms.

Noah leaned on the railing and pointed, "there were some rabbits in the field by the machinery this morning."

Blaise came out of the trees as the others bolted in another direction.

"Rabbits," Noah said.

Blaise turned and took off after them.

"That was," he had no words to describe it.

"Yeah, I'd say you get used to it, but I don't know if you ever do." He jerked his chin toward the direction they had gone, "most of them have known and been around shifters since birth, so this is just normal to them."

"I don't think it will ever feel normal." He rubbed his hand over his head, "I can't even get used to having this upsized body."

Noah blew out a breath, "yeah at least I didn't have to contend with that." He looked at him for a second longer, "how's your shoulder?"

Griffin rolled it slowly and couldn't help but grimace, "a little better."

"At least your bear is helping with the healing; otherwise, you'd still be in a sling."

"I think the pros outweigh the cons." Griffin smiled, "but I'm still assessing the situation fully."

"The strength must be nice."

Griffin chuckled, "I could have used it over the years."

"Hey, thanks." He gave him a serious look.

"For?"

"Calling him, stirring it all up so we can get moving again."

Griffin could see the haunting look back in Noah's eyes, "is that what you do when it gets to be too much? Go out and hunt down Aiden's sins?"

"Something like that." Noah pulled out his phone he looked at it. "Gage and Kelsey will be back over here shortly."

"Are they part of the teams?" Griffin grinned, "Kelsey is a fireball and Gage is a very big man."

Noah smiled, "I don't know if the teams could handle Kelsey." He shook his head, "they're not; with Blair and I going out so much, they stay here and watch over all three places," he shrugged, "and Gage is one of Devin's seconds, along with Calum, so I guess having one in the action all the time means the other one has to stay where it's safe just in case."

"Seconds?" Griffin hadn't heard that before.

Noah nodded, "when Devin is King, they'll basically be his personal bodyguards or something similar."

"That's interesting, they're not the same clan."

"I think that's the idea; having it be different clans assures that one big event doesn't take it all down," He lifted his hands and let them drop, "I'm still learning all the bits that go with this life."

"You're miles ahead of me there. I'm still working on the fact that I'm a bear. I haven't even considered the hierarchy and monarchy parts."

Noah rolled his head from side to side, making Griffin wonder if he was lying about needing to go for a run and had just hung back with him so no one else had to. "When you figure it out, let me know."

A truck pulled in and Griffin followed Noah's nonchalant stance and didn't panic. When it stopped, Kelsey hopped out of the driver's seat. From around the other side came Gage, that was something else he had to adjust to, the fact that females could do whatever they wanted. Right behind Gage was the little one, Daisy, he thought her name was. She skipped along in the snow like it wasn't even there. She saw Noah and ran faster, sliding right into him.

"I asked mom if I could go over and play with your kids and she said yes, but Kelsey has some things to do here first. Is that okay, that I wait here until she is done?"

Noah squatted down to her level and it amazed Griffin that he wasn't guarded at all as he looked at the girl, "it's fine. When you go over, what's the rule?"

Daisy's shoulders slumped, "don't go down the slide face first anymore, it's too slippery with the snow."

Noah smirked, "that's right." He tapped her nose gently with the tip of his finger, "we don't want this cute face all marked up."

Daisy smiled and then turned to him, "I'm Daisy. I heard you were a bear."

Griffin glanced at Kelsey for a second, then back to the child and nodded.

"That's cool. We could use a bear at home."

Kelsey chuckled, "his bear is not a pet, Daisy."

Daisy turned to her, "but I can't have a dog because they don't like the cats, and Thera hasn't come back to visit," she looked up at Noah, "the cats wouldn't care about a bear."

Noah tried not to smile, but Griffin could see it in his eyes anyway, "Griffin has to come to help us with some things."

She spun back toward him, "I think with a name like *Griffin*, you should have been a griffon, not a bear." She shrugged, "but it doesn't work that way because Bear is really a lion." Before anyone could say a thing, she bound back off the porch and slid through the snow.

Griffin glanced from Noah to Kelsey and then Gage, "I'm not uh," he waved his hand in her direction, "equipped to deal with that."

Kelsey laughed, "I don't think any of us are equipped to take on Daisy most days."

Calum came walking out of the trees, fully clothed and back in his man's body. "That was fun."

"You cheated," Blair came out behind him.

"He did." Kobie caught up to them.

"If I'd known there was vendetta to settle, I might have wandered in the other direction." Blaise looked happy as well.

Calum shrugged, "there were no base rules."

"What did he do this time?" Gage even looked entertained.

"He scared any animal that might be nearby."

Calum gave Gage a wide-eyed look, "blame my cat, he had something to say."

Gage started laughing, "he does that when he's not in the mood to defend his 'title'" he made marks in the air.

"I'm sorry, I don't believe he holds the best tracker anymore." Blair put his arm around Kobie's shoulder, "that title belongs to my amazing mate now."

Calum rolled his eyes, "we'll do a rematch next year when Tomas' goons aren't closing in on us." He glanced at Griffin for a second, "by spring he shouldn't ever be a problem again."

"Deal." Kobie smiled and went toward the house, "we're

going home for a few to round up some clothes, text us when you're heading out."

Blaise glanced at her truck, "can I gas up here? Once we're moving, I don't want to stop until we have to meet up with Leyton for our supply package."

Gage nodded, "take what you need." He pointed to the large buildings, "there are some gas cans in the shop if you want to take some backup fuel."

Blaise nodded her head, "not a bad idea." She smirked, "my truck gets very thirsty."

"Do you need anything else?" Kelsey motioned to the stairs, "we have quite a few packs that Zain sent here for emergencies, with so many arriving in the area." She went up the steps and opened the door, "come take a look."

Griffin watched Blaise go into the house after her and then turned to Blair, "so the plan is to stay on the move?"

Blair nodded and gave Calum a brief look, "for now."

"No one will know where you and Blaise are going, just Blaise." Calum motioned to the house, "it can't leak if no one knows."

Griffin turned to go in, "am I being foolish to hope this is all over in a week?"

Noah walked by him, "at least you get to see the country."

"That's true." Griffin went in after him, he hadn't seen much of anywhere in his life, but it would be more enjoyable if he didn't have to worry about a bullet finding his head every second of every day.

Chapter Forty

Blaise stabbed the call button before she changed her mind. At the second ring, she almost hung up.

"Hello?"

"Hi—mom."

There was a pause. "Blaise?"

She scowled at the floor; the woman had one daughter. What other female would call her mom? "Yeah," she wanted to smile, to feel that connection she was told mother and child had, but it wasn't there. "I just thought I'd touch base with you and see how everyone is."

"Oh. Well, everyone is fine."

"That's good." As awkward moments went, this was off the charts.

"Your brother has a new position in the clan, we're all very proud."

"Great." Of course, it was about the perfect brother. "Aunt Esina, she's doing good?" The only person that never used to look at her like she was a mistake.

"Yes, you know her; she'll never change."

She wanted to say, 'hey, remember Emersyn? We found her,' but didn't know if it was safe to do that. Blaise knew her aunt stayed in touch with those back home.

"How is your work going?"

She looked out the window where Noah and Griffin were standing. "It's going good. I'm on the road a lot."

"Seeing the sights is nice."

"Yeah, well, haven't been seeing much since that storm."

"No, I imagine not. We got quite a bit of snow here."

Blaise nodded, wanting to tell her that her truck was finished, about her job and her home, but it didn't feel right. "So, ah, I don't know if I'll make it home for the holidays—the Alliance is keeping me pretty busy."

"Oh, that's fine, dear."

She nodded again; it always was. "Okay, I won't keep you, I need to get back to work."

"All right."

"Tell everyone I said hey, and I'll call when I can."

"Okay, Blaise."

She stood there waiting for something. The things she knew weren't going to happen.

"Love you, mom," she blurted out.

"Be safe, Blaise." The line went quiet.

Blaise wrapped her arms around her waist and looked out the window again. She refused to acknowledge her view was blurred by wet eyes. Taking a deep breath, she nodded to herself, wiped her hand over her face, and then turned on her heel to go out with the men.

They'd be heading out soon, and she wanted to make sure they had enough drinks and things to get through so they didn't have to stop to eat.

She may not have a family that doted on her, or cared enough to call, but she had a team that counted on her, and she would never be their weak link.

Chapter Forty-One

"With mates, is there this constant need to see them? I don't know if that's why I can't stop looking at you or if it's because you're the first woman I've been around that doesn't look at me with fear on their face."

Blaise looked at the door, wondering when the others would be back. Dragging her gaze away from it, she glanced at Griffin, who stood in the middle of the room. "I guess it's the mate thing because I feel it too, my cat wants to be *right* beside you all the time." She could have lied, probably should have, but that wasn't how she was made.

"You were upset earlier, I knew it, or my bear did. What happened?"

Moving away from the table with the map, she sat on the arm of the couch and looked down at her hands. She might tell the truth, but that didn't mean she wanted to look at it too. "Just a call home."

"You miss your family. I'd say I understand, but the only family I know, I'd rather stick a knife in their heart than talk to them."

She grinned fleetingly, "I get that." She blew out a breath, "uh, no, not really missing them—they, uh, are happier when I'm not around," she motioned to the darker side of her neck, but still didn't look right at him. "I'm embarrassing."

"That's ridiculous. You're an amazing woman. You're on a team that I assume isn't easy to get on—male or female. Your family should be singing your praises."

Blaise smirked, "no, it's all about my brother with them." She looked back at her hands, turning them side by side. She'd always thought it looked like hands from two different people. She heard him move across the room but continued to study her hands.

He stopped before her and touched her chin, so she looked up at him. His eyes were that of man and not his bear, it was good he was getting his animal under control, even though he didn't think he was.

"I'm proud to know you." He told her softly, "some families are overrated."

Blaise licked her lips and tried to find a way to change the subject, "I think our families fit into the cruel and unusual category."

"They do." The warm touch on her chin was hard to ignore. "Stand up."

She gave him a wary look but still got to her feet.

"Don't stab or shoot me," she could see amusement in his eyes, "I just want to hug you."

Blaise tried to clamp down on her emotions so he wouldn't see how surprised she was.

"I don't know if you need one, but I feel like you need one." He held his hand behind her but didn't force her to move.

She wasn't sure if she moved or if he did but found herself in his arms with her face resting against his collarbone, and her arms were wrapped around his waist. It felt good, not in a sexual way, but in a way that calmed her cat and seemed like it rejuvenated her soul. It was odd that a hug could do that, but it did. Blaise closed her eyes for a moment, telling herself that the hug was over when she opened them. She couldn't afford soft emotional moments; it had taken her too long to build the shield that protected her.

Griffin didn't squeeze her or grope any part of her, he just stood there and gently held her. She could hear his heartbeat, and considering the strength, it was beating with, she thought it was amazing he was just standing still.

Taking a deep breath, she opened her eyes. He smelled like home like a place she needed, and the realization shook her to the core. Her cat was still and watchful and it was one of the rare moments that Blaise wasn't sure what she was thinking. Stepping back, she placed her palm over his heart and patted his chest lightly a few times. "We should take the other bags out, we're going soon."

He placed a hand over hers, and she felt him inhale deeply. "Okay."

When he stepped away, she felt like a coward. Who was afraid of a hug? A hug that could break all of her defenses and dissolve her strength. The biggest problem with Griffin having lived as he had, was that he didn't know he was supposed to be a big jerk like too many men were. Blowing out a breath, she turned away from him and walked to the kitchen.

"Blaise?"

She glanced at him when she reached the door.

"I'm here if you need another hug," he shrugged, "or to talk. I don't know most answers, but I have ears."

He was a jerk for saying the right things. "I'm aces, Griff, but thanks." She looked away before he could see her lie. How was she going to do infinite days with him, secluded and on the move? She had no idea, but it was her assignment, so somehow, she'd get it done.

Chapter Forty-Two

They'd driven straight through after picking a random location on the list they were given. Blaise checked that Griffin was still sleeping and then stepped outside. It was early, but she knew that the teams would either be on route to safe houses or getting things ready. It had taken her a day to work up the nerve to make this call, so she needed to get it done before it drove her crazy.

Opening Illias' message, she tapped on the number and then jabbed the phone symbol when the call screen came up.

On the third ring, someone answered, and her nerves had her talking before they got a hello out. "Sorry to call you so early, Prince…"

"My son is out for a run right now."

Son? It was the king. "Oh," come on words, "it's Blaise—sir, Blaise Morgan."

"Maybe I can help you, Blaise."

"Uh, yeah, you would probably have the answer I'm looking for."

"I will try to."

One-on-one, he didn't seem like the same man on the group call. "I'm calling about Griffin Ballard, sir." She closed her eyes at the use of his last name, of course, he knew who he was;

everyone did now.

"Is he all right?"

Her eyes popped open, "Yeah, he's fine. He's still asleep."

"Thank you for keeping him safe, Blaise, as you know he's a very important man right now. The operations taking place later are all thanks to him, bringing us closer to ending all of it."

She nodded, "that's kind of why I'm calling, sir." How did she word this? "After, you know, when we shut down Tomas for good because we will…"

"Yes, we will." He agreed.

"Yeah, so after we do that, what's in store for Griffin? I mean, I know he has a clan, but he doesn't know them and," she was rambling, dammit, "and even if at some point they can be contacted, the fact that he's," she frowned, "a bear," did that sound right? She hoped so, "they may not be so accepting, especially because the other half of him is Tomas DNA—"

"You're worried he will be rejected from a clan?"

She nodded again, "clans can be like that, sir," she scowled at the ground, "I'm living proof that being different isn't accepted."

"Mmm."

"So-so, what happens with Griffin?" She'd never stuttered and mumbled so much in her life before.

"I don't have a definitive answer for that right now, Blaise, he may want to try his clan ties, or simply disappear and attempt to have some sort of normal life. I can't say for sure."

Disappear? She looked at the door. Would he do that? "So-so, he's free to make his own decisions then."

"Of course, as soon as we realized he wasn't a participant in what his family did—" he paused, "did you think he was a prisoner?"

Blaise shrugged, "to be honest, sir, I haven't been sure about much lately, which is why I'm asking, so I can be clear." She liked clear and decisive, none of this second, third and fourth guessing things.

"Blaise, don't take this the wrong way, I don't know you

very well, I wish I did know the team members better—"

"I get it, you're a very busy man."

"Yes. It seems like you've grown quite fond of Mister Ballard, which is to your credit that you can look past his previous situation…"

"Sir," she bit her lip and then decided she was all in, she needed answers, and if this was the only way to get them, "he's my mate." There was a pause and she tensed.

"That's interesting." Was what the man that led the entire collective of clans—around the planet said to her confession.

"It is?" This was not what she thought would happen.

"Yes. I was talking to the research team recently, and they were hypothesizing about mixed DNA and if there was even one drop of shifter blood, would it still be enough for mating to occur? Of course, we didn't have any instances to back it up."

"I'm not following." She wasn't going to be some kind of science experiment.

"With your mixed DNA and his, we now have the answer. It was suspected to be possible after Deacon Parrish and Gia Marin were mates, but the human factor was in question—we have many being freed that aren't of one bloodline…"

Blaise hadn't known that. Deacon and Gia? What was that about? "This is not the conversation I thought I'd have, sir."

Shepard Addison chuckled. The *King* chuckled at her. "I suppose it's not, yet I think you've answered your own question, Blaise, as to where Griffin belongs or what happens to him when we shut down Tomas."

She scowled at the ground. "I did?"

"If he wants to be part of the Alliance, he needs a connection within, whether it's a clan or mate."

"I didn't think that I'd ever—"

"That you'd have one because of your mixed blood? I'm sure that is a surprise then."

"Surprise is putting it mildly." She felt like someone had decked her in the brain about eight times.

"I supposed you have some decisions to make now." He

cleared his throat, "this could take years to clean up, the various factions helping Aiden Tomas' organization, you and Griffin will both be valuable assets with that."

Blaise stood there looking in front of her but saw nothing. Years? She hadn't thought of that. It made sense, there was no quick and easy way to shut it down with how far spread it was worldwide. She cleared her throat when she realized she hadn't replied to him. "You know I'll do whatever needs doing to get them all, sir, and," she glanced at the door, "Griffin is very committed to helping."

"Everyone appreciates that. I will have to let you go, I have a few more calls to make before the teams get set up for the operations. "Are you at a secure location?"

She looked around, "we are, but I might move us every few days just to be safe."

"Wise plan."

"Thank you, sir, for taking the time to speak to me."

"I wish I could with more. I'll talk to you soon, Blaise, about a new project we're working on, but I can't share the details right now."

"Oh. Okay. Thank you for considering me." She had no idea for what, but even to be acknowledged by the King was a big deal to her.

"I'll be on the call later during the operations. I'll talk to you then."

She nodded, "yes, sir." The line went quiet.

Blaise looked at the phone. She had no idea what had just happened. Jamming it back in her pocket, she went inside and closed the door quietly. She stood there looking at Griffin, after watching the rise and fall of his chest for a few minutes, she relaxed. He was still asleep. She wasn't sure of the scope of his hearing, but the thin walls of this little cabin probably wouldn't be much of a challenge for him.

Slipping her boots off, she went over and sat in the chair by the fireplace. The King spoke like mixed DNA was no big deal, her kind or Griffin's. She shook her head; too bad everyone didn't think like that. She needed to ask Deacon what was up with him, because she didn't know what the King was talking about.

Her cat was prancing inside her; Blaise settled her thoughts so she could try to figure out why. As she sat in the dark, trying to translate what her animal wanted, she realized Griffin was awake now and looking at her.

Chapter Forty-Three

"Everything all right?"

She glanced over her shoulder to see Griffin sitting in the chair in the corner. "Everything's good."

"Okay, then why are you refolding the clothes for the fourth time?"

Blaise looked down at her bag. Had she? "Just trying to make some space." It was a good reason. "We have to go meet up with someone and pick up more supplies."

"Are you going to put them in your bag?"

Keeping her head down, she put the clothes back in, "no." She was being ridiculous, she knew that, but she was going stir-crazy with nothing to do but think. "How's your shoulder?"

"Much better, just a dull ache."

"Good."

"What supplies are we picking up?"

"Extra food, stuff that won't go bad." She zipped up the bag and set it on the floor, then stood there looking around the room, trying to figure out what to do next. "Equipment, so you can see the rescued people or," she shrugged, "otherwise."

"We'll see what your teams are doing as they're doing it?" He stood up and stretched slowly, and she watched his movement to see if he was lying about his shoulder.

"I guess we will." She knew how important it was to keep him on the move and off anyone's radar, but she would have loved to be on one of the breach teams right now. There was nothing like the simplicity of it. No chit-chat; everyone knew their part, and if she was lucky enough to come across someone that was uncooperative, all the better. She had a lot of internal baggage that she'd love to unload on someone in the form of physical aggression.

He just stood there looking at her. Did he know about her conversation with the King? If he did, then he knew she was holding out on him. If he didn't, then she knew she was. There was no winning right now. Lifting her hands, she let them slap down on her hips. "Grab a seat." She motioned to where he'd just got up from. He sat down and didn't even question her. That bugged her. After everything he'd been through, she would have demanded to know why before even considering sitting down. "I, uh, spoke to the King earlier." She shook her head quickly, "I was actually calling Devin, but he was out for a run and his father answered the phone."

"He told you something that isn't sitting right?" He waved his hand around, "you've been moving non-stop like you can outrun it if you stay in motion."

She snorted, huffed out a breath, and sat on the end of the bed. "Something like that, I guess. I'm restless, I don't do stop very well and with the teams going out…"

"You wished you were going with them and not babysitting me."

"Yes. Well, no, I don't mind keeping you safe from that maniacal monster." She shrugged, "I like my job, with the teams."

"You've very good at it, from what I saw when they found us at Raymond's cabin."

She smirked, "yeah, I'm good with physical stuff, not," she looked around the room, "the sitting still stuff."

Griffin nodded his head slowly, "I understand. I've always been confined to small areas, so I suppose I'm better adjusted to it." He held her look, "which I suppose is good with my future not looking like it will be free, wide-open spaces."

"About that." She saw the guarded look replace his relaxed one. "I asked the King what was next for you," his expression didn't falter at all, "once we take down Tomas and all those in the country, so to speak." She rolled her head from side to side, trying to release some of the tension, "he said it could take years to shut everything down worldwide."

"It's going to be a long game."

"Yeah." She sucked in a breath, "he says after those here are shut down, you can make your own decisions. You can contact your mother's clan, or," She shrugged, "do what you want."

He was quiet for a moment, "really?" Rubbing his hand over his head, he blew out a breath, "I wasn't expecting that." His shoulders slumped in relief. "I don't know what I want to do." He looked out the window, "I've never had the choice," he glanced at her and smiled, "sure, I've thought about thousands of things, but," he leaned back in the chair and stared at the floor, "what would I do? I have no skills to speak of."

"There are always jobs at the Alliance."

Griffin gave her a surprised look, "I'm not a warrior."

She was going to argue, the way he handled things when they'd been taken, that was fighter trait. "There is more than just fighting jobs, there's a lot of people at the headquarters that do things." She didn't want to tell him the other part of doing what he wants. It would be like lying if she didn't though. "Uh, to be part of the Alliance, you have to have a connection…"

"A connection?"

"Yeah, be part of a clan—or-or mates of someone that is."

"Right. Otherwise, you're a rogue." He nodded his head slowly, "that's what Sloane told that Alpha before I was shot."

"Yeah." She cleared her throat, "the King said you could go off and do something else, but you wouldn't have Alliance protection."

"On my own?" His brows creased, "what would I do?"

Blaise didn't know what to suggest. If it weren't for the Alliance, she had *no* idea what would have become of her.

"I supposed hanging out with you is off the table," he looked around, "once we're done playing hide and seek and Aiden is just a bad memory."

It hit her then, what was bothering her since she spoke to Shepard Addison. It wasn't about missing the ops or keeping Griffin safe. It was that when things finally settled down for the whole shifter community, he could leave. It explained her cat's odd silence and why Blaise couldn't stop moving. He sat there watching her, no emotion showing in his expression. "Right now, I can't think past getting Tomas and all of those working with him."

"It's not going to be a quick thing." He mused.

"No, it's not." She was happier with this conversation.

"A lot of plans and things could change twenty times before it's done."

Blaise got up, "yeah, everyone will have to adapt fast as they go." It was true. Things could get crazy and hectic once they started closing in on all the people working for Aiden Tomas.

"We could be driving around for months."

She shrugged, "it wouldn't surprise me." If she thought about this long enough, she knew that both of them were prolonging what was happening.

"I could take a turn driving now and then."

Blaise quirked an eyebrow at him, "I don't know if I'm ready to let you drive my truck."

"I'm a good driver."

"I'm sure you are, but she's my baby."

Griffin grinned, "I will win you over."

She gave him a skeptical glance, "good luck."

"What time are we leaving?"

"I'm just waiting on the when and where from Illias."

"Okay." He motioned to the door, "go run. Your constant motion is making me anxious." He frowned, "actually it's my bear, but today we seem to be on the same page."

She looked out the window.

"Go. Run around the cabin if you have to, just give me a little breathing room for a few minutes."

Going over to the chair, she grabbed her run pack. "I won't be gone long."

She went to the door and almost walked out without putting her boots on. She had some serious thinking to do and some decisions to make. She glanced back at the cabin, so did he. Turning to stand behind some bushes, she decided she wasn't going far.

From this vantage point, she could see for miles and the cabin. Her cat's vision helped to see in the window and what Griffin was up to. He was pacing. Not doing anything, just in constant motion. It must be hard when you and your animal were plagued with thoughts and couldn't shift to run them off. She watched him go to the little kitchen table and lean down on it. Was he talking out loud? It looked like he was talking out loud. She couldn't judge, she talked to her cat that way sometimes too. He hunched his back and dropped his head forward. Was he thinking about what she'd told him? If it were her and she'd been stuck somewhere for years, she would have her bag ready to go when everything was done. Is that what he was going to do? He stiffened and moved away from the table. He walked over to the window and looked right in her direction. She knew he saw her, it wasn't hard to see a tiger sitting on a rock in the snow. They continued to look at each other, for a lot longer than she should have. She needed to burn off some thoughts so she could focus on driving. Standing up, she stretched and gave him one more look and then bound down off the rock and took off through the snow.

Chapter Forty-Four

Griffin had been quiet for the whole drive, and it bothered her. Blaise didn't know what was going on with her; normally, silence suited her just fine. Pulling up behind the black SUV, she turned off the truck and looked at him. "I don't know how much they brought, so come give me a hand loading it up."

He nodded and opened his door.

Blaise couldn't help grinning when she saw Leyton get out of the vehicle. He was one of her teammates, and she liked working with him. He was polite with absolute resolve when on task. "Hey, Ley." She closed the door and walked to the back of the SUV.

Ley was a big man, but he didn't use his size to intimidate others unless they needed it. "How are you doing, Blaise?"

She shrugged, "Aces."

The second man appeared along the passenger side. She'd never worked with Nox, but knew he was solid when it came to his job. She nodded at him as she opened the back of their ride. She was just about to introduce Griffin when Nox turned and gave him a once-over.

"Shouldn't he be in cuffs?"

She watched Griffin shut down, the pleasant expression on his face blanked and he had closed himself off, that fast. "No."

She went over and looked at the bags and cases in the back, "why would he be?"

The look Nox gave her basically said she was an idiot. Her opinion of him was about to change. "He's Aiden Tomas' brother." Nox stated in a clear voice, "and," he looked Griffin up and down, "a half-breed."

All the good intentions Blaise had vanished in a heartbeat. "And you're an Alpha's kid, but we overlook that." She leaned on the back of the vehicle, waiting to see if he was going to take this further and then changed her mind, "The *half-breed's* other self is a bear, Nox, a Kermode spirit bear and if you have any questions about his animal, ask Tripp, he'll tell you all about it."

"A bear?" Leyton grinned, "grizzly," he tapped his own chest. "I don't think I've ever seen a Kermode bear." He motioned up and down Griffin, "I'm guessing a big breed."

"What does him being half bear have to do with the fact that he's from—"

Something inside Blaise snapped and she moved before she could think it. When she was face to face with Nox, she growled a low quiet warning, "who cares where he's from. He saved my life *three* times since I met him." She scowled at him, "Shot one of Tomas' goons before they got the drop on me, busted us out of a metal container when they came for him and," she glared at Nox, "took a bullet meant for *my* back," she shook her head and huffed out a breath, her cat was too close and it was breaking all the rules to attack an Alliance team member, "and it's *his* information that is going to hand us Aiden fucking Tomas and shut it *all* down." She waved her hand in the air, "the ops tonight," she pointed at Griffin, "all thanks to him." She nodded and then sneered at Nox, "the information that's handing us their transportation routes and contacts? Him. So, you need to show some god damned respect and be thankful I don't cut you tongue out—"

An arm wrapped around her waist from behind, pulling her away from him.

"Blaise," it was Griffin, but she already somehow knew that, "it's fine. *That* is the reaction I'm prepared for when meeting people from the Alliance."

"It isn't right." She glared at Nox, even as Leyton got in his face and straightened him out.

"That's what I thought when those kids were disrespecting you." He leaned closer to her ear, "do I kiss you now to thank you?"

Her shoulders slumped, and she shook her head, "no, you do not. I have a rep to protect here."

"All right. Rain check, but you could take it down a notch. I'd appreciate it, but my bear is unhappy that you're upset."

She spun around and looked at him, his eyes had changed color, and his jacket looked tighter. "Hey," she put her hand on his chest and rubbed it, "tell the big guy I appreciate his concern, but we don't have time to smack people with trees and tables right now."

Griffin gave her a lopsided grin, "I didn't hit him with a tree."

"Tell that to that guy's head."

He took a deep breath and exhaled slowly.

"That's it." She was surprised she was able to settle him down when she was internally trying to wrangle her cat from taking a chunk out of Nox.

"Everything good?"

They both looked to see Leyton standing there with his hands in his pockets. "Sorry about that." He pulled his hands out, walked over to Griffin, and held one out, "thank you," he jerked his head toward Blaise, "for having her back. She's a huge asset on the team, and we'd be lost without her."

Blaise snorted, "he means that literally," she smiled at Griffin, "he can't read a map to save his life."

Leyton laughed, "there's that too." He studied Griffin, "ornery things, bears. Don't let yours bully you like that." He motioned to their vehicle, "let's get this unloaded; I've got doors to kick down in four hours."

Blaise looked around and didn't see Nox. She smirked.

Leyton must have put him on a time-out in the car. She went over and grabbed one of the bags and looked in it. Illias had sent every kind of snack from the look of it.

"So it's true?" She turned and handed Griffin two bags before looking at Ley, "what?"

"That the end is in sight because of Griffin?"

Blaise watched him put the bags in the back seat of her truck, "it is."

"Excellent." Leyton stacked two of the cases on top of each other and went toward her truck. "So do you just drive around with him?"

"We have to stay on the move. No one knows our location when we stop." She watched Griffin for a moment, making sure he had his animal under control. "Tomas has gone after him twice so far," she smirked, "and Griffin called him, and he freaked him out, so he's desperate now."

Leyton handed her a case and then grabbed the last two. "You'll keep him safe. I'm just a call away if you need backup."

Blaise set the case in the back seat and took the bags from Griffin, "I appreciate it." She shrugged, "I think we'll be okay."

Leyton nodded, then pulled out his phone, "we have to get moving." He walked backward toward the SUV, "I'll talk to you soon, Blaise," he saluted Griffin.

Blaise closed the door and looked up at Griffin, "pick a direction and we'll see where the next safe house is."

Griffin looked around and then pointed East.

"East it is." Blaise smiled at him and went around to the driver's side.

Chapter Forty-Five

He'd been quiet again and it was getting on her last nerve. She didn't think she liked the chatty version of him, but she definitely didn't like the silent one. Getting out, she looked around, "I guess we have some shoveling to do." She pointed, "key is supposed to be in that little shed. See if there's a shovel there too."

It was weird that a little house was in the middle of nowhere. She turned in a circle. It was in the open, which should make it easier for her to keep watch, but it made her feel uneasy at the same time. They'd be heading out in the morning again.

Griffin came back and unlocked the door, and then started shoveling toward her.

She grabbed some of the bags from the truck and started for the door, she didn't care how deep the show was. She had to go through everything before it was time for the ops and hoped Illias sent instructions on how to set up the gear without leaking a signal or whatever it did.

"You're quiet," she walked by him.

"A lot to think about."

She set them inside the door and turned back to get more. "You can't talk and think at the same time?"

He stopped shoveling and looked at her, "you don't like chatting."

"I don't like heavy silence either."

"You're very hard to please." He mumbled and went back to shoveling.

Blaise glared at him and then turned and went back to get more out of the truck. On the way back she stopped and looked at him, "we need to figure this out; we're going to be stuck in each other's faces for," she jerked her shoulders up, "who knows how long."

He paused with the shovel full of snow, "this?"

She nodded and started walking, "us."

Setting the things down, she turned to go get more, and he was *right* behind her.

"I didn't know there was an us."

"You know what I mean." She waited for him to move, but he didn't, he just continued to stand there like a wall and block her from leaving. Puffing out her cheeks, she blew the breath out, she turned and picked up the things she had just set down and walked across the room, she'd clean up the wet floors later, she decided.

"I don't know what you mean." He was standing at the door, blocking any space she could have used to go back out. "You tell me we're mates, but we don't talk about it." He lifted his hands and let them drop, "you tell me I can leave when this is all done but skirt the issue when I inquire about the chance of staying with you." He repeated the motion, "you tell me to stop chatting and then get upset when I do that." He made an exasperated sound, "I can't stand up for you, but you can flip out on some guy for saying what everyone else thought." He lifted his arms again and held them out, "so what do we do, Blaise? You tell me."

She scowled at him and then dropped the cases on the table, wincing, she hoped whatever equipment was in them, it would be padded, and she didn't just damage the system they needed to be a remote part of the ops. "Look, it's not like this is something that happens every day," she motioned between them, "finding a mate was never on my to-do list." This was not the way she wanted to talk about this. She didn't know how to talk about this but knew barking at each other wasn't the way to go.

He snorted, "being free from Aiden was never on mine, but it happened."

He had a point. "The way I see it, we have three choices." She went over and stood a few feet from him, hoping to clear this up and then get on with the things she had to do.

"What are they? The choices." He had a very guarded look on his face.

"We do what we've been tasked and keep moving around and help the teams bring it all down, just like we are, nothing changes, and then you go do your thing or figure out what your thing is."

"Isn't that what brought us to this discussion? Nothing changing?" He put his hands on his hips and just stood there staring her down.

She gave him a hard look, "I can get someone else to do this," she motioned out the window, "drive you around to safe locations." She didn't like the idea, but it was an option.

"No." That was it. No explanation, just no. He crossed his arms over his chest and stood there.

She snorted, "option three is ridiculous."

"What is it?"

"We seal the deal." She had to stop herself from jolting at her own words, which hadn't once been in her thoughts. Not once.

"Become mates? That deal?"

She wasn't sure how long she stood there looking at him; she was too busy trying to figure out why she'd said that. Did she want someone stuck to her side for the rest of her life? She gnawed her lip, she'd never had a close relationship with anyone since she was a child, and that had only been Emersyn. Could she even function with all that mushy crap that, from observing others, seemed to go with mating?

"Blaise."

She blinked.

"Get out of your head and answer me."

She frowned, not sure what the question had been.

"Do you want to be mates?" Griffin tilted his head to the side, "obviously, we already are, but do you want it to be a done deal?" He stepped toward her, and she had to force herself to stand her ground and not back up. "Cat got your tongue?" He smirked; she glared back at him. "Okay, let me tell you what *I'd* like." He stopped with only two feet between them, and Blaise felt like she was suffocating as she stood there. "I'd like to have someone in my life that doesn't hate me, look down at me, or is embarrassed that I am what I am." The expression on his face softened, "I think that's something you've also never had."

Her head seemed to nod all on its own; she wasn't in control of whatever was happening here. Her cat was silent, so she must have been having some sort of out-of-body experience.

"I don't know the first thing about mates, or being one," he searched her face, "I don't even know what it's like to have someone to talk to, the longest conversations I've had since the camp with Noah are the ones I've had with you, so I can't even tell you a bunch of lies about how great it all will be, because I don't know."

Her brain was stuck. She couldn't even think of the conversations they'd had. "I've always been alone. I probably suck at having someone around me all the time."

"We have that in common."

She realized what they did have in common, and it surprised her. Never had she ever dreamt that someone out there would understand what she'd been through by not being the perfect shifter specimen. "I don't know anything about mates."

"Ditto."

She gnawed on her lip again and stood there staring at him, watching her. "We need to get our stuff out of the truck."

"We *need* to finish this conversation. Whenever we discuss something, and it heads somewhere *emotional*, you run like your tail is on fire."

"You're getting pretty cute with the shifter references."

He smirked briefly, "what's the saying if you can't beat them..."

"Join them." Putting her hands on her hips, she studied him, "are we really talking about this?"

"You started the conversation."

She was just about to deny it but realized she had.

"You said we need to figure *us* out." He moved closer, "this is us figuring it out, not running away from it."

She scowled up at him, "I can't say I'm having any soft feelings for you right at this moment."

He smirked, "Noah told me that your mate is the person that helps you learn many lessons about yourself." His eyes searched hers, "and accepts you regardless of your own opinion *of* yourself."

That was the first time she'd heard mates described as anything but the 'they complete me' crap. "Makes sense, I guess."

"Being mates sounds like a good partnership to me." He reached over and put his finger under her chin, forcing her to look at him.

She wanted to close her eyes, but her cat managed to get her opinion in on it and she wanted the bear in front of them. "So, you want to do this?"

"Do you?"

All she could hear was the two of them breathing. *Accepts you* kept playing on repeat in her mind. Her brows furrowed, "are you going to kiss me or what?"

"Kissing I can do that; it's the *or what* part, I don't know what I'm doing."

"Don't expect a user manual from me."

He smirked, "of course not."

She bit her lip and looked at his mouth, "just do what feels right." She lifted one shoulder and let it drop, "we'll see if this works." It sounded shallow the way she'd said it like it was a tryout for some position or something. Her brain wasn't working with her right now and her cat, well, she was all for team bear.

"Do you expect it not to work?" He rested her chin between his thumb and finger, she could feel the warmth of his hand cover the whole side of her face. "We've been staring at each other for over a week now."

Had it been that long? She didn't even know what day it was. She hadn't slept since meeting the man, and now he wanted all these answers she didn't have. "This," she gripped his forearm, "talking now, is not necessary."

He leaned down, and she could feel his breath on her mouth, "what if I want to tell you what I want to do to you before I do it?"

She could taste him, and her cat wanted in on it now, "or-or you could just do."

"You'll tell me if I need to do more or less?"

"Mmhm," His mouth brushed against hers, barely a whisper of a kiss. Her cat wanted to bite him. *Shit*. Leaning back, she looked up at him, "if um we're doing the whole deal—you know that involves bites, right?" She was really going to do this. And then what? Take the half-breed home to meet her folks? That was *never* happening.

He pulled off her hat and worked the tie out of her hair, "I've seen them on the others. It's an important part?"

His fingers threading into her pulled-back hair sent shivers over her body, "yeah, it is. It's uh," she licked her lips, "basically like a wedding band, but very permanent." He leaned down, and she felt his breath on her neck, she tilted her head to the side, "so, you need to make sure you want that because it doesn't wash off or anything."

Griffin straightened and looked down at her, then clamped his teeth together and rolled his lips back. "I can't call on animal teeth to do that."

Blaise's cat was trying to come out through her chest to be near the man. "You don't know you can't." She ran her tongue over her teeth, checking to make sure her cat would at least let her run their body. "Whatever is meant will be, Griff."

"That would make a good greeting card." He grinned.

The man had a warped sense of humor, how had she missed *that*? Oh, yeah, because she'd been running like her tail was on fire. "Griff?"

He cupped her face in both of his large hands and for the first time in her existence, Blaise felt like one of those tiny women. "Mmm?"

"You need to kiss me." Stick with the facts; suited her and her cat just fine.

"You stopped me to explain about bites."

She nodded as best she could when her face was sandwiched between his big paws, "now you know." Her cat moved through her. *Shit.* "Oh yeah and there's another part."

"What other part?" He grinned, "the part I don't know anything about?"

She smirked, "no, uh, you can't touch me until I mark you." She shrugged her shoulders, "it's so the woman has control, and the decision is hers."

He leaned down, pressed his mouth gently to hers, then dropped his hands away and straightened up, "after what I've witnessed, I agree, one thousand percent."

Blaise blinked and then looked him up and down, "I didn't mean right this second. I meant," she flapped her hand in the air, "when we get there."

His grin was quick as he moved and pulled her closer to him. "This is awkward."

She frowned, "we haven't done anything yet."

"Not that," he tilted his head to the side, "I still don't know how to drive this new-sized me." He gripped her waist in his large hands, "I don't want to hurt you."

"You won't." Her cat was ready to come out and bite him, so he'd shut up and do something.

"Can we take off your weapons? I don't think getting stabbed would be very enjoyable."

"Shit." She stepped back and undid the belt for her holster, then reached down and undid the strap around her thigh. She held it out, and he took it, then she went to work pulling the various knives out. Back, hip, thigh, she bent down and pulled one out of her boot, then paused, trying to remember if that was all. Nodding to herself, she turned and set them on the table and then looked down to make sure she'd remembered everything.

"Only four?"

She shrugged, "the rest are beside my seat, too uncomfortable to wear them while driving."

"Of course," he smirked and then sobered quickly. "My bear is being weird." He rolled his eyes, "well, weird for him."

Blaise nodded and moved back to stand in front of him, "my cat wants out to claim you."

He raised an eyebrow, "but she's not coming out, right?" He motioned between them, "this is between us, with only two legs, right?"

Blaise snorted, "no, she's not. Some things I'm definitely in control of."

"Good to know." He put his hands on either side of her face and leaned down and brushed his mouth over hers, "I like your taste almost as much as the way you smell."

"Mmm," she really didn't want to talk all the way through this. Reaching up, she wrapped her arms around his neck and pulled his head back down to kiss him again. His kiss was slow and gentle, and she was okay with that, for now. She didn't want to rush him and make him self-conscious about his lack of experience, but she wouldn't be able to do this if the speed didn't accelerate. He cradled her into his body. They fit together like no one ever had with her, making her cat come closer to the surface.

As the kiss deepened, she could taste blood and it set her on fire. Reality hit her and reminded her that blood meant someone was bleeding; she pulled her mouth from his and ran her tongue across sharp teeth. "Sorry, she's not behaving."

Griffin licked the blood from his lip and held her look. "I'm not bothered by it. Quite the opposite, actually." His voice was deep and husky and vibrated through her.

She grabbed a hand full of his hair and pulled his head back down while walking backward and hopefully aiming them for the sofa she'd seen by the window. When her foot hit something, she broke the kiss. It was the bags she'd brought in. "Truck is wide open out there."

"Are you concerned about it?"

"We don't want our stuff taken."

He straightened up and glanced at the window, "you figure there's a lot of traffic out here?"

She knew there wasn't; half the roads on the way here hadn't been traveled in days. "No."

"Is this you having second thoughts?"

Blaise cocked her head to the side and looked at him, that sounded like *coward* to her ears. She shook her head, and then her cat was so close that her vision changed, and she knew she was looking at him with eyes that were more her feline's than her own. Her cat was done waiting, and there was nothing Blaise could do to persuade her to behave.

Grabbing the side of his open jacket, she pulled him toward her, then turned and used her foot to pull his. He stepped back and then sat on the couch. Blaise followed him down and straddled his lap. She shoved his jacket to get it off him.

"Go close the door." He sat forward and worked the jacket off.

She looked over to see the door was wide open and huffed out a breath. "Don't move." Getting up, she ran out the door to the truck, sliding to a stop when she reached it. Closing the two doors, she patted her pocket for the keys. Locking it, she paused and looked around. Nothing in any direction but snow. Perfect. Her cat prodded her to get back in the house.

Running back in, she shut the door a little harder than necessary, but she didn't care. Bending down, she undid her boots.

As she kicked the second one off, she looked over to see Griffin was still on the couch. He'd taken off his boots, jacket, and shirt. Her cat moved through her and something else— she was going to label it lust.

Yanking her jacket off, she tossed it toward the table and didn't care if it made it or not.

Pulling her shirt over her head, she realized she'd never had sex when it wasn't her cycle. That startled her, making her pause for a second. She couldn't start thinking about that. She started to take off her bra.

"Leave it for now." Griffin's voice was so deep it didn't even sound like him.

She looked down at him.

He shrugged one shoulder, "If I'm not supposed to touch you, stop tempting me."

She smirked and walked toward him. "Tempting you?"

He held out his hand, and she found herself taking it. "Thirty-year-old virgin here—too much skin all at once will be an overload."

She grinned and straddled him, "overload, huh?" He continued to hold her hand. The heat from his bare skin against her waist felt so good. She'd never paused to think of the feeling of skin on skin before and had to wonder if mating was full of other surprises she'd never thought about.

He put his hand behind her and pulled her tight into him. "Can I kiss you before I'm not allowed to touch you?"

She got lost in the way his eyes were changing and felt breathless. Her mate was a spirit bear. She sat there and looked at him, really looked at him. His hair was a mess, he had scruff from not shaving for the last few days and he looked perfect. He was no longer that clean-shaven, evenly parted hair man she had seen when she'd walked into Raymond's cabin. "Yes." She whispered and feathered her fingers through his hair.

His kiss was slow and gentle like he was tasting her. As he did, his fingers worked her braid out and she felt her hair fall around to curtain around their faces.

Her cat was content with this, so far, and she knew that was going to end shortly. It was as if she knew that he needed more time to explore her and take her breath and taste inside him. Blaise was surprised how he tasted like something she'd been looking for her all these years and had never been able to find.

He brushed his tongue against hers, and heat shot through her. Now her cat was right there. Before she did something unexpected like take a chunk out of his tongue, Blaise lifted her head and kissed her way down his jaw. He grasped her hair but didn't pull or guide her head. She licked over his throat, and he growled. She knew the rules, no touching, but didn't care about it. This was her choice, and he wasn't doing anything to hurry her. She lifted her mouth from his skin, "I accept you as my mate, Griffin." Just saying the words felt right; she knew she'd found something she hadn't even been looking for. Without hesitation, she opened her mouth against his skin and felt her cat step up with the teeth just as she bit into him. The taste of his blood filled her mouth and never had something tasted as good as it did. Griffin gasped, and she felt his hand grip her hair tighter. He wasn't trying to move her away; he was holding her closer. Releasing his flesh, she licked over it and then paused for a second to watch the blood roll down over his skin. Leaning down, she followed it with her tongue.

"I'm marked?" He was breathless.

"Mmm," she licked up the blood.

"My turn." He grasped her hips and stood up, taking her with him. She felt her back hit the couch, and his hands tugged at her jeans. Reaching down, she undid them and then lifted her hips so he could pull them off.

His movements weren't desperate, and he looked into her eyes the whole time. When the jeans were off, he leaned down, grasped her bra, and ripped it apart. Her breath caught in her throat. Reaching, she undid his jeans. He stood up and got rid of them before she had a chance to help.

He knelt on the floor and leaned down to pull her head up. He claimed her mouth in a hard rough kiss, and Blaise felt like her insides were on fire. She moaned against his and found herself lifted in his arms until she was sitting up again. His mouth and hands seemed to be all over her at the same time.

She ran her hands through his hair and down over his back. She could feel the muscles beneath her touch and knew his bear was close. Jabbing her tongue into his mouth, she felt his sharp teeth and pulled her head back, breaking the kiss. "Mark me," she was breathless, and her words were barely whispered, but he heard her.

"Do I have to say words?"

"I don't care. Just bite me." It came out as a growl, and she knew her animal was done waiting.

He moved closer and pulled her to the edge of the cushion, she could feel the tip of his erection resting against sensitive folds. She clamped her teeth together, so she wouldn't rush him, but he needed to hurry up, or she was going to lose it.

His hot breath was against her throat as he brushed her hair out of the way. He gripped her hips and pulled her onto him at the same moment his bite pierced her skin. It felt like her body exploded in every direction.

When she tried to gain some leverage to move, he put his hand underneath her bottom and lifted her whole weight for her. His teeth were holding her in place still and she couldn't have moved away if she wanted to. He may not have been raised with shifters, but the male possessive part of their specie was very much present. Her cat submitted and was loving it. Blaise held on, unable to process as she climbed higher with each movement of his body.

When he released her neck, she wanted to object, but she found herself on the couch again. He lifted her legs up and thrust into her, and she gasped. Later, when her brain returned, she would have to tell him that the other part he was worried about was not a problem.

Every time she thought she was going to crash over the edge, he changed speed or position, leaving her a quivering mess, unable to communicate that she was going to lose her mind any second. He lifted her again and they were on the floor now. She didn't know how he was doing it, but he had his arm between her back and the hard floor.

She could taste the salty sweat on his skin, which drove her closer. When he started to suck on his bite mark, she lost all touch with her body. The screaming was her own, and she didn't care if she had no voice for a week, it was worth it.

He tensed, and she clung to him, remembering through the fog of what he'd done and that this was his first time. His growl sent shivers through her, and she waited for him to collapse on her, but he didn't. There was a three-second pause and then she was lifted up and found herself in his lap as he kept moving.

"I feel like purring."

He chuckled, "can you? Purr?"

She frowned, "I don't know, but I'm not going to."

He grinned and pulled her closer. His mouth moved over her throat, and he pulled his head back. "I did it."

Blaise gave him a blank look.

"The mark," he rolled his eyes, "the other part too."

She grabbed his hair and turned his head and then looked at the teeth marks on his neck. "You did the other part with excellence."

He smirked, "Regrets?"

Lifting her head, she licked over her mark and was rewarded by him pulling her tight against him. "Only if you get all mushy."

"Mmm," he rested his face where her shoulder and neck met, "no mushy stuff, got it."

Her phone buzzed, and she lifted her head trying to see where it was. Her pants were halfway across the room. "The op. I don't know how much time we have left."

Griffin released her and flipped to his back, "I'll make coffee."

She sat up and looked down at him lying there sprawled and naked, "first time I wish there was no op." She blinked and got up before she changed her mind. Her whole body was still buzzing, and for the first time in her life, she felt a peace inside her.

"Hey, Blaise?"

She pulled the phone out of her pants, "yeah?"

"Can we try a bed or something softer next time?"

She looked at him, examining his knee, and grinned, "I didn't flip us on the floor." She looked at the phone. "We need to set up the laptop, Illias is calling in five with instructions."

"We should probably go out and get the rest of the stuff then."

Blaise looked at the door, her eyes wide. "This distracted brain better not be a permanent thing or I'm going to get grumpy." She yanked on her jeans and looked around for her top.

Chapter Forty-Six

Griffin leaned over and inhaled Blaise's scent right beside her ear. She smirked but leaned away from him.

"Work."

"You smell different, still sweet and spicy, but the floral is not the same..."

"That's you." She turned and looked at him, then got up and went over and jerked the curtain closed, "we don't need anyone seeing what we're watching."

Griffin shook his head, "I don't think the squirrels will care." He pointed to the other window that had a view of the mountains. "We're in the middle of nowhere."

Blaise grabbed a water bottle and shrugged, "I'm taking no chances." She opened it and jerked her chin toward the screen, "how much time is left."

"Ten minutes if they're on time."

Blaise sat down, "they'll be on time." She smirked, "too bad it's only ten minutes," she looked at the bed, "there's not enough time."

Griffin looked at the bedroom door and then at the screen again, "after."

Her phone buzzed. She looked at it and then did something on the keyboard. The screen went live, and instead of blank space, there were people on it, moving along a building quietly.

"Showtime. The team Noah is on is the first breach." Blaise sounded hyped. She pointed to a key. "If you need to tell them anything, push that."

Griffin leaned closer to the screen as they went inside the building. He wasn't sure if their mics were muted or if they moved that quietly. Whoever had the camera on went through a doorway. The room was darkened, but he watched as a man was approached. He looked like he froze where he stood; if armed people snuck up on him, he'd probably be no better. The man looked left and then right. Griffin held his breath.

Lights were turned on, and one of the teams appeared beside the man. Griffin leaned closer and glared at the screen, he hurried to press the button, "Noah, it's Al."

"Where?" There was no mistaking Noah's growl into the comm.

"With, uh," he glanced at Blaise.

"York," she supplied.

"He's with York in the kitchen."

There was a crashing sound, and then someone was in front of York, blocking the view of Al.

"Who's Al?" Blaise whispered.

Griffin moved his hand from near the button but didn't look away from the screen, "he's the one that whipped Noah."

"Oh." She leaned closer and took his hand; he felt better for it.

Seeing Al and knowing where they were brought back many memories he didn't ever want to think about again.

"Son, you will control yourself right now. Get him under control, Calum." Raymond barked into the call.

Griffin stared at the screen and watched Calum and Blair peel Noah off the other man. They continued to hold him when Raymond's voice came over the call again.

"York, give me a clear view of *Al*."

York moved, so his camera wasn't blocked by the two men working hard to contain his friend.

"*That* is Allen Dunlap, the Global Coordinator for the

Alliance," Raymond stated with venom in his voice. "He has worked for the Alliance for *fifteen* years."

"Holy shit."

Griffin turned and looked at Blaise; the shock was clear on her face.

"He's from Shepard Addison's clan, and he's been working for the Tomas family."

The seriousness of who they had just gotten hit Griffin, "he whipped Noah." He whispered. He needed to ask why his picture hadn't been in the ones he'd looked through. The Alliance needed to share *all* of them with him, even the ones that had been with them a long time.

"Noah, son, I know your story and understand your drive to end Allen's existence, but we need him for now. I need him in a cage in front of me to find out who else betrayed us."

There was a growl over the mic.

"You can have him after, Noah; I'll make sure of it," Griffin recognized Blair's voice. "You had my back with Lindon, I'll make sure you get retribution."

"As will I," Raymond added, "but we need him breathing right now."

Griffin watched Noah shake off Blair and Calum and back away. He could see the hatred on his face as he turned and looked at Al, but he still found the control to turn away and leave the room. He didn't think he could have done that if it had been Griffin.

"Graham, you escort Allen to HQ, I want him paraded in wearing chains for all to see."

"Will do, boss."

"York, get us a view of the others." Wynter's voice was loud through the earbud.

"On it," York replied.

Griffin leaned back, he wanted to throw up or crush something, the inclination for both was strong. He continued to sit there because he needed to see the other faces.

"I can't believe he's part of the king's clan," Blaise whispered and then was behind him, wrapping her arms around him. "And because of you, we got him."

Griffin leaned back, so their cheeks were touching, "we have to get every last one of them, Blaise."

"We will."

He watched the faces as York stopped in front of each one momentarily. "Yes, *we* will," he whispered. He wasn't going anywhere, if he had to devote the rest of his days to traveling the world and searching for faces that haunted his every thought, he would do it.   With his mate beside him, he felt like he could accomplish anything.

"Okay, people, the next breach will live in thirty seconds. Mister Griffin, you keep your eyes on that screen." Illias said, "you are our secret weapon, and it's feeling like the tides have finally turned."

There were a few agreements over the comms, and Griffin closed his eyes for a moment. It may have taken thirty years, but he'd finally found his people. He didn't expect everyone to accept him, but even if a few did, it was better than it had ever been. He pressed the button, "you good, Noah?" He didn't care if he wasn't supposed to do that, he needed to check on his friend.

"Yeah." Noah finally replied. "Maybe we'll get Mylar tonight too."

Griffin nodded, "save him for me."

"Will do, Griffin."

"We need to keep comms clear, people."

Griffin wasn't certain, but he thought that was Nox's voice. He leaned forward to apologize for breaking their protocol, but Blaise hit the key before him.

"Ten seconds before the next breach, and FYI, Griffin is my mate, so if anyone has a problem with that or him, they can tell my fist."

Griffin grinned and looked at her. She looked so fierce. He pulled her into his lap and wrapped his arms around her.

"Duly noted," there was no mistaking Calum's amused voice over the speaker.

"Going live now," Illias informed everyone.

Both of them turned to look at the monitor. Blaise's phone buzzed again.

"The King wants us to go somewhere after this."

Griffin looked at her phone at the time, "tonight?"

"Yeah."

"Must be important." He kissed her cheek, "we can take turns driving."

Blaise leaned back and smirked at him, "nice try."

"And team two is live." Came from the speaker and made them both turn to look at the screen again.

"Because of you, we're going to get them all, Griff." She whispered and sat forward to watch what the camera was showing.

"Because of us." He whispered back.

KEEP READING FOR AN EXCERPT OF

Honor

Animal Senses Series Book 11

By Jacqueline Paige

Chapter One

Slinging his bag over his shoulder, Asher stepped outside and closed the door. The snowbanks were a lot higher than in the last few years. The storm had been insane, it was the first time he'd been happy not to be driving. He'd been stuck here for two days because of the weather and was more than ready to get back on the road.

Going over, he opened the van and tossed his bag inside. He should probably spend some time cleaning it out, but there was always time for that when waiting at safe houses and when the teams were gathering to take down more of Tomas' places. Jesse told him that things were on the upswing now, and they were going to be able to tear down what Aiden Tomas' family had built, finally. He looked forward to that.

Closing the door, he glanced across the road at the house. He started toward it and then stopped three steps later. He still couldn't bring himself to go inside. That house was filled with happy moments as long as he stayed out of it. As soon as he stepped inside, the empty space would remind him of reality. It wasn't as if he could forget, still eighteen years later, he could see his parents and brother lying in their own blood.

It had been a family outing as they'd always done together. As hard as he tried, he couldn't recall the reason. Was it berry picking, or were they just going for a hike, he wasn't sure. A few families were there, so it must have been for berries. He had been chasing his little brother and annoying his mother by doing it when the first screech had paralyzed their movement. His mother rushed over, scooped up Cyrus, and told Asher to run and hide. Even a child knew when the tone in a parent's voice told them it was of the utmost importance to listen. He'd listened without question. He couldn't hear her voice anymore, and he missed it.

How far he'd run, he didn't know. He'd hidden in the base of an old hallowed out tree and had stayed there until he heard the sounds of creatures around him. Had they really stopped during that time? Were no birds or critters making a sound, or had the adrenaline blocked out everything? When his patience ran out, he emerged and wondered why his father hadn't come and gotten him. He checked in shrubbery and overgrowth for his mother and brother as he retraced his steps back to where they had been.

They hadn't gotten away or hidden. They had barely made it fifty feet from where he'd been when she told him to run. He was behind a tree, watching the men check the bodies on the ground. He didn't know if they were looking for one in particular or what they were doing. For a fleeting moment, he had thought they were there to help until the wolf with the blood all over its face strolled over to one of the men and growled. The men spoke to it, and then they left. Asher had almost died that day too. He'd started to rush to look for his mother when someone grabbed him from behind and covered his mouth. He hadn't known until they spoke to him that it was his clan's Alpha. Others had come running, and the only glimpse he'd gotten of his family was looking over Alvin Cain's shoulder as he carried him back to their village. Four had vanished that day, the rest were slaughtered.

"I guess you're leaving now that the roads are open."

He spun around to see his grandmother standing on the steps, a big blanket wrapped around her shoulders. He loved her dearly and was glad his Aunt and Uncle were still here, so she wasn't alone. "Yeah, I'm just waiting on word of which way I'm going." He hoped that Zain or Illias would get back to him soon. He just couldn't be here. "Listen," he went over and looked down at her weathered face; she was his sunshine in the otherwise dark world he lived in, "about the house." He watched her look over at it and could see it still got to her. "I think, with all those we've been finding, we should clean it up and let some move into it."

"I always thought you'd want it someday." She looked at him and nodded, "Okay, I'll tell Alvin."

"Tell Alvin what?"

They turned to see their Alpha coming toward them.

"If it has anything to do with a shovel or a snowblower, I don't want to hear it." He smirked.

Asher couldn't help but grin, he'd had his fair share of shoveling in the last few days, along with most of the clan.

"Asher wants us to open the house to those in need." She looked up at him, and he thought it was pride in her eyes but couldn't think why, "give some family a little more space than bunking in with others."

Alvin stopped and studied him, "you sure, son?"

Asher nodded, "I'm on the road, I don't need a big house."

His Alpha was the only reason he was alive today, and sometimes Asher wasn't sure if that was a good or bad thing. "All right, I'll get someone in there to clean it up." He nodded, "we'll store anything that's personal."

Asher shrugged. He didn't need it and doubted he'd ever want it.

Alvin inhaled slowly and then blew it out, "I'm looking for Journee, have you seen her?"

"Journee?" His grandmother frowned, "I haven't heard that name in—" Her eyes widened, "she's here?"

Asher knew the name was familiar, but he wasn't sure who she was. His grandmother told him of all the comings and goings, her words, but he couldn't keep it straight.

"You remember her, don't you?"

He looked at Alvin.

"She was with the group the day…" Alvin cleared his throat, "she showed up in the middle of the night, I was over helping Len get his generator going. When I got back, she was sleeping on the couch, and Maeve told me to leave her be until morning." He rubbed the back of his neck, "she said she had something important to tell me."

"Did she say how she got back? Where's she been?"

Asher realized this girl had gone missing the day his family was killed. He looked around, there were too many traitors to trust she wandered into the village after eighteen years.

"I have no details yet, Inez. That's why I'm looking for her."

"Alpha Cain." One of the men came running over. "There's a hurt cat at the bottom of the river hill." He held up a worn backpack, "I'm guessing she's one of ours by this."

Alvin took the pack. "It's Journee's." He started walking toward the hill.

Asher looked down at his grandmother, "go inside and stay warm, I'm going to see if I can help." She nodded.

He caught up to his Alpha, "so she just showed up? Has anyone heard from her all these years?"

Alvin glanced at him, "I know what you're thinking, but Maeve says she looked soul weary tired, her clothes were tattered, and her eyes were haunted by demons."

Asher sucked in a breath. "We shouldn't share too much with her, just in case."

The Alpha nodded, then stopped and walked slowly along the path across the top of the hill.

"Just down there." The man caught up to them and pointed.

Down at the bottom lay a cheetah. Her coat was paler than most, but that wasn't unheard of. She wasn't moving at all. Asher moved by the men to find the trail she'd taken down. He stopped and watched a small wolf pup circling her. "There's a wolf down there; if the parents are nearby, we need to hurry."

"That's her pup."

Asher jerked his chin and looked back at him.

Alvin smirked, "Maeve said the pup lay on the porch while Journee was in the house."

Asher looked down the incline again. A cheetah shifter with a wolf pup that was new. He wouldn't have any problem getting down there in cat form, but then he wouldn't be much help in that way. "I'm going to zigzag down to see how bad she's hurt."

"Be careful. I'm going to call Jag and see if he's got that old sled he used to pull the kids around on."

Asher nodded and started down. His boots were great in the snow, but this was going to suck as far as frozen feet went. He slid a few times and had to drop to stop himself from landing down there with her. Now he had snow in his jeans, jacket, and sleeves. Yeah, driving sounded good right now; a heated vehicle and miles of no people, and no chatting was what he longed for.

As he reached the bottom, the pup started going crazy and barking at him. Asher guessed he was around four months old, judging by the teeth he was seeing. They were not milk teeth, that was for sure. "Hey, bud, I'm here to help her." He kept his hands at his side and did not move them around as he walked slowly in that direction. The pup crouched and snarled at him. "It's okay." He kept his tone soft and even.

When he got closer, the animal ran back to her, whining and licking her face. "I'm Asher, Alpha Cain is at the top of the hill." She lifted her head and looked at him. He could see the pain in her amber eyes. "Let me take a look. Don't try to get up yet." He crouched down a few feet from her and waited for the pup to decide if he was allowed near her. Journee turned her head and looked at the wolf and the pup laid down by her head.

Creeping closer, he saw her back leg sitting at an odd angle. "Can you get up?" When she moved her front paw, he held his hand out, "whatever you do, don't try to shift." He wasn't trained, but he'd been around others that had gotten hurt in their animal form and knew that shifting back if something was broken could permanently disfigure them.

She lifted her weight until she had both paws under her chest and started to rise slowly. He could see the shaking.

"You know what, don't try to get up." He knelt and reached over to run his hand along her back leg. He stopped when he felt the sharp point of bone. "Stay down." He leaned back and rested his weight on his heels, "I think it's broken." He glanced to see her watching him, "I have no idea how to set it so you can shift, so we're going to have to get you up out of here and let someone more qualified do that."

She huffed out a breath and dropped her head back down. The pup inched closer and rested his chin on her shoulder.

Asher couldn't imagine being hurt and stuck in one form. He pulled out his phone, "I might know someone with answers." He had no idea how he was going to get a hold of Calum's mate, but Jesse could. He brought up the number and saw that he had no signal. "I can't call until we're back up top."

The pup jumped up and started growling. Asher turned to see the Alpha and the other man coming toward them with a long plastic toboggan. It was ideal for transporting her, but it would work.

He stood up and turned to go get it when she groaned. Asher's cat was immediately there and tense. The pup started barking and growling. His cat probably wanted to eat the vicious little furball. Walking around her, he squatted, "come here." He held out his hand to it. "Come on, we can't help her if we're tripping over you." He paused to wonder if the pup had tripped her up on her way down. He glanced around and couldn't see the tracks. How long had she been lying here? The pup came closer and inched further, dragging his belly in the snow.

"How bad?"

He kept his eyes on the pup, "I think there's a break in her back leg, but I'm no expert."

"Okay, we'll get her to the top, and then I'll have to call around and see if any of the clan doctors are nearby. Ours is off helping the Alliance."

"I can call someone once we back up top and have a signal."

The pup was only a few inches from his hand now. Asher wondered if it would be okay with his scent. Then again, he was running with another shifter, so he should accept him. When he was close enough to grab, the wolf darted in the other direction and stood ten feet back, watching their every move.

"Let's get her on this." Alvin looked back up the hill, "it's going to take all three of us to pull her up."

245

Concealed

The Solrelm Series Book 1

By J. Risk

Chapter One

Early evening was one of Bastian's favorite times to watch humans. The low light made their souls so easy to see, but that wasn't the only reason. As nighttime approached, they changed. The polite, carefully composed people that smiled innocently during the day, turned into entirely different people once the sun went down.

He was sitting on the roof of a five-story building, looking down at them moving along the busy sidewalk. Picking a location with coffee shops and fast food always ensured his entertainment.

With the vast number of years he'd been alive, *his* entertainment was very important. Without it, the years, decades, the centuries dragged out and it was mind-numbing. The previous century, he'd been assigned to other areas, but then they'd—as in whomever it was that made ridiculous decisions about what was best, without ever asking those doing the work—decided each authorized watcher would be placed in *one* area going forward, so the chances of missing any souls in need of aid would lessen. It had made for some very tedious decades for him, but he'd also gotten to know the area better than his own home, which was useful at times.

Leaning over the ledge, he looked down and smiled. There

were so many of them down there right now, if he'd been higher up they'd look like ants in their colony. The addition of cell phones into society made for some humorous moments. One of them would stop dead and stare at their phone and the entire flow of the group would change to move around them. Of course, the collision of two watching their phones instead of where they were going happened too often to have any entertainment value now.

A waning soul caught his attention. It wasn't pulling at him yet, but the body it was in wasn't long in this world. He'd been seeing it soon, or one of his kind would be—Bastian couldn't be everywhere all the time. It was disappointing his kind couldn't teleport with a thought as the Alterealm royals could. The things he could do if he had that power were countless and probably illegal.

He held his breath as another bus moved down the other side of the street. The main reason he'd chosen this location tonight, was the bus terminal was only half a block over. Studying any females close to it, he looked carefully, not having a clue of what or whom he was looking for. The seer princess in Alterealm could have at least supplied him with a rough description. A woman and bus are what she had said. He *had* to find the woman. None of it was helpful.

Not one of those women, or rather their souls struck him with any sense of urgency in any way, so hopefully, he didn't miss *the* one he was supposed to save. Of course, if the bus-woman scenario meant for him to be *at* the bus station watching those boarding and departing buses, the mystery woman was good and truly screwed because the tedium of *that* held zero entertainment value, so he was here instead.

Many from his realm complained about the modernism of the human realm, there were too many to watch over now, they traveled too quickly and many more obscure grumblings. Bastian, he loved the fast pace of this current time. *So many souls, so little time.* He chuckled. Although lately, he'd been busier than he cared to be with a lot more than watching for souls to help cross to their next life, it was— Pausing, he turned and looked back the other way again. The darkness of a soul popped out like a flashing nefarious sign. One from the lawless faction was down there and they were coming down the street in his direction.

"Won't be a fruitless trip after all." He watched as the man impersonating a normal human paused a moment before moving again in his direction. "That's it, come to Bastian, you traitorous cur." He rolled his eyes at the word from long ago, then shrugged, he was allowed to think in any time period, he'd been around for many of them. Too many some days.

He glanced along the sidewalk, trying to find the soul the lawless traitor was after. It wouldn't be the sickly one whose time was almost up. They didn't highjack those. They liked the strong souls with many decades left in their current bodies. There were too many strong ones in the area. Most were just human with very little hints of anything otherworldly mixed into their genes. Maybe he was going to pick some random soul, that was happening far too often lately. Headlines of people's sudden, unexpected deaths were far too common. Although, the lawless ones weren't behind all of them. After all the human body was fragile and sometimes unforeseen things did happen. He'd been on morgue detail a lot recently and after tracing the soul's signature in the corpses, he knew many were being taken by the unsanctioned soul suckers from his own realm.

Standing up, Bastian glared at the other side of the street. Another dark-souled bastard was on the other side. Two in one area was not a whimsical coincidence. They were hunting a specific soul. "Now, I'm intrigued, boys. Thank you for keeping things interesting." He exhaled slowly and focused on making himself invisible. Of course, if his brothers knew he often perched in very visible, precarious locations where the chances of being seen were high, they'd have monumental conniptions. Did he care what they thought of his habits? Not in the slightest. Being invisible was necessary this time though, it wouldn't do if these lawless spotted him, then he'd have to run. Being a prince and somewhat a celebrity among his people, made him *very* memorable. But he still wasn't fond of running.

Keeping them both in his sights, he quickly moved down the fire stairs. Getting both of them was going to be a challenge, but nothing spiced up an endless day better than an impossible task.

He was on the last few steps when his heart practically did a flip inside his chest. He looked around with a feeling of urgency. He didn't have time to help a soul pass right now, he really didn't. He glanced around, looking for the soul calling out to him and then he saw *her*. Stopping, he put his hand over his heart, which now felt like it was going to beat right out of his chest. She was breathtaking. Miles of pale blonde hair, high cheekbones—Bastian wanted desperately to see her eyes. It wasn't a myth that you could see a person's soul through their eyes. Of course, Bastian could see it regardless, but the view from those intriguing orbs was always better. That and his people had black, without variation irises and humans' eyes were so pretty with the flecks and differences in color. She glanced behind her and much to his disappointment, she was wearing sunglasses, which was odd for the fading light, but each to their own. He more than agreed with that. He was the epitome of *that*.

There was something more important than her beauty and no doubt lovely eyes, that made him dizzy with joy, she housed the very soul that haunted his every dream and all his nightmares. The soul he had chased through time since his own began. He'd never felt drawn to a soul that wasn't close to passing on or burning out, just *this* soul that was now in her fragile human body had many times over the years given him the motivation to carry on. He wanted to rush to her, touch her skin, and feel that she was real. He wanted to kiss her. Take her breath of life into his body—

Movement caught his attention, and he remembered the lawless ones. They were both moving in *her* direction. All the pieces clicked together in his head like cogs on a gear. They were here for her and now he knew why. Grabbing his phone, he knew he should call Tor or at the very least Trendan for backup, but did he? No. He dialed the first number on his call list. Chase, one of the kings from Alterealm.

"Bastian?"

Scowling, Bastian watched her look over her shoulder again, over the rim of the glasses covering her light-shaded eyes, she was afraid. She knew she was being hunted. He remembered the king, "yes. Where is the little seer? Is she there?" He'd hoped to bring these bastards in alive to question them, but that probably wouldn't be happening now. Pulling the wand from his pocket, he decided he was sucking their souls right the hell out of those bodies. He'd have to send in clean up afterward, couldn't have any of his kind ending up in a morgue somewhere to terrify and amaze some coroner when they sliced them open to discover the secret inside.

"I'm here." Princess Crissy said.

"The woman—the one with the bus, what did she look like?" Jerking his head in the other direction, he looked one way and then the other, checking for a bus.

"I-I didn't really see her."

The woman started to hurry along the edge of the sidewalk, to avoid collision with others, she was barely staying on the curb. A loud hissing drew his attention. A bus was coming along the same street.

"I think I've found her. This can't happen. Kings, I may need that favor soon." An ambulance went blaring past, the bus moved over into the other lane to get out of the way. It was very close to the curb now. They weren't getting her. "Someplace secure in your realm. It can't be here, and it will have to be guarded."

Bastian ran down the steps, then jumped over the last few. "Damn, why didn't I see this?" Another ambulance went by "The easiest way to take down the leadership of my realm…" He was such an idiot. He froze, trying to decide the best course of action. Then remembered he was on the phone, "would be to take out the soul I can't live without, the one that I live for—

" How did she know she was being hunted? He could count on one hand the number of times in all his life when a human knew one of his were nearby. He ran, trying to avoid the people on the sidewalk and was failing. "I'll call you later." Hanging up, he shoved the phone into his pocket and ran toward her.

He felt the pull of a hot soul and stumbled, debating for a moment if he should see who it was from. He couldn't, not this time. One lost soul was worth the answers. Answers he'd been looking for since that first time many centuries earlier. He'd end up doing penance later for losing a soul, but he needed to save her.

Bastian rushed through those coming toward him on the crosswalk and then started looking, searching—she had to be here. He couldn't be too late. He just couldn't, not for her. Spotting her, he sucked in a breath, she was going to step off the curb. It couldn't end this way. He jumped out onto the street, not caring about the cars flying past him. "Stop." He bumped into someone and didn't care that now he was no longer invisible and would also be a target for the lawless—if they didn't run the other way after seeing he was also in the neighborhood. He hopped back up on the curb when she paused and looked in his direction. Dammit, he wanted to see her eyes, *needed* to, but the glasses covered them.

Tires screeched as a van lost control for a moment, swerving. If she had stepped off that curb, it would have hit her. The glasses slid down her nose and revealed to him the most beautiful pale eyes he'd ever seen. They were huge as she realized the near miss she'd just had. She was all right. His shoulders slumped in relief. For the briefest of moments, she looked at him and he held his breath for fear she would look away if he moved. A horn honking brought them out of the hypnotic moment and then he remembered those after her.

Before he could take a breath and search for those two bastards, he found himself standing in the command center of Solrelm. He hadn't taken the link off his wrist. *Dammit.*

"Have you completely lost your mind?" Trendan growled at him from the other side of the desk.

"Forever ago." Bastian slapped his wand onto the desk and then hopped over the table to stand beside him. Why was he monitoring him during his downtime? He'd ask in a minute, right now he needed to get some guards to that location and find those two soul-stealing bastards.

Bastian's brother watched him tap the screen with more force than necessary as he brought up the location, then hit Tor and Ulric's badge numbers. Dragging them to that location, he leaned over the mic switch. "Two from the lawless faction." He scowled at the screen, "I need them alive to question." He had to know how they knew about her. Huffing out a breath, he turned to look at his older brother. *One* of his two older brothers. This one standing here looking at him like he'd lost all touch with reality, he trusted. "I was visible when you jerked me back here." That ought to be fun for some human counselors when their clients tell them about the disappearing man. He wanted to laugh but was still annoyed.

Trendan rubbed his hand over his short, well-trained blond hair and frowned. "You had two closing in on you. You know they're only visible on here," he tapped the screen, "for a few moments and there you were running around like a madman." He gave his head a quick shake. "Was there a reason for that?"

Bastian looked around the control room, noting a few curious glances their way. "Yes. Was there a reason you were in the control room during your downtime?"

Trendan scowled at him. "I was looking for you." He gave those monitoring the screens a quick side-eye. "We need to talk."

Glancing down at the screen, he saw Tor and Ulric's markers moving around the area he'd been yanked out of. She *had* to be all right. "Yes." Bastian clicked his teeth together, "we do. Next time try phoning me instead."

He messaged Tor as we walked to his quarters, telling him to text as soon as he was back. Opening the door, he went in, leaving it wide open for Trendan to close.

Shrugging out of his leather jacket, Bastian tossed it to the sofa and then took off his link bracelet and set it on the table.

He ran both hands through his hair as he went over to the black cylindrical shelf in the wall. Opening it, he looked inside. It was empty.

"You're about six hours early for that," Trendan said, sounding amused.

Closing it, Bastian blew out a breath and went over and dropped down onto the sofa. "I don't even know what day or time it is."

With his ever-serious expression on his face, his brother sat on the arm of the chair across from him. "You need some downtime."

Bastian snorted, "I need something all right." Leaning his head back, he looked over at him. "Why did you need me?"

"I found three more."

Bastian didn't need to ask three more what, he knew exactly what he was talking about. The men that had been taken, their minds wiped and then records of their human realm visit erased. But it was so much worse than they thought. "How long ago?"

"Two from a dozen decades ago, one of them from this decade."

Bastian sat up so quickly, he almost slid right off the cushion. Holding his hand out he narrowed his eyes at him, "this decade? So," he jumped up and paced to the other side of the room, "so," he spun around and looked at him, "we might have a chance in hell on tracking this one?"

Trendan nodded.

"Holy hell." He put his hands on his head and blew out a breath. "Answers," he mumbled, "we could actually get answers." Dropping his hands, Bastian looked back at him. "We might be able to reverse what was done to him, restore his memories with it being so recent..."

"That's my thought too." Trendan looked guilty, "I still think we should discuss this with—"

Bastian shook his head, "no. Mother and Father can't be brought in until we know more." Neither of them wanted their parents to be in on the wicked scheme of hiding the fact their kind could indeed have a mate and child from outside this realm, but until they knew more, they couldn't risk revealing their hand.

"They can't be part of it." Trendan slid down off the arm of the chair and sat in it properly. "Being able to have children with others outside our realm would be a blessing, the female…"

"No. We can't chance others knowing." Bastian rushed over and sat on the table. "I have the powerful royals from Alterealm assisting me, as well as FaTerra…"

"You spoke to the FaTerra princess?"

Bastian nodded, "yes, there's some serious magic," he waved his hand around, "juju in play here and no one has the juice like they do."

"That's true."

Blowing out a breath, Bastian closed my eyes. "Can we get to him? The dad?" He looked at Trendan.

"Most likely. We'll have to enlist Tor and Ulric's help and come up with a good plan."

Bastian waved his hand around, "they know." Trendan's eyes rounded; Bastian smirked. "We grew up with them, they've been attached to our hips as our guards since puberty, if we can't trust them there is no hope in life left."

"Ulric is solid."

Bastian nodded, "as is Tor." Getting up, he went into the kitchenette area and opened the fridge.

"What about Sigor? We could call him back."

"No." He perused the contents. "He's still chasing down the barrier issue." What was he in the mood for? "I think he's in Aridon, helping them figure out where their barrier might be breached, or might have been," he paused, "blown up or whatever that lunatic Arwan was trying to do."

"Yeah. Elyas is thrilled being the acting commander of the guard while Sigor is taking *personal* time."

"Now do you want to tell me what you were doing? Was it for the Alterealm Royals? The reason you were running about the human's space."

Bastian grabbed a bottle of juice and then put it back and looked at the coffee maker. Did he need caffeine? Probably not, but it wasn't like he was going to die from drinking too much. "No." Did he tell him? Picking up the coffee pot, he went to the sink and glanced at him. He already knew how he was going to react to this, they'd run this gauntlet many, many times. "I found that soul again." Bastian had honestly thought it was gone forever. Watching the liquid as it filled the pot, he closed his eyes for a moment. She had to be all right.

Trendan didn't jump on him, which was a first. Usually, when he brought up that haunting soul, he scoffed. The coffee was brewing before his brother spoke again. "The same soul you've been chasing through the centuries, across the universe? How *do* you know that this is the soul intended for you?"

"I don't. All I know is I *must* find it each time it is reborn. I feel more of a connection to it—more than anyone I've ever felt in my life. Even you."

"I'm missing something. *We're* missing something. Why that soul?" Trendan leaned back and looked relaxed for all of three seconds before he tensed again. "Could it have been one of ours at some point?"

"No." Bastian frowned, "ours don't…"

"Wait." Their cousin Aliria bolted out of Bastian's bedroom.

Bastian spun around, Trendan reached behind him and pulled out a knife.

"Seriously, Liri, how many times do I have to tell you to *announce* when you're hiding in here." Bastian put his hand over his heart and tried to settle his breathing.

"I could have stabbed you," Trendan mumbled as he put the blade away.

She shrugged, "it's close to banquet time, you should *know* I'm here hiding."

Both his brother and he nodded, all of them made themselves scarce when the banquet season was near. Endless dinners, luncheons, and parties leading up to the parade of new eligible females. He'd offered her his suite as refuge years ago when she'd come of age. How she was still single, and his aunt hadn't tied her to a partner, he really didn't know. She might be better at avoidance than even he was.

"What were you talking about?" She went over and perched on the sofa, sitting more on the top of the back than the cushion. She flipped her red 'mermaid' hair back, "what dad, what soul," she gave Bastian a hard look, "what is so special about this soul?"

Bastian crossed his arms over his chest and turned to look at his brother, silently telling him they weren't going to get out of explanations, not with Liri. He adored her, she was a fellow rebel that bucked the system as hard as he did, but she was viciously tenacious when she set her mind to something.

Trendan sat down and heaved a loud sigh. "We—"

She dropped down onto the cushion of the sofa and leaned forward, "don't say can't. You know I can keep a secret." She motioned around the space they were in. "I've been using Bast's place for years to hide and never once told anyone about the things he's up to."

Bastian raised an eyebrow at her confession. "I don't hide my rebellious streak."

She gave him a blank look, "no, *you* have a penis, you don't have to."

He conceded she was right with a shrug. "She could…"

"No." Trendan glared at him, "just knowing any of it puts her at risk."

"Don't I have a say?" She looked from Trendan back to him, "I need some other purpose than primping and preening to attract a partner that I don't want—yet."

Trendan's expression softened, "I know it's hard, Liri, but all of us have a duty.

Bastian snorted, "Attending the never-ending luncheons with the females of the realm can be trying. Everyone looking at you with that watchful look." He scowled at him, "I don't see you going to a lot of these, Elyas goes to even fewer—why is it all falling on me?"

He shrugged, "I have to…"

Liri laughed, a little louder than necessary, "you avoid them just like both of us." She flopped back and made a pouty face, "if there's a chance I don't have to be tied to a stranger…"

"Your parents would never allow it." Trendan looked at Bastian for backup.

Liri was on her feet, hands on hips, and glaring at him before Bastian could open his mouth, "You have *no* say because last I checked, I was the only one here with a womb to procreate more *females* for the realm." She crossed her arms over her chest, "*my* womb, *my* choice." She threw her hands up, "I just want to do something. *Anything* for once that doesn't feel like I'm selling myself to the highest bidder."

"You are watched more than we will ever be." Trendan's tone told Bastian he was slowly caving, and he waited for that opening to jump in.

"You could tell them I'm needed to do something." She smiled at him, and Bastian felt sorry for him, he'd been on the other end of *that* look before with her and ended up giving in to some crazy ideas. Prince or not he could still be reprimanded in many unpleasant ways for doing some things.

"The little seer princess in Alterealm could use some help finding those mixed souls for us." Bastian shrugged.

"Are you crazy?" Trendan's harsh look returned in a snap. "How do we explain she's in Alterealm or the human realm?" He stood up and glared at Bastian, "you are talking about finding humans that are part Solrelm, aren't you?"

"Yes—or any souls that are half ours." Bastian rubbed his hand over his hair and looked down at the floor. Tor should have been back by now. Feeling his pockets, he realized he'd left his phone in his jacket. Going over, he pulled it out of the pocket.

"I don't understand this, like completely human or part of our DNA or other DNA?" Liri looked from Trendan to him, "is that even possible?"

Bastian grinned, "very possible and I have the proof." He checked for messages. There weren't any. "We've also found some of the Solrelm dads responsible for those mixed offspring and someone has known about this miracle and gone to great lengths to hide it."

Liri's eyes rounded to the point it had to be uncomfortable. "We can have children with someone not from here? Do-do they have our abilities still?"

Trendan blew out a breath, "yes." He rubbed his hand over his jaw, "the only ones that know right now are us," he pointed to himself and then Bastian, "and our two guards."

Bastian wondered for a moment where *her* guard was, how was it she could dip on her guard so often? Tor was in on most of his plans, but he doubted her guard, what's his name, knew half of the things she did.

She nodded, looking completely animated, "okay," she nodded again, "good idea, too many knowing would be bad." She sat back down, "have you interviewed these fathers?"

Trendan glanced to him before answering, "no, they've had their memories wiped."

"Wiped? On purpose? Like someone knew and is hiding it?"

Trendan blew out a breath, "yeah."

"Holy shit. This is huge." A few expressions crossed her face then she nodded, sending her wavy locks bouncing on her head. "I want in on this. I want to help."

"We should work on getting to the dads," Bastian turned to Trendan, "she could help the seer."

"Isn't their seer a little busy with…"

"That prophecy of the Alterealm royal family, it's been fulfilled."

Trendan cocked one eyebrow at him, "the nine brothers?"

"Yes." Bastian grinned wide, "and most of their true mates were half-human, well, except for the one that is half Solrelm."

"Shit." His tone was contemplative.

Bastian glanced at his phone, he needed to find Tor. He looked at Liri and then to his brother, "we need to find all the dad's locations, find the traitorous bastards that were involved in that secret," sucking in a breath, he continued, "find the traitorous bastards from here that were helping the insane mage, not to mention the lawless faction jerks were after the soul that's mine—"

"How are *we* going to do all of that?" Liri asked quietly. Neither Trendan nor Bastian missed that she was making sure she was included going forward.

"We can call the Alterealm royals, one princess can hear thoughts, one of their kings can get inside heads—"

"You want to bring them over here? Wouldn't it be safer if we met in the human realm?" Trendan was on the edge of the chair now.

"I don't know." Clutching the phone in his hand, he crossed his arms. "I don't know. I just know we need to do something *now*."

"This has to end." Trendan stood up.

"It does."

Trendan looked at his phone, "Ulric says they'll be back shortly." He looked back at Bastian, "meet me at interrogation?"

Bastian nodded, then motioned to Liri, "I'll fill in a few blanks for her and then meet you there." Why hadn't Tor messaged him?

About Jacqueline

Jacqueline Paige lives in Ontario in a small town that's part of the popular Georgian Triangle area.

She began her writing career in 2006 and since her first published works in 2009 she hasn't stopped. Jacqueline describes her writing as *all things paranormal*, which she has proven is her niche with stories of witches, ghosts, physics and shifters now on the shelves.

When Jacqueline isn't lost in her writing, she spends time with her five children, most of whom are finally able to look after her instead of the other way around. Together they do random road trips, that usually end up with them lost, shopping trips where they push every button in the toy aisle, hiking when there's enough time to escape and bizarre things like creating new daring recipes in the kitchen. She's a grandmother to nine (so far) and looks forward to corrupting many more in the years to come.

Jacqueline also writes under the pseudonym of J. Risk

Jacqueline loves to hear from her readers, you can find her at

http://jacquelinepaige.com/